RAY HARRISON

HARVEST OF DEATH

BERKLEY BOOKS, NEW YORK

HARVEST OF DEATH

A Berkley Book / published by arrangement with
St. Martin's Press

PRINTING HISTORY
First published in Great Britain by Quartet Books Limited
St. Martin's edition published 1988
Berkley edition / February 1990

ISBN: 0-425-11979-3

A BERKLEY BOOK ® TM 757,375
Berkley Books are published by The Berkley Publishing Group,
200 Madison Avenue, New York, New York 10016.
The name "BERKLEY" and the "B" logo
are trademarks belonging to Berkley Publishing Corporation.

PRINTED IN THE UNITED STATES OF AMERICA

10 9 8 7 6 5 4 3 2 1

To Varian and Jon

HARVEST
OF
DEATH

PROLOGUE ───────────

'Do you think the landlord really did have it put on him, sarge?'

Detective Sergeant Joseph Bragg, of the City of London police, glanced irritably at the face of Detective Constable Pratt, bovine in the light of the street lamp.

'Why should we doubt it?' he asked shortly.

'Well, it's the sort of thing that goes on in Stepney or Limehouse, not the City.'

'There is always a first time for anything.'

'It's just that the George is a managed house. It might go down better with the brewery, if the place had been smashed up because he refused to give in to demands for money.'

Bragg grunted non-committally. He must resist the urge to put Pratt down all the time, he thought. It wasn't his fault that Detective Constable Morton was streets ahead of him, in every respect. This was a conscientious enough lad; he had risen to the rank of corporal in the army, so he must have something about him. It was just that they didn't strike sparks off one another, as he and Morton did.

1

'I tell you one thing, sarge. Inspector Cotton won't want to hear anything about a gang demanding money with menaces.' Pratt chuckled throatily to himself.

It was true, without doubt. It happened often enough in the Metropolitan police area, though from what Bragg could make out, they were casual affairs. But it would be a new departure if it were coming into the City. Mind you, it was logical enough. There were plenty of pubs in the square mile; a lot of them taking more in one lunch time than an East End pub took in a week.

'I don't know, constable,' Bragg responded. 'It might be right up Inspector Cotton's street. If he got a tip-off, he would be able to throw a cordon round the pub, then go in and arrest them all single-handed!'

Pratt laughed appreciatively. He well knew the hostility that existed between Bragg and his superior; and Cotton's ability to make a cock-up of any operation was legendary.

'Let's go up Garlick Hill,' Bragg said. 'I had better let the desk-sergeant at fourth division know how we made out. You might as well cut off home.'

'Did you see that, sarge?' Pratt grabbed Bragg's arm.

'See what?'

'In that warehouse . . . between the two gas lamps.'

'What about it?'

'I could swear that I saw a light.'

'Where? What sort of light?'

'On the first floor. Like the beam from a lantern.'

'Keep in the shadows. Let's get a bit closer.'

They crept up the opposite side of the street and concealed themselves in a doorway.

'It will be a fur warehouse, in this neighbourhood,' Bragg muttered. 'I expect they will have got new stock in, ready for trimming ladies' autumn coats.'

'There! Did you see it?'

'Yes! . . . What is behind these buildings?'

'Angel Court, sarge.'

Bragg bit back his growing annoyance at this lax mode of

address. Once this absurd cricket tour by the Australians was over, he would have Morton back with him.

'They'll be screwsmen,' he said. 'Picked the lock of the back door. Can you see the beat constable anywhere?'

Pratt peered into the darkness around them.

'No, I can't.'

'Then we will have to tackle them ourselves. If we try to whistle up men from Cloak Lane police station, they will have gone. Come on . . . and keep it quiet.'

They crept back down the street to Angel Court and tip-toed along it, counting the yard gates as they went. Bragg stopped at the fifth, and gently pushed. It opened before him. He beckoned Pratt to follow and sidled along the shadow of the wall, till they got to the back of the building. The back door was at the top of three shallow steps. In the darkness, it looked secure enough.

'We could do with a lantern ourselves, constable,' Bragg muttered. 'Right, this is what we'll do. If the door is unlocked, we will creep up the stairs to the first floor, and surprise them. You are a bit younger than me, so I want you to rush in and grab the first one that comes to hand. The others will try to escape down the stairs. I will be on the landing to stop them.'

'And what if the back door's locked, sarge?'

'Why, then I stay here, while you go up to Cloak Lane and bring some of the lads.'

'Right.'

Bragg eased himself silently along the wall and up the steps to the back door. He turned the knob and the door swung inwards. Pratt followed him inside. They found themselves in a wide corridor leading to the front of the building. Enough lamplight came through the fanlight over the front door to reveal a flight of stone steps leading upwards.

'After you, constable,' Bragg whispered. 'And when you go in, make enough noise for a platoon!'

Pratt's teeth gleamed in a smile, then he turned and began to lead the way upwards. By the time they reached the upper

landing, the light from the street had dwindled, and they
had to pause while their eyes became accustomed to the
shadows. Then Bragg nudged Pratt and the constable burst
through the door, shouting at the top of his voice: 'Police!
Stay where you are. You are under arrest!'

Pratt lumbered around like a bullock, colliding with
trestle tables and upending furniture. Suddenly, Bragg was
aware of a shadow stealing along the wall, towards the
door. When he judged himself to be beyond Pratt's reach,
the man flung himself through the doorway and on to the
landing. Bragg grabbed him round the chest and the two
men crashed to the ground. The screwsman thrashed around
him frantically, but he was light of build and, choosing his
moment, Bragg managed to heave him on to his face. He
twisted his arms behind his back and clicked the handcuffs
on him. As he did so, the door crashed open again. Pratt's
voice, from within, shouted: 'Stop him!' Crouched over his
prisoner, Bragg was a couple of yards from the doorway,
but he lunged sideways. He felt a blow on his arm, then the
man was past, clattering down stairs.

'Sorry, sarge,' Pratt loomed in the doorway. 'There
wasn't room to move in there . . . I see that you got one
of them.'

Bragg rose to his feet. 'Take him to Cloak Lane, and get
him charged. He will soon tell us who the other man was,
if he knows what's good for him.'

Pratt dragged the screwsman to his feet and pushed him
unceremoniously down the stairs. Bragg followed and
closed the back door behind him. The police station would
have the name of the keyholder. He would not welcome
being rousted out of bed to lock up again, but that was his
bad luck.

Bragg followed Pratt and his captive up Garlick Hill. He
felt unaccountably weary. The struggle had been violent,
sure enough, but it had not been prolonged. His left arm
was smarting too, where the second man had struck
it . . . Smarting and yet warm, a bit like thawing out after

throwing snowballs as a lad. He turned into the police station.

'God Almighty, Joe,' exclaimed the desk-sergeant. 'You are bleeding like a stuck pig!'

Bragg looked down at his arm. There was a long slit in his sleeve and blood was running down his fingers.

'We shall have to get you to the hospital,' the desk-sergeant said firmly. 'Here, Jim, get a cab quick!' He pushed a shirt-sleeved constable through the door and rushed over to Bragg.

'Best thing we can do is bind it up as it is,' he said. 'A knife, was it?'

'I expect so,' said Bragg dully. 'It was dark.'

The sergeant took out his handkerchief. 'It's not very clean,' he murmured apologetically, as he knotted it around Bragg's arm. 'Hold it up a bit, if you can, Joe. The blood just spurts out, if you let it hang down.'

There was a clatter of hooves outside and Jim dashed in. Bragg felt Pratt's arm around him, guiding him towards the door. Dizziness was coming over him in waves. He dimly heard the cabby protesting at the blood, and Pratt threatening him with the loss of his licence. Then he was propped in the corner and the cab was rattling away. He wondered dully how long it took from Cloak Lane to Bishopsgate . . . the clatter of the horse's hooves was getting more and more remote . . . he could barely feel the shuddering of the cab as it raced along. He steeled himself to stay awake, then dizziness overwhelmed him and he knew no more.

When he recovered consciousness, it was full daylight. He peered around him with half-closed eyes. An iron bedstead . . . a row of them opposite, curtains between each bed. He tried to move his feet, but they were imprisoned by tightly drawn bedclothes . . . He must be in the police hospital. He lay quietly, taking in the situation. His head was splitting, as if an Irish navvy was pounding it with a rammer. His mouth was dry and he felt that, if he moved, he would vomit. He heard brisk footsteps and

closed his eyes. The last thing he wanted was a nurse
bullying him into getting better . . . What had happened?
He could remember the struggle with the burglar . . . then
there had been a second man; he had struck out as he ran
past.

Bragg moved his left hand and a jagged pain shot up his
arm. God! He wouldn't do that again in a hurry . . . He
remembered now. He'd been bleeding, dripping blood over
the charge room floor. Well, he was still alive, if only just.
Best to lie doggo, till he knew which way it would go. His
mind drifted back to the borders of unconsciousness . . .
He was a brawny youth again, helping to feed the thresher,
tossing down the sheaves with his pitchfork. Faster and
faster went the machine . . . he couldn't keep up with
it! . . . Why was no one helping him? Why were they all
grinning derisively at him? With the sweat running into his
eyes, he laboured frantically, thrusting the corn into the
monster's maw . . . He was falling behind again! Exhausted, he gave a despairing heave—and couldn't withdraw his fork! He was being dragged into the thresher,
along the chute, towards the beaters . . . 'No!' he shouted
and on the instant was wide awake, eyes staring.

'Ah! You have come round. Good!' The nurse walked
purposefully across the polished floor towards him. 'How
do you feel?'

'Terrible,' Bragg mumbled.

'It is only the effects of the chloroform. It will soon pass.'

'Can I have a drink, nurse?'

'Of course.' She smiled cheerfully at him. 'Come on, sit
up.' She ripped back the bedclothes and thrust her arm
under Bragg's shoulders.

'I . . . I don't think I can manage it,' he protested
feebly.

'Nonsense! You have only got a scratch on the arm.
Come along!'

Bragg wriggled up out of his cocoon and balanced
precariously, while the nurse piled pillows behind him; then
he sank back thankfully. He looked at his left arm. It was

heavily bandaged. The hand had been cleaned perfunctorily. There was still caked blood between the fingers and round the nails.

'Here is some water for you.'

It went down a treat, thought Bragg. Better than any ale. Yet, immediately, his stomach felt queasy again. Still, his head wasn't throbbing so badly. You couldn't have everything. He lay back on his pillows and drifted into a doze.

'Wake up, sergeant.' The nurse was back again, carrying a bowl of steaming water. 'We must have you tidied up, before matron comes round.'

With a groan, Bragg submitted to having his bristly face washed. Then the nurse began to clean up his hand. She was gentle, but every movement sent a stabbing pain up his arm. Despite his entreaties, she persisted until every speck of blood was gone. Then, placing the injured arm on the coverlet, she tucked in the bedclothes like a strait-jacket again. Worn out by her ministrations, Bragg slept. He was dimly aware of a tall blue figure with a severe face inspecting him and making some remark to her respectful acolytes. When he awoke, his head was clear and he was glad to consume the plate of pallid boiled fish they brought him. He had barely finished, when a white-coated doctor approached his bed.

'Well, Sergeant Bragg, and how are you feeling?' he asked, taking his pulse.

'Not too bad, now.'

'You are a lucky fellow, d'you know that?'

'If I'd been really lucky, I wouldn't be here,' Bragg countered grumpily.

'Was it a pub bawl?'

'No, a couple of screwsmen after some bunny-rabbit for their girlfriends.'

'Well, you have got quite a nasty wound there.' The surgeon took Bragg's uninjured arm, and pushed up his sleeve. 'The blade slashed across the middle of the inner forearm, about here.' He drew a short line with his fingernail, about three inches below the crease of the elbow.

'It sliced into the muscles and tore the radial artery. That is where all the blood was coming from.'

'It was really spurting out. I thought I was done for.'

'You will soon make it up, don't worry. We had to excise the damaged portion of the artery and tie the severed ends. It's all right! You will get plenty of blood to your hand through the ulnar artery. Apart from a little loss of sensation on the arm, where the superficial nerves have been cut, you will be as good as new. You are lucky, though, that the knife missed the median nerve. If that had been cut through, you would never have been able to use your hand properly again. As it is, in time, you will hardly know that it has happened.'

'In time?'

'Oh, yes. You cannot rush these things.'

'I don't doubt you are right, doctor. But how long?'

'We shall have to see. There is no question of your going back on duty for some time. I shall want to see you in three days—that is Friday morning, at ten o'clock. In the meantime, there is no reason why you should not go home. Your wife will be able to look after you, I take it?'

'I am a widower, sir.'

'Ah. Do you live in the section house, then?'

'No. I have lodgings in Tan House Lane.'

'Hmn . . . Perhaps we should keep you here.'

'No,' said Bragg hurriedly. 'Mrs Jenks, my landlady, will take care of me all right. She had a spell looking after her husband with a bad cut.'

'Very well. We will put the arm in a sling for you, but I do not want you to keep it rigid. A little gentle movement will do no harm—and it will soon let you know, if you are overdoing it!'

The surgeon walked off with a grin and chatted briefly with the sister in charge of the ward. Before long the nurse brought his clothes and helped him into them. Bragg was half surprised that he could stand up so easily. Four hours ago he would have been happy to die. Nevertheless, an orderly was deputed to get a cab for him. The journey home took but a few minutes, yet when they arrived at Tan House Lane, Bragg had some difficulty in getting down.

'You all right, guv?' the cabby asked, as he took the fare.

'Yes. I'll be fine, thanks.'

Bragg mounted the front steps and unlocked the door. He leaned against the passage wall, while his strength returned, then began to go slowly down the back stairs, to the basement kitchen. As he opened the door, Mrs Jenks swung round.

'Wherever have you been, Mr Bragg?' she began querulously, then took in his grey, haggard face and the jacket thrown over his shoulders.

'Oh, my God! Are you hurt?' she exclaimed.

'Yes, Mrs Jenks.'

'I'll send for the doctor.'

'No. I have just come from the hospital.'

'Come and sit down.' She set his armchair by the fire and he sank into it gratefully.

'They have no right to send you home in that state,' she said shrilly.

'It's only a knife wound. They say it will be all right in time.'

'Huh! That is what they said about Tommy, and look how it ended with him.'

'I know, Mrs Jenks. But they say it is a clean cut. All I have to do is rest for a few days till my blood builds up again, then I shall be able to knock around all right.'

'Well, see you do rest. That was the trouble with Tommy.'

'I promise I will.'

Mrs Jenks's husband had been a prosperous dustman, with his own horse and cart. He had cut his hand on a tin can and shrugged it off. He'd had scores of cuts like that, he said. But it had taken bad ways, and scepticaemia had set in. They'd amputated the hand, but it had been too late to save him.

'Let me take your jacket . . . Why, it's covered in

blood! Fancy sending you back like that. I shall have to wash it.'

'I wouldn't bother, Mrs Jenks,' Bragg said weakly. 'They cut up the sleeve, to get it off me.'

'What would they want to do a thing like that for?' she asked. 'I shall never be able to sew it up again.'

'It can be thrown away.'

'It was as good as new. Really!' She stalked off with the jacket and Bragg could hear her bustling about upstairs. Then she returned.

'Here, put this shawl around your shoulders, it's lamb's wool, so it will not be heavy on your arm, and it's warm.'

Bragg leaned forward compliantly, and she tucked the ample folds around him.

'Now, you stay there,' she admonished, 'while I tear up that old sheet for bandages.'

For the next week, Mrs Jenks fussed around him, ordering every detail of his life, watching his face anxiously for confirmation that he was recovering. By the time that he had to visit the hospital for the second time, he was feeling much his old self. The surgeon seemed pleased with his handiwork, too, and after what seemed like a perfunctory glance at the wound, he chatted about the century that Jim Morton had scored at Lord's against the Australians. Bragg merely grunted at the doctor's enthusiasm. To him, it was a stupid notion that prowess on the sportsfield could raise the standing of the police in the eyes of the public. He felt like saying that if Morton had been on duty that night, instead of Pratt, there would have been two screwsmen laid by the heels and he would have come off unscathed.

At his next visit, Bragg professed himself as right as rain again. But when the surgeon undid the bandages, his face showed concern. The area around the cut had become red and shiny at one end. He pressed it gently and Bragg caught his breath in pain.

'Hmn . . . We shall have to keep an eye on that,' he said. 'I think that the internal sutures may be giving you trouble. The inflammation may subside spontaneously, of course. Come back in four days and I will have another look at it.'

'I can barely feel it,' Bragg protested. 'I've always had good healing flesh . . . Can I go back on duty? I want to catch the bastard that did it.'

'You are as likely to lose your arm, as catch your criminal, sergeant,' the doctor said sternly. 'You will have to leave your private vengeance to others. I will see you on Tuesday morning.'

By the time he returned to the hospital, Bragg's arm felt swollen and painful. The slightest jolt sent it throbbing sickeningly. When the surgeon examined it, he sucked in his breath in concern.

'The first thing we have to do,' he said, 'is to remove the stitches.' He took a pair of needle-pointed scissors, then smiled reassuringly. 'I will not hurt you more than I have to.'

Bragg gripped the arm of the chair and looked away, as the surgeon started to snip the sutures. He began at the outer end of the cut, where the inflammation was less. After the first two, however, he seemed to have to dig the points of the scissors into the swollen flesh. Bragg ground his teeth, to avoid crying out in pain. By the time it was finished, he felt spent and sick.

'Almost certainly, there is an abscess forming. We shall have to get rid of it,' the surgeon said. 'Can your wife . . . ?'

'Landlady,' Bragg interrupted.

'Your landlady. Can she poultice it for you? If not, we shall have to admit you again.'

'She can do it, if needs be.'

'Very well. A simple bread poultice will suffice, it is the heat that does the trick. Come back in three days, unless it becomes very painful.'

Bragg found it impossible to decide whether it was the abscess itself, or the treatment prescribed, that hurt most. Mrs Jenks seemed intent on compensating for any short-comings in her nursing of her late husband. The kettle was always steaming on the hob, thick slices of bread lay in muslin ready to be scalded. It seemed that no sooner was his arm becoming easy, than she was clapping another boiling-hot poultice on it. Her thin shrewish voice would overbear his protests. It was for his own good, she would castigate him. She wasn't going to let him go the way that Tommy did . . .

Morton visited him frequently over the next few days. He was back on duty, between test matches, and could not have been more concerned. Yet Bragg could not get it out of his mind that it was Morton's fault he had been injured. He was short and rude with him—indeed with everybody. He snapped at the surgeon, when he pointed out with relish the white spot forming under the skin, and told him to continue with the treatment for a few more days. It was as much as he could do not to lash out at Mrs Jenks when she advanced on him with yet another steaming poultice. At last, worn out with pain and loss of sleep, he dragged himself to the hospital again. This time the surgeon seemed pleased at the large purulent head that had gathered. He poked about in an enamel tray and picked up a lancet.

'You touch me with that,' Bragg snarled, 'and I'll knock your bloody head off!'

The surgeon smiled reassuringly then paused, his knife in the air. His eyes were fixed, staring over Bragg's shoulder. 'Oh my God!' he muttered.

Bragg turned his head to look. He felt a slight touch on his forearm and jerked back, to see yellow pus oozing out of the abscess.

The surgeon grinned. 'That was not too bad, was it? Now I am going to clean the area, and we will see what has been causing it. I promise you that it will not hurt.'

Bragg's clenched right hand was only inches away from the surgeon's midriff, but he worked unconcernedly, conjuring the pus away from the abscess with gentle pressure.

'There, you see?' he said, pointing to a couple of brown specks on his gauze. 'Those are the remains of sutures.

They are the little fellows that have been causing your trouble. You should be all right now.'

'No more poultices?' asked Bragg.

'No more poultices. It should heal up quite quickly on its own.'

The surgeon's prediction was fulfilled. By the time that Bragg went to the hospital again, the wound was virtually healed and he could move his arm without too much discomfort. He was hoping to get back to work, on light duties perhaps, but his hopes were dashed.

'Not yet, sergeant,' the surgeon said firmly. 'We shall have to get some strength into those muscles first. You are going to have to work on them, to get them into trim. You need graduated physical exercise, and good food. I have a mind to send you away from London for recuperation. There are too many virulent germs around at this time of year. Have you any relations in the country, you could go to? It would be an official convalescence, so you would get an allowance to cover the cost.'

'I've got relations in Dorset, sir. That is in the country.'

'Excellent! Dorset would be ideal. One stipulation I would make is that there must be a doctor in the village, so that he can keep an eye on you.'

'Then I shall have to stay with my cousin in Bere Regis. They have got a doctor.'

'What is his name?'

'Dr Lys.'

'Good, I will write to him. Now, how long shall it be for?' He studied the calendar on the wall. 'Let us say that you will return to duty on Monday the eighth of September. I think that I can hold Inspector Cotton in check till then.'

Bragg was up in his sitting-room at the back of the house, a few evenings later, when he heard feet on the stairs. Then Morton poked his head round the door.

'I am sure that you are sufficiently recovered to receive a distinguished newspaper reporter,' he said lightly and stood back to reveal Catherine Marsden.

'I didn't know that you had been hurt, until James told me this morning,' she said in concern. 'How are you?'

'I am coming on now,' Bragg replied with a smile of pleasure. 'It was a bit rough for a time.'

Catherine looked closely at him. 'You have lost weight,' she pronounced. 'Your face is quite thin . . . I have brought some flowers to cheer you up.' She placed a bunch of roses on the table.

'That is kind of you. But I am going away tomorrow. The surgeon is making me leave London for convalescence. It makes me feel like an invalid, but he says that I might be bitten by some unspeakable bug if I stay here.'

'Then Mrs Jenks shall have the flowers,' Catherine said. 'I am sure that she deserves them.'

'Where are you going to?' asked Morton.

'I have arranged to stay with my cousin, in Bere Regis. That's a village in Dorset. I don't know if it will be much of a rest, he owns a busy carrier's business. But it will be a change, and I have not seen him for donkey's years.'

'I thought that you came from Dorset,' Morton said.

'So I do; from not very far away. But my mother still lives in the area so, when I go down, I stay with her.'

'I am sure you will enjoy that,' Catherine said warmly.

'I hope so, miss. And what have you been doing, these last few weeks?'

'She has been busy keeping her admirers at bay,' Morton said teasingly.

'As a matter of fact I have been working very hard . . . I have been asked to join the *Star*, as their society correspondent. It is a great compliment, of course.'

'And undoubtedly deserved,' Morton interjected airily.

'However, I do not think that I shall accept.'

'Is the job of society correspondent lacking in *gravitas*?' Morton gave a disarming smile.

'You know full well it is not that,' Catherine retorted crossly . . . 'I know that a London daily newspaper is much more exciting than the poor old *City Press*, but I fear that it might bring too much pressure.'

'Can I believe my ears?' Morton cried. 'Is our beautiful feminist refusing a challenge?'

'There is little point in a woman's demonstrating that she is superior to a man, if she derives no satisfaction from the work. The *City Press* suits me and, since it comes out only twice a week, there is time to concentrate on work of high quality.'

'Well, I would not have you turn into a drudge,' said Morton. 'Think what it would do to your amiable disposition!'

'And what are you doing, lad?' asked Bragg, intervening.

'I am doing work of the lowest quality. Since my afternoons are spent practising for the Oval test match, I am sentenced to copy out personnel records every morning!'

'Serves you damned well right,' Bragg said sourly.

'No doubt.'

'When is the match?' Catherine asked carelessly.

'The fourteenth to the sixteenth.'

'Oh.' A look of disappointment crossed her face. 'I shall be away.'

'Don't say that you are becoming interested in cricket!' exclaimed Morton incredulously.

'Why should I not? Is it something that only men can appreciate?'

'No, of course not, but . . .'

'I went to the first day of the Lord's test . . . I was really quite proud of you.'

Morton looked astounded. 'Did the Prince of Wales command your presence?' he asked sardonically.

'I was escorted by someone of much more importance to me.'

'Who is that?'

'Papa, of course.' She turned to Bragg. 'How long will you be away?' she asked.

'I am reporting for duty on the eighth of next month . . . that is, if I don't get bored stiff before then.'

'You ought to take all the time you need,' Catherine asserted. 'After all, the Commissioner will only realise that he cannot run his force without you, if he is compelled to try.'

CHAPTER ——————
—————— ONE

Bragg looked at his outline in the long speckled mirror. Without his jacket, he looked unwontedly slim. His face certainly was thinner, too. If it had not been for the strands of grey in his hair and moustache, he thought, he might have passed for thirty-eight. But it was a damned steep price to pay for renewed youth! He finished transferring the contents of his portmanteau into the chest of drawers. Mrs Jenks had folded every item with meticulous care. She had been full of advice and admonitions, up to the very moment he had left. She obviously did not believe that he could be taken care of properly, in the depths of the country. He hung his coat in the closet, next to a girl's party dress. He had been put in fifteen-year-old Ada's room, by the looks of it. He combed his hair and put his frock-coat on again, then sat by the window and looked out.

Oddly enough, he had never stayed at the Old Brewery before. He and Ted Sharman had been as thick as thieves when they were lads; but, living so near, there had never been any call to sleep in each other's houses. It was a rambling collection of buildings, but the old brew-house made an excellent shed for the carts. There was plenty of room in the house, too, particularly as the boys had left home. It was a pleasant place to live, that was for sure . . . Funny thing to build a brewery right next to the east window of the church. Mind you, there must have been some ripe, yeasty smells at times, to liven up the services!

Bragg had worked for a time in his father's carrier's business, over at Turner's Puddle, and he looked around him with interest. The yard was tidy enough, but the buildings looked a bit dejected. Paint was peeling off some of the windows and a slate had come adrift from the stable roof. It was lodged in the gutter, still whole. Perhaps, when he was feeling up to it, he would get a ladder and replace it.

He went down to the kitchen, where Emma Sharman, big and jolly, was making buns for tea.

'Will you be comfortable there?' she asked, with an easy smile.

'Yes thanks, love. It's as good as the Savoy.'

'I will make us a cup of tea, and we can have a chat.'

She bustled round the big deal table, setting out cups and sorting a handful of tempting biscuits from a tin.

'What are you playing with, Uncle Joe?' asked eight-year-old Kittie, perching on his knee.

'Why, it's a soft rubber ball. I hurt my arm and I have got to keep squeezing this, to make it better.'

'Can I try?'

She took the ball into her own dainty hand. 'It's not very soft,' she said. 'I can hardly press it at all.'

'Don't bother your uncle Joe,' said Emma equably. 'Go out and play for a while.'

Kittie looked at them shrewdly, then, deciding that nothing of interest was likely to happen, jumped down and ran into the sunshine.

'Your family is growing up,' Bragg remarked.

'Goodness me, yes! I'm a grandmother now, did you not know? Robert has a little son. He will be three months old, next Wednesday.'

'Has he, indeed? He cannot be more than twenty.'

Emma smiled sheepishly. 'Well, you know how it is,' she said.

'Who did he marry?'

'Molly Preston. She's a towny from Dorchester, but she is right enough.'

'Let me see, Robert was the eldest, wasn't he? What is Peter doing?'

A shadow passed over Emma's beaming countenance. 'He has gone to work in Poole docks,' she said. 'He gets good money, but we don't see much of him. At least, I don't. His father sees him sometimes, when he is collecting a load there.'

Bragg wondered what Peter had done, to be out of favour.

'And there was another girl before Ada and Kittie, wasn't there?' he asked.

'Rose! Come on Joe! You were her godfather; only you had to do it by proxy, because you couldn't get away from London.'

'That's right.' Bragg decided to face out his appalling lapse of memory. 'Is she still at home?'

'No, she is in service, just up the road at Shitterton Manor. A parlourmaid, she is, and getting all la-di-da!'

'I would like to see her, while I am here,' Bragg said diplomatically.

'Oh, you will. The cook often sends her shopping in the village, for bits and pieces. She is always popping in.'

'That must be nice for you . . . Now look, Emma, I am getting an allowance for the time I spend here, so I am going to pay it over to you. I know that was not in your mind, when you said I could come; but it would not be right for you to be out of pocket, and me in pocket.'

'All right, Joe,' she smiled warmly. 'I won't pretend it'll not come in handy.'

Just then, Ted came in and Emma hastened to pour him a cup of tea. He was shorter than Bragg, but broad and strong. As a boy, he had been light-hearted and full of fun.

Yet throughout their journey from Dorchester station, he
had been quiet, almost taciturn. Bragg wondered if Ted had
been against his coming, despite the frequent invitations,
and had been overborne by the generous nature of his wife.

'I hear you have a grandson, Ted,' Bragg remarked,
pulling out his pipe.

'That's right—Alfred.'

It was an acknowledgement of kinship, rather than an
expression of pleasure. Bragg looked across at Emma, but
she was her usual beaming self. The child was not the cause
of friction, then. Indeed, why should it be?

'Well, the succession to the business is assured,' Bragg
chaffed him.

Ted made no answer but, draining his cup, got up and
clumped outside.

When he had got his pipe going to his satisfaction, Bragg
sauntered out into the yard and strolled around. In the old
brew-house was a large two-horse van and a Norfolk
dogcart. Ted was busy grooming a colt of about twelve
hands—much too light for serious work, though it would
look well in the trap. Bragg peered into the stable. A big
shire stallion was contentedly munching hay, and there was
hay in two more of the mangers. More than half of the
stable was empty. It was all of a piece with the run-down
look of the buildings. He crossed over to Ted and stood
watching him.

'How many men have you working for you?' he asked.

Ted glanced up. 'Just Robert,' he said shortly.

'I suppose that he is out on a job?'

'Taking a load of planks to Milton Abbas.'

'I see . . . I think I will have a walk up to the Cross,'
Bragg said and strolled out of the yard. A load of light
timber would mean a cart—probably a flat—pulled by one
horse. So Ted had two shires for a cart plus a big van. That
was dangerously inflexible. If the cart was out, you hadn't
enough horses to pull the van—though you would have to
have a big load, to justify using a van of that size. Yet, with
the cart out, there was always one horse idle, eating its head

off. At the other end of the scale, the trap was hardly big enough to carry more than parcels . . . Funny. He had always had the idea that Ted had a thriving business. Not that he had been here for many years . . . Come to think of it, his sister's letters had not mentioned Ted, recently. But then, they wouldn't. Briants-puddle was all of two and a half miles away. That was another world, down here.

Bragg stood for a time at the roadside, breathing in the earthy smell of the cow-parsley and gazing about him. The village lay wholly to the west of the cross-roads, for the eastward extension of the Dorchester road, to Poole, had been constructed not many years before he was born. Odd that they called it the Cross, as if it had existed from time immemorial. There had never been a cross there, that he could remember . . . To the east, there was nothing but open country, with a few farmsteads huddling in the folds of the hills. After the hot summer, the countryside was already dappled with the soft hues of ripe corn. The gentle contours of Woodbury Hill were hung with a mesh of green hedge-rows. On the sunny slope, he could see a line of reapers scything down a field of oats; their slow progress followed by the ant-like scurryings of women and children binding the sheaves and stooking them. A hundred yards to the south of him, the Bere Stream ran in its wide, shallow bed and beyond was the heathland of Black Hill. It was just as he remembered it, from thirty years ago. Then, if the harvest was late, he would play truant and help the farmers in the fields. He smiled to himself and strolled on.

'Hey! Mister! Wait a minute!'

The shrill shout was coming from the other side of the main street. Bragg looked round and saw a slight figure detach itself from a doorway, and start to cross the road. It was a man, but one so undergrown that he seemed like a youth. His left arm was deformed and drawn up into his body. His left leg was twisted inwards and upwards, so that he balanced on his toes. Nor could he have much use of his right leg, because he was not able to take anything approaching a step. Instead, he progressed by swivelling from side to side, his right arm flailing the air. He finally reached the low wall in front of the Royal Oak and, with a practised twist of his body, perched himself on it.

'Are you the London bobby?' he asked.

'That's right,' said Bragg genially. 'And who are you?'

'Ernie Toop—Ernie the cripple,' he said waspishly. He had a long chin and his cheeks were unshaven; but he was clean and his clothes, though dusty, were not ragged.

'And where do you live?' Bragg asked.

'Over yonder, with my ma and da.'

'I see . . . I was going to have a glass of beer out here. Can I get you one?'

Ernie's eyes gleamed. 'Aye, you can,' he said.

Bragg brought out two glasses. Ernie seized his as if fearful that Bragg would change his mind.

'Good beer,' Bragg remarked, wiping the foam off his ragged moustache with the back of his hand. 'A bit more yeasty than we get in London. I can see that I shall put a fair bit of this away.'

'There's nothin' in London that we haven't got better,' Ernie said aggressively.

Bragg smiled. 'You could be right there,' he said.

'What're you doin' up there then?'

'Somebody has got to keep them in order.'

At that moment, a woman in late middle-age came down the street. She was rushing along, her black coat flapping open. Ernie gave a chuckle and, putting his glass down on top of the wall, rubbed his hands together gleefully.

'Go on, you old crow!' he shouted, as she came abreast of them. 'You will be late for your own funeral!'

'I'll lay you out, Ernie Toop, that's for sure,' she riposted and hurried on, while Ernie sniggered to himself.

'Who was that?' Bragg asked.

'Tabitha Gosney,' Ernie said with satisfaction. 'She's the midwife, and she lays dead people out. She's the nearest thing we've got to a nurse.'

'You have a doctor, though.'

'Old Lys?' Ernie said with a sneer. 'He's only for the

nobs. Ordinary folk have to make do with the Old Crow. They only send for Lys when there's no hope. Waste of money, it is.'

'I see.'

'Tabby will be off to Doddings, about the little maid that got hurt.'

Bragg remembered that Doddings was a hamlet, half a mile to the east. He and Ted had often walked down there, looking for trout in the stream.

'It is very quiet in the village,' Bragg remarked, since Ernie seemed to have run out of conversation.

'They're all in the fields. I shall be up there, when they start bringin' the corn in. Somebody will give me a lift on a cart.'

Bragg drained his glass. 'Will you have another?' he asked.

'No. They won't let me pee against the wall, and it's hard work gettin' back home.'

'All right.' Bragg went back into the pub. The bars were deserted and, as soon as he had served him, the barman also disappeared. In frustration, Bragg took his beer outside again. A tall sinewy man was talking to Ernie. He was smartly dressed in a tweed lounging jacket and knicker-bockers. He wore shiny brown boots, and was tapping a switch against his leggings impatiently. He made a remark to Ernie in a hectoring voice, then strode across the road.

'Is that the squire?' Bragg asked.

Ernie tittered. 'That's mister Big Boots.'

'Who is he?'

'George Ollerton. He's a foreigner, from the north somewhere . . . It were one of his carts that knocked down Anna Dyer.'

'Is that the little girl from Doddings?'

'Yes.'

'So he is a carrier, then?'

'Damned nearly the only carrier,' Ernie said peevishly. 'He won't let his drivers take me with them. Says it makes them waste time.'

'He is not an easy-going man, then?'

'Not him!' Ernie spat emphatically into the dust. 'He sacked Dick Tyson, because he got back ten minutes later than he reckoned he should have done, and couldn't take out another load that day. After the harvest, Dick'll be sittin' on the wall by me, and that won't fill his kids' bellies.'

'Was the little girl badly hurt?' asked Bragg.

'She's not come round since, and that's four days now . . . Big Boots is keepin' quiet at the moment.'

'Was he to blame, then?'

'Some would say so. I saw it all, sittin' here. One of his carts was bringin' a load of coal, from Poole docks to Tolpuddle. It was halfway down the hill there, when a bunch of kids ran out of a field gate into the road, right in front of the horses. They were startled and pulled across; the cart overturned and the little maid got a knock on the head. One of the horses had to be put away as well.'

'Do the village people say that it was Ollerton's fault?'

'Some do, and some don't. Alf Dyer says that it wouldn't have happened if there'd been two men on the cart. That way one of them could have held the brake on, instead of trustin' to the horses to hold it back.'

'And yet I can see Ollerton's point,' said Bragg. 'It is not much of a hill, and it's the only one between Poole docks and Bere Regis. Two big horses would be able to control that load in the ordinary way.'

'That's not what Ted Sharman is sayin'!' Ernie gave a malicious grin and, slipping off the wall, began to shuffle across the road again.

Bragg started to walk along West Street, the main axis of the village. Then, on a whim, he turned down Church Lane—little more than an entry leading to the parish church. For once, the tower seemed to have all its pinnacles. As far back as he could remember, it had been missing one or other of them. Come to think of it, in one of his sister's letters there had been mention that this church had been closed for restoration. That generally meant ruination, or so some people would say . . . A young woman emerged from the side gate of a large house on the left. She was slim and tall. He raised his hat to her and received a pleasant smile in return . . . He had had his doubts about this trip. Indeed, he would not have come, if the surgeon had not virtually compelled him to. But now he began to feel that he might enjoy it. He would be able to relax in the slower pace of life, gormandise on the good food and drink. Beyond that, he would be able to rediscover his roots. He was country born and bred, after all. Perhaps he would be able to slough off the thick skin of cynicism and detachment that his years in London had given him.

He opened the iron gate and passed into the churchyard. A line of clipped cylindrical yews stood sentinel over the rows of lichen-covered headstones. Behind were more recent graves, some with elaborate marble monuments, incongruous and jarring. Living in London, Bragg had become accustomed to churchyards that had been turned into public open spaces, their gravestones removed or propped against the walls. This was a real living church-yard, not a secularized promenading area. Over there, were a couple of low mounds, with fading flowers still on them . . . It must be comforting to know that you were going to rest here, in the shadow of this ancient church, among people who had known you, instead of an anonymous public cemetery out in Essex.

'You must be Sergeant Bragg, from London.'

A tall, gangling man of around forty, in clerical garb, was advancing towards him hand outstretched.

'That's right, sir.'

'I am Francis Ryder, the vicar here. We have all been looking forward to your visit. You are something of a celebrity, you know, after that counterfeiting case last year. You quite put Bere Regis on the map!'

'But I was born in Turner's Puddle, not here.'

'Ah, but you went to school here, so you are at least an honorary Bere Regian, if that is the correct possessive form.'

Bragg smiled. 'That is true enough. I used to bring my

school penny, tied in the corner of my handkerchief, every Monday morning.'

The vicar looked solemn. 'Thank goodness that those days have gone forever,' he said.

'I don't know. The children might not agree with you. If you had not got your penny, they would not let you in. So young tearaways, like me and Ted Sharman, could be turned away and have something to spend into the bargain!'

'I trust that you received due parental chastisement!'

'Oh, we did. I expect that that was why my father made me stay on till I was eleven, instead of leaving at eight like a lot of them. I don't know that it did me much good, though.'

'I fear that a great number of parents in the parish would echo that sentiment,' the vicar said sadly.

'It's not that I am against education. One of my constables has a Cambridge degree, believe it or not. I can see that his education has sharpened his brain far beyond my capacity. And I don't doubt that he gets a deal of satisfaction out of things like art galleries and music, that are a closed book to me. But then, he has always had plenty of money to indulge his fancies.'

'One of which is, presumably, working as a constable.'

'That's right. But while there are so few openings for children from the country, I cannot see a fat lot of point in making them stay at school.'

'I have heard that argument so often,' the vicar said ruefully. 'It astonishes me that the least privileged people in society are the most resistant to changes that would improve their lot.'

'You are not a countryman then, sir?'

'No. I was born in Bristol and went to school in London—St. Paul's. But I would never want to live in a town again.'

'So you are an honorary rustic?' Bragg said with a grin.

The vicar looked uncomfortable. 'I certainly love this area,' he said. 'I count myself fortunate to have been presented to this living. It is in the gift of the Master and Fellows of Balliol College, Oxford, where I was educated . . . I must admit that it was not so much my ecclesiastical promise, as their indulgence towards my antiquarian interests, that secured me their patronage.'

'Antiquarian?' Bragg repeated in surprise.

'I became fascinated with the ancient world when I went to help at an excavation in Norwich, during my first long vacation. It is an exceedingly enjoyable and, some would say, important activity. Unfortunately, in our Philistine society, it is the province of wealthy amateurs. As one comparatively unprovided with this world's goods, I must confess that entering the church was a necessary means to obtaining a modest participation in unearthing the secrets of our forebears.'

'Well, there is plenty of ancient history around here,' Bragg said cheerfully. 'I once went to Maiden Castle. Amazing, to think of all that earth being dug out and lugged up the hill, with not much more than their bare hands.'

'Ah, but you do not need to venture out of Bere Regis to find sites of archaeological interest,' the vicar said enthusiastically. 'It is a very ancient place of habitation. In human terms, the Romans were comparative newcomers to the area . . . I had not realised that you were interested in the subject. I am sure that you can spare a moment. I am just engaged in preparing a plan of the ancient pathways. I know it would interest you.'

The vicar set off at a shambling walk and Bragg, willing to humour him, followed. They crossed West Street and went up a steep driveway to a large stone house, overlooking the centre of the village. Then they passed through an open French window, into what Bragg assumed to be the vicar's study. A large mahogany bookcase took up most of one wall, while the centre of the room was occupied by a desk, littered with books. The vicar took the swivel chair and pulled a bundle of papers from a drawer. In the bottom of it was a litter of knapped flints, a piece of bronze and several fragments of pottery. Ryder unfolded a large piece of paper and smoothed it out on the desk.

'That red line is the parish boundary,' he said eagerly. 'Here is the Bere Stream and, to the south of it, the river Piddle. Now, the green lines are the ancient pathways, insofar as I have been able to determine them. You will see that they bear but little relationship to the roads as they exist today.'

'Why is that?' Bragg asked indulgently.

'To answer that, we have to visualise the area as it was three and a half thousand years ago. In those days, the valley floor would have been overgrown with trees, and was probably marshy also. For that reason, as you can see, the east to west road followed the crest of the chalk downland, by Woodbury Hill, the camp of the ancient Britons on top of the hill.'

'When would that have been constructed?'

'I suppose five hundred years before the birth of Our Lord . . . There is one section of the north to south trackway that I have not yet established. Would you like to walk it with me?' the vicar asked with a boyish smile.

'Why not? The doctor said I must have plenty of exercise and good food. It sounds as if you can supply half of the prescription.'

'Good, good! Shall we say some time next week?'

That evening, after supper, Ted and Bragg were left together in the parlour, while the womenfolk were making raspberry jam. Bragg engaged in reminiscences that failed to raise an answering spark in his cousin; yet Ted was too preoccupied to make conversation himself. Bragg was about to ask if he would prefer him to go back to London, when Ted looked across challengingly.

'I supposed that you have noticed the state of the business,' he said.

Bragg was caught unprepared. 'I realised that it couldn't be going too well,' he mumbled.

'I'm near finished, that's what,' Ted exclaimed angrily. 'And it is not for want of hard work.'

'I'm sure.'

'Ever since that bastard Ollerton set up, it has been on the slide. Why, I don't know.'

'I saw him up in the village,' Bragg said. 'He looks a rather disagreeable man.'

'He is that—and he's from Yorkshire. By rights, he should have fallen flat on his face. But he didn't.'

'Perhaps he has the capital to ride out the hard times.'

'Capital!' Ted sneered. 'When he came down here, he had a pregnant wife and hardly a chair to sit on . . . I grant you that he worked every daylight hour, all that spring and summer; but he was only labouring on the farms. They said that he was trying to get a job at Roke Farm as a horseman. Then, all of a sudden, he buys himself a horse and cart, and sets himself up as a carrier.'

"How long ago is this?'

'Fourteen or fifteen years ago.'

'And, in that time he has built up a sizeable business?'

'He has six men working for him—and he still does some trips himself . . . I'm buggered if I know how he's done it.'

'Why don't you sell the big van? It doesn't seem a lot of use, in the circumstances.'

'Who would buy it?' asked Ted irritably. 'It needs four new wheels, for a start, and the left mainside is rotten . . . The only buyer would be that sod Ollerton. I would be that much nearer bankruptcy then.'

'I'm sorry, Ted. I had not the least idea of this. If there is anything I can do . . .'

'Do you think I haven't tried everything?' Ted burst out. 'I tell you I cannot explain it. I had to let Peter go. His mother kicked up a fuss about that, but the business could not support us all, once Robert had got wed. At the moment, it is not even keeping me and him.'

'I am not saying that you haven't done everything you can,' Bragg said carefully. 'But there must be a reason, even if we cannot see it.'

Ted visibly fought to control his anger. 'You know full well, Joe, that there is not a lot of trade coming from the village itself. Bere Regis is just handily placed between Poole and Dorchester, Wimborne and Wareham. So we have been able to pick up a load in one, and take it to another, more cheaply than a carrier based in any of them.'

'I have done plenty of trips from Turner's Puddle, for my dad, in the old days.'

'Right. So you know that the most profitable business is taking coal from Poole docks to the merchants in the towns . . . Ten years ago, every coal importer switched to Ollerton—one after another. I don't move a single lump of coal now. The same happened with timber. If it wasn't for Baker & Fox, nobody in the timber trade would be using me, either. Why? From what I hear, Ollerton is not undercutting my prices—at least, he wasn't when the business went over to him.'

'You have tried to get the trade back, I suppose?' Bragg asked quietly.

'Of course I bloody have! I've licked arses till I could spew, but it's always the same tale. "We are quite satisfied with our present arrangements, thank you, Mr Sharman." I could shoot the Yorkshire bastard!'

'How long can you keep the business going?'

'I am about at the end of my tether. The buildings are mortgaged—I did that three years ago, stupid sod that I am. I might have been able to start it up as a brewery again. But the bank would never agree to that. If I don't pay the interest at the end of the year, and I cannot see how I shall, they will turn me out. You can understand how desperate I am.'

'I have a bit of money put by . . .' Bragg began.

'Keep your money! You would only be throwing it away, lending it to me!' Ted jumped to his feet, and stamped angrily out of the room.

CHAPTER ———————
——————— TWO

Bragg got up late next morning and, by the time he went
downstairs, Ted and Robert had gone out. Emma chatted
brightly as she bustled about cooking his ham and eggs and
brewing a huge pot of tea. As he ate, she kept asking him
if he remembered so-and-so; then, whether he did or not,
she would launch into an account of their whole history.
Half-listening, Bragg realised that he did not know all that
much about Emma herself. He had been in London when
Ted took up with her. He had not long been in the police. He
was infatuated with the great city, puffed up with the
importance of his new job, scornful of his village past. His
wife had been four months pregnant when they heard that
Ted was going steady. Next thing, he and Emma were
married and a child on the way. Well, it was the way of
things in the country, and only to be expected with Emma's
warm nature . . . It was odd to think that his own son
would have been the same age as Robert, if he had lived. It
was something he no longer thought about. He had put all
that behind him, concentrating on his work, avoiding all but

31

superficial relationships, living on the surface—for twenty years. Staying for a while in Dorset would not only be a pleasant, nostalgic holiday; it might open emotional wounds that he thought were long healed.

He escaped from Emma's prattle and walked up to the village. As he approached the cross-roads, Ernie began shuffling across the street.

'Where's your missus?' he asked sharply, hoisting himself on to the wall.

It was almost as if Bragg had projected his train of thought to the cripple. Yet, in a village, everybody knew everything about everyone—or wanted to. If you tried to keep a bit of privacy, you were condemned as standoffish. He would have to endure a good bit of prying and questioning, in the days to come. Whatever he told Ernie would be round the village in a twinkling, so he might as well go along with it.

'She died in childbirth,' he said evenly.

'Oh.' There was no trace of sympathy in Ernie's voice. It was just a flat acknowledgement of a common happening.

'Can I get you a beer?' Bragg asked.

A sly smile crossed Ernie's face. 'Aye, you can!'

Bragg brought the foaming glasses to the wall and sat beside Ernie, the sun warm on their backs.

'They say Londoners live under the ground,' Ernie said abruptly.

'Some do,' Bragg conceded gravely. 'It's only the very poor, but quite a lot of them live in basements.'

'Half a dozen to a room.'

'It does happen, in the worst areas.'

'And the houses are like rows of rabbit hutches.'

Bragg smiled. 'When a couple of million people all crowd into the same place, it makes land dear.'

'How big is London, then?'

Bragg sought for a meaningful standard of comparison. 'It would easily cover the area from here to Dorchester, and south to the coast.'

It was clearly beyond Ernie's comprehension. He spat in the dust. 'I'll stay here,' he said.

'Ernie!' The angry figure of Ollerton came striding across the road. 'Have you seen Harry Green?'

'Not this mornin'.'

'Bloody layabout!' Ollerton tapped his switch against his leggings with irritation, then turned to Bragg.

'You'll be the policeman from London that everybody is making a fuss about,' he said.

'I don't know about the fuss, but I am certainly in the London police,' Bragg replied mildly.

'Well, we could do with a few more police around here. They are a thieving lot of buggers in Bere Regis.' He turned abruptly and strode off.

'Nice chap, our George,' Ernie said caustically.

Ollerton was under a handicap from the start, Bragg thought. The accent of the villagers was relaxed, unemphatic, almost slovenly. His speech stressed every syllable, the vowels pure and unslurred. Everything he said would sound dogmatic and aggressive to the locals . . . On top of that, he seemed a particularly unpleasant person. It was hard to understand how he could wrest business from a native like Ted Sharman.

Ernie twisted round and looked along South Street. A cart was coming down Rye Hill, towards the village.

'That'll be Robert,' said Ernie. 'I wonder if he will be going on.'

He watched the cart intently, as it crossed the bridge and approached the Old Brewery. Robert waved when he saw them, then brought the horse to a halt on the roadway. He jumped down and sauntered into the yard.

'He's going on, he's going on,' Ernie chanted gleefully.

'Will you be going with him, for the ride?'

'Oh, yes. He's not like Big Boots.'

Nevertheless, Ernie kept peering anxiously over his shoulder, until he saw Robert emerge again and climb up on to the cart. Then he slipped off the wall and leaned against it, waiting. After a few moments, Robert pulled up in front of them.

'Want to come to Milborne St Andrew, Ernie?' he asked.

'Aye, I do!' With a triumphant grin at Bragg, the cripple shuffled over to the cart and was hauled up on to the box.

'Sorry, Uncle Joe,' Robert called. 'There isn't room for you, too.'

Bragg laughed. 'Don't worry, I know Milborne well enough. I might have come with you if you'd been going to Poole. I have not been there for twenty-five years. I should think it has changed a deal.'

'All right. See you later.' Robert shook the reins and the cart rumbled off.

Bragg sat on the wall a little longer, then decided to walk the length of West Street to the other end of the village. It was a glorious day, the heat of the sun tempered by a gentle breeze from the south-east. A perfect day for harvesting; the cut corn would be drying in the stooks a treat. They had nearly finished reaping the field of oats on Woodbury Hill and there was plenty on the valley bottom ready for cutting . . . They talked, in books, about the idyllic way of life in the country, Bragg thought sardonically. People like that had no conception of the endless toil that made up these people's lives. Milking morning and night, caring for the horses, feeding the hens and geese, driving the sheep to fresh ground; ploughing, harrowing, sowing; never a remission from the endless labour. Hay-time and harvest were extra back-breaking burdens, not the bucolic festivals that writers and painters made them out to be. And what could such folk look forward to, when their working days were over? Living with their children, in everybody's way; or, if they were lucky, allowed to stay on in a damp cob cottage, with a leaky thatch . . . He looked up. Dear God! What had happened to old Dicky Smith's place? It used to have a beautifully rounded thatch, with a scalloped decoration at the ridge. Now, the walls had been raised a couple of feet, and it was roofed with corrugated iron! Bere Regis could not have been counted a pretty place, at the best of times; but corrugated iron! As he walked along, Bragg saw several more cottages that had been treated in the same way. Grudgingly, he admitted that they would be more weather-proof, that the occupiers had a right to be cosy; but surely there was enough ugliness about, without people's houses looking like cow-sheds? He went on grumpily to the edge of the village and stood for a while, looking at West Mill straddling the stream, its wheel still. Before long, they would be grinding the new season's corn; carrying the white sacks of flour into the towns, to sustain their scurrying life. Bragg mentally kicked himself for being as mawkish as any poet. Nobody scurried in the towns around here; their pace of life was placid, compared to London. They were merely the focus of the country life around them, operating to the same rhythms . . . Blast it! If he didn't stop philosophising and romanticising, he was going to spoil his holiday. He decided to walk back again and, as he did so, came up with a man who was emerging from the lane to Shitterton. He was around fifty-five years old and was dressed in a Norfolk jacket and knickerbockers, with heavy stockings and stout shoes. A springer spaniel was snuffling in the hedgerow in front of him. In the crook of his arm a shotgun drooped. The man at first hesitated, then decided that a meeting was inevitable.

'Good morning,' he said, in a dry, cultured voice. 'You must be Bragg.'

'That's right, sir,' said Bragg genially. 'And you?'

'Er . . . I am Charles Jerrard, from Shitterton Manor.'

'Ah, the squire.'

'I suppose so . . . Yes.' There was a moment's silence, then: 'They say that you were educated in the village, Bragg. I suppose that I ought to remember you. I would have been back home from school by then.'

'People shouldn't think of me as a Bere Regis man. I lived in Turner's Puddle till I was fourteen.'

For the first time Jerrard turned his head to look directly at Bragg. Of slight physique, he had cool, grey eyes and pepper-and-salt hair. With his longish nose and little moustache, he seemed to Bragg rather nondescript for a big landowner.

'Did you go to work in London at that age?' he asked.

'No, no!' I was in a shipping office in Weymouth, until I was eighteen.'

'Ah, I see.'

Again the conversation languished. Bragg glanced at the fine twelve-bore shotgun the squire was carrying, its stock glowing in the sun like a newly picked chestnut. It was a pity that they had to get knocked about; but then, they were made to be used.

'Are you going shooting?' he asked.

'Er . . . No, not really. I am taking the dog for a walk . . . or he is taking me, I am not sure which.' He managed a brief smile at the laboured pleasantry. 'I generally bring the gun. I sometimes get a pot-shot at a pigeon or a rabbit . . . Well, I am turning off here. Good day.'

He swung across the street and hurried up Butt Lane. Bragg had the feeling that the effort of conversation had become insupportable to him. He smiled to himself and wandered back to the Old Brewery at a leisurely place. When he walked into the kitchen, there was a slim seventeen-year-old girl perched on the end of the table. She was carefully dressed and her hair was pinned up in an adult style that made her look saucy.

'Hello, Uncle Joe,' she said with a bright smile.

'And how is my favourite goddaughter?' Bragg glanced across at Emma and she pursed her lips chidingly.

'I am all right. How are you?'

'Your mother is stuffing me with food, and I do nothing but stroll round the village, so I should be improving.'

'Show me where you was hurt,' Rose said eagerly.

'You bloodthirsty little baggage!'

'Go on!'

Bragg took off his coat and pushed up the sleeve of his shirt. Rose drew in her breath at the sight of the puckered red scar on his arm.

'Ooh!' she cried sympathetically. 'Did it hurt?'

'Not all that much, when it happened. But I went through it, all right, when I was getting better. You see this artery?'

He pointed to a knotted swelling under the skin. 'It was so damaged, that they had to tie off both sides of the cut.'

'Oh, Uncle Joe!' Rose shuddered. 'But you'll be all right?'

'Oh, yes. As long as I keep squeezing my little ball, I shall get back to normal again . . . And what about you? I hear you are working at Shitterton Manor.'

'I'm second parlourmaid, now,' Rose said proudly.

'Do you like it?'

' 'Course I do.' She tossed her head. 'I get five shillings a week, and all my keep.'

'That is very good. And what about the work?'

'It's all right. Mrs Jerrard is a bit of a tartar, mind. She thinks nothing of going down the banisters with a white handkerchief, after you've dusted them. But if you do your work properly, she's not bad. I wouldn't want to be her lady's maid, though, especially when there is a dinner party on.'

'I have just met the squire in the village,' Bragg remarked.

Rose laughed. 'Poor old Charlie!'

'Rose!' her mother cried, in a shocked voice. 'You will get the sack if anyone hears you talking disrespectful, like that. You know how things get back in this village.'

'That's what we all call him,' Rose said airily. 'She leads him a dog's life; always nagging at him and complaining. He's out most of the day to get away from her; but she makes up for it at night.'

'Do they quarrel, then?' Bragg asked innocently.

'He hasn't got the spirit to quarrel properly,' Rose replied contemptuously. 'She just goes on at him and, if you ask me, he tries not to listen.'

'What do they quarrel about?'

'Oh, if he won't take her to London for a new dress, if she can't have her friends to dinner, if she has to have his friends for dinner, if one of the tenants is behind with his rent; most often it is when she thinks that someone has been rude to her . . . She's short of some children, that's what my da says.'

'Rose! You'll get us into trouble,' her mother exclaimed.

Rose slipped off the table. 'Well, I expect that the butcher will have finished boning the joint, so I'd better be off. We have some unexpected visitors for dinner. I'll see you again, Uncle Joe.'

She crossed over and kissed him dutifully on the cheek, then skipped out into the yard.

'I told you that she was la-di-da, didn't I?' Emma remarked ruefully.

'Get away with you! It is just high spirits. She's a beautiful young woman. You ought to be proud of her.'

'Oh, I am, but I mustn't let her know it!'

That evening, Ted seemed particularly morose and touchy, so, after supper, Bragg decided to go to the Drax Arms for a drink. This pub was older than the Royal Oak, with low ceilings and heavy oak beams. He stood at the bar with his pint. There was a fair crowd of customers but, though some of them nodded to him, no one engaged him in conversation. Surely, there must be someone here who had been at school with him? He searched each new face for some spark of recognition, but was disappointed. It was not that he wanted congratulation, or flattery. This local hero business seemed to exist only in the minds of the nobs. But it would be pleasurable to meet somebody with whom he could talk over old times. He asked the barman about a couple of people whose names he could recall, but he did not seem even to know of them. It must be because he was a policeman, Bragg thought. You could never shake it off. Even when you were a hundred miles from your patch, you were still a policeman first and a human being a long way second. Disappointed, he drained his glass and walked back home.

Next morning, Bragg stayed in bed till nearly ten o'clock. It was not that he felt unwell. On the contrary, he felt his vigour increasing every day. But the more energetic he felt, the more the emptiness of the day would weigh on him. He really must take to riding out with Robert, on his deliveries. He would be more congenial company than Ted at the moment. Of course, that would mean that Ernie would be unable to go. Bragg was irritated at his feeling of guilt. Blast it! Everything was so ossified in the country; they were so jealous of their relationships. Well, Ernie would have to give way for a week or two, that was all.

Over breakfast, Emma burbled away in her usual happy vein, heedless of his monosyllabic replies. After it, he offered to wash up—but that was Ada's job. So he went into the yard, thoroughly out of sorts with himself. Looking across, he could see the sun shining down on the east end of the church. He could fill an hour or so by looking round it. He called through the kitchen doorway that he would have a bite of lunch at the pub, then walked slowly up to the Cross. For once, Ernie was nowhere to be seen. Probably he was out with Ted or Robert. He went past the Royal Oak and turned down Church Lane. There was no comely young woman, this time, to raise his hat to; but nor was the vicar in sight. Bragg strolled along between the lines of yews and went into the porch. Over the arch were the enormous hooks used for pulling down burning thatches. He pushed open the church door, wondering if they still kept the old fire-pump under the gallery, at the back of the church. Then he checked in amazement. The west gallery was gone! . . . So were the old box pews. And he could swear that the organ had been in a different place. His visits to the church had been limited to three school services each year, but he could remember the interior well enough. He had spent most of the time staring around him, while the parson droned on. He walked to the back of the church and parted the curtains at the tower arch. Yes, there it was! Looking more decrepit than ever. It was pitifully inadequate for its task, no more than a hand-pump on a barrow. But they would never get round to finding the money for something more modern . . . Bragg smiled. One summer holiday, when they were bored, he and Ted had tied old Mrs Shave's goat between the handles and given it a whack. It had got halfway down West Street, before the twine broke and the terrified goat got free! They should have got a new fire-engine then, instead of mending the old one.

He turned and strolled up the aisle. At least they had not altered the roof of the nave. Indeed, the magnificent old timbers looked more impressive than he remembered. The twelve apostles had had their paint touched up as well. In his childhood, they had always seemed to lean grimly over the congregation, ready to smite an unruly pupil. Now it was possible to identify one or two of them. That one, with the key, must be St Peter; while the end one on the other side, clutching his money-bag, must be Judas Iscariot. Odd, that old Cardinal Morton should have wanted to honour him in his new roof. But he must have been content with the result; his chubby pink face still looked down serenely, from one of the bosses.

'You are admiring the roof, I see.'

'Good morning, vicar. I must say that the restoration has transformed the church.'

The vicar sighed. 'Yes, and yet there is still so much to do.' Then he brightened. 'I do not suppose that you could blow the organ for me, could you? I like to keep in practise, but every able-bodied person seems to be involved with the harvest, at the moment.'

'Well . . . I suppose I could.'

'Good! Through the little curtain, there . . . You will see the handle.'

Bragg smiled wryly at the ability of everybody connected with the church to put on people—and their willingness to be exploited.

'Be careful!' the vicar called after him. 'The floor is rotten, round there.'

Bragg stepped cautiously into the little alcove. A brace had been inserted between the wall and the organ case, apparently to keep it upright. Bragg moved a loose piece of floor-board with his toe and revealed a gaping hole. Be careful, indeed!

'Ready?' called the vicar.

A handle projected from the organ case; obviously you just moved it up and down in the slot. 'Yes,' Bragg replied and, squatting on the narrow seat, began to pump. The bellows sucked and sighed like a sleeping animal, and the vicar began to play. As Bragg pumped, a little lead weight slid down the panelling, beside him. When he stopped pumping, it would crawl up again. If he pumped too hard, it would stop its descent and there would be the hiss of excess air escaping. The first time this happened, Bragg thought something had gone wrong. He stopped pumping, till the organ squealed like a strangled bagpipe and died. He quickly got up pressure again and the vicar went on with his piece. Whatever was it, anyway? It sounded damned dry. There wasn't a proper tune to it; the same bit was repeated over and over again, first high then low, twisting round each other like puppies in a basket. It was not Bragg's idea of music. Marie Lloyd wouldn't be able to make much of that! He tried pumping with his left arm and was gratified to feel the pull of the muscles again. But after a time, the wound began to ache and he resumed with his right. One thing was certain, he was not going to be bamboozled into doing this again . . . The vicar was letting rip now, making a real old racket. A row of grey wooden pipes at his elbow began to groan; the music slowed perceptibly and ended in a grand chord. To Bragg's ear, that was the best part of the whole performance. He could hear it, still echoing round the church, long after the organ had ceased to sound. Then there was a thud, as the lid came down over the keyboard. Bragg abandoned his position and emerged into the aisle.

'Thank you, Mr Bragg, I am most grateful.' The vicar smiled boyishly. 'I think that Bach is the supreme composer, don't you?'

'I don't think that I have ever heard him before.'

'You are not a churchgoer, then?'

'I can't say that I am.'

'We will have to change that while you are here! Why not come to tea sometime . . . ? I will confer with my wife.'

'I would like that,' Bragg replied insincerely. 'Well, I must be off. I am late for my lunch already.' He consulted his battered watch and hurried away, before he got trapped into any more good works.

Turning out of the porch, he came face to face with the nice young woman, and someone he took to be her mother. He half put his hat on, so that he could doff it to them, then compromised by holding it to his chest.

'Good afternoon, ladies,' he said affably.

'Good afternoon, Mr Bragg,' the mother said in a commanding contralto voice. She was a head shorter than her daughter and of stocky build. Her clothes looked expensive, but she might as well have saved her money, Bragg thought. She still looked like an ill-packed parcel. Perhaps she felt that, too, for she had put string after string of beads around her neck—jet, moonstone, turquoise, amber.

'My name is Amy Hildred,' she went on. 'And this is my daughter, Fanny.'

Bragg courteously pressed the gloved hand of each.

'It is a change to have a new face in the village,' Amy said. 'Particularly a man who had done something in life.'

'I have done little enough, ma'am,' Bragg protested.

'Nonsense! That is not what the *Star* said. If you ask me, what you did was quite exceptional.'

'It was no more than my duty.'

'And how many men do their duty, nowadays?' she asked sharply. 'We have a vicar here, who is more interested in digging holes in the ground than ministering to his flock. And his sermons are about as stimulating as a heap of wet washing . . . We live at The Retreat. You must come to tea.'

'Thank you, ma'am.'

Amy turned away, but Fanny seemed disposed to linger. She was older than Bragg had thought: about thirty-six. Her face was pleasant, without being pretty, her complexion fresh and clear.

'We are putting some roses on papa's grave,' she said, then turned her head to listen.

Bragg could hear heavy footfalls, and a voice shouting: 'Help! Police!'

With a muttered: 'Excuse me,' he dashed to the end of the lane and intercepted a panting youth.

'What is the matter?' he demanded.

'George Ollerton's gone and shot hisself!'

'Where?'

'By the stile into the seven-acre field.'

'Where is that?'

'On the path to Doddings.'

'Right. I'll go down there. You bring PC Bugby.'

The lad stumbled off, while Bragg pounded round the corner and down South Street. He hopped over the stile by the bridge and ran down the footpath, his arm throbbing. This field was a meadow, but over the hedge he could see the ripple of oats. He raced up to the stile and clambered over. A man and a boy were standing together, on the bank of the stream; in the distance was a flutter of black. On the ground, some six feet into the cornfield, was Ollerton's body. He was crumpled up, on his left side. A double-barrelled shotgun was lying against his hip, his right hand clutching the barrels, above the fore-end of the stock. There was a shocking wound in his right temple. It seemed as if that side of his face had been blown in.

'Who found him?' Bragg asked.

The man looked mistrustfully at him. 'I did,' he said.

'And what is your name?'

'Alf Dyer . . . I sent my lad for Bugby.'

'Did you see what happened?'

'No. I heard the shot from up the field. I came and found him like this.'

'Have you touched anything?' Bragg asked.

'No, we haven't,' Dyer said emphatically.

'Who was that going down the path?'

'Old Tabby Gosney.'

'Did she see anything?'

'She only came up after we'd found him.'

Bragg tried to remember the shooting cases that he had been involved in. Professor Burney, the chief police surgeon to the City of London, was something of an authority on gunshot wounds. He revelled in pointing out the features of a case that interested him, dwelling ghoulishly on the factors that influenced his judgement. Bragg tried to clear his mind of his instinctive revulsion and examine the body objectively. It certainly looked to be in a natural enough posture, given a violent death. The wound itself was in the middle of the right side of the head, between the ear and the eye. The neck and forehead were pock-marked with shot, also. There had not been a lot of bleeding, for such a horrific wound. But Ollerton would have died immediately. Bragg peered at the skin of the face. He could see no sign of scorching, or powder traces. He was still crouched over the body, when he heard voices behind him.

'And what might you be doing?'

Bragg straightened up to find a uniformed constable, helmet in hand, glaring at him from the stile.

'Ah. Constable Bugby, isn't it?' he said in a friendly voice. 'I'm Bragg.'

'I know full well who you are, sir.'

'I thought I would take a look.'

'So I see.'

'I am a police sergeant, as you no doubt know.'

'Not in this force, you're not . . . sir,' Bugby said pugnaciously.

He climbed down from the stile and examined the body perfunctorily.

'Did you find him?' he demanded of Dyer.

'Yes.'

'Then I shall want a statement from you.' He took hold of the gun and opened the action. 'Silly sod,' he remarked, removing the cartridges. 'He would go around with the safety-catch off. It was bound to happen sometime.'

He waved at some men who had appeared with a hurdle.

'Leave it on that side,' he called, 'and we will lift him over.'

'Surely you are going to wait for the police surgeon?' Bragg asked, aghast.

Bugby swung round. 'You can't leave bodies lying around the parish,' he said didactically. 'Our police surgeon lives in Winterborne Kingston. It might be tomorrow before he can get here. You are among the country clodhoppers now, and you would best help by keeping from under my feet . . . sir.'

He motioned Dyer to take the shoulders, and they lugged Ollerton's body over the stile. They deposited it on the hurdle and the men carried it towards the village. Bragg decided to keep out of the constable's way by having another look at the scene of death.

CHAPTER ———————

——————— THREE

The death of Ollerton seemed to have stunned the village.
For the rest of that Thursday, and the following day, people
were subdued—even ordering their groceries in a hushed
voice. There was none of the morbid excitement often
generated by another's misfortune. Bragg encountered few
signs of genuine sorrow; but many people had seen the body
as it was carried to the mortuary behind the police station,
and everyone seemed shocked by the terrible manner of his
death. Out of respect, people picked their way round the
patch of pavement that Mrs Ollerton scrubbed every day in
front of her door; the Friday whist drive in the village hall
was poorly attended. By Saturday, however, the gloom was
lifting. When Bragg walked up to the Cross, in mid-
morning, he was joined by Ernie Toop, as usual.

'Bad do about George,' the cripple asserted.

'Yes.'

'There'll be some changes there.' His eyes were glinting
with private satisfaction.

'What will his widow do?' Bragg asked.

'They say she's goin' to carry on. They reckon that she's made Harry Green foreman.'

'Was he not the man Ollerton was calling a layabout, the other morning?'

'Oh, he'll work hard enough now. He will fancy his chances,' Ernie said with a prurient smirk. 'He's a widower; he'll be thinkin' he'll get his leg over, before long—though he'd better shut his eyes!'

'You are a revolting person,' Bragg said.

Ernie tittered gleefully. 'Why shouldn't he? It's a good business.'

'I suppose it would not be the first time it had happened.'

Ernie cocked his head. 'There are some as says it weren't an accident.'

'There always are,' Bragg replied non-committally.

'There are plenty of folk will be glad to see him out of the way.'

'That hardly means that they would kill him.'

'Ted Sharman, for one.' Ernie looked up at Bragg's face mischievously. 'He'll be looking to get some business back now.'

'Talk like that, and you will not get many more rides from Robert!'

'I don't care. Somebody will take me.'

'Well, I happen to know that Ted was out with a delivery at the time.'

Ernie's face fell. 'Perhaps the Old Crow did for him, then.'

'Tabitha Gosney?'

'They say she was down there. 'Twould be a brave man that would cross her.'

Bragg laughed. 'She could never overpower a man like Ollerton,' he said.

The twisted grin was gone from Ernie's face. 'Maybe she has other power,' he said in a low voice.

'Are you saying that she's a witch?' Bragg asked in astonishment.

Ernie's voice was harsh. 'I didn't say it—you did!' He

squirmed off the wall and shuffled across the road as fast as he could go.

Bragg strolled home pensively. Were there others in the village who shared his unease? Probably not. More likely, they were trying to extract the last drop of excitement from the death of someone who had been widely unpopular.

After lunch, Emma suggested that he should go to the cricket match. She said that, in the last few years, it had been one of the highlights of the summer. A team of local farmers and tradesmen played a team from the gentry round about. There was a beer tent, and tea was served in a marquee. Since Robert was not working and Ted was mucking out the stable, Bragg decided that he might as well fall in with the suggestion. He had watched the Weymouth club's matches, as a youth. It might be a pleasant way of passing an afternoon.

He strolled up North Street, past the squat cob cottages and, turning down a narrow entry, found himself in a large field. It was level and well grassed, with several tents round the roped-off cricket pitch. He was looking for the beer tent, when he heard a voice calling his name. He turned towards the pavilion and saw the young woman from Church Lane, beckoning to him . . . Fanny Hildred, that was it. She was sitting in a deckchair and gesturing to a vacant one beside her. Well, perhaps the beer could wait . . .

'Welcome to our annual tournament,' she called as he approached.

'I thought it was a nice friendly cricket match,' Bragg said with a smile.

'It always seems to me like a medieval tourney, with one champion hurling the ball, while another tries to hit it out of the ground.'

'I can see that you are a connoisseur of the game, Miss Hildred.'

'Not at all! This is the only game of cricket that I watch, but it is such fun.'

'Well, the weather could not be better. Who is going to win?'

'For the last six years the players have won . . . They call it the "Gentlemen v. Players" match, like the real one in London.'

'I see.'

'But this year they will not have poor Mr Ollerton on the team, so it could be a very even match. He was a stalwart batsman!'

'And which side do you support?' Bragg asked.

'Neither. I come because it is an occasion, and it relieves the tedium.'

'You are not over-enthralled with life in a Dorset village, then?'

'Now you are cross-examining me!' Fanny exclaimed with a teasing smile.

There was a tentative cough and the squire appeared in front of them.

'I was wondering, Bragg, if you er . . . would agree to play for the gentlemen. I am afraid that we have been let down and can only muster ten men.'

'But I don't know that I could,' Bragg protested. 'I have never played a real game of cricket in my life.'

'You must have knocked a ball about in your youth,' the squire persisted.

'Well, yes.'

'That is good enough. You will be the last man in, so, with any luck, you will not need to bat at all. We will find a quiet place for you, when we are fielding.'

Bragg hesitated. He hated making a fool of himself.

'Oh, do play, Mr Bragg,' Fanny said eagerly.

'I only have these clothes, though.'

'You need not worry.' The squire raised a thin smile. 'Most of the other side will be playing in black boots and braces.'

Though he was irked by the condescension in the squire's tone, Bragg could not ignore the challenging look on Fanny's face.

'Very well, then. So long as you realise that I am useless at it.'

'Good. We are fielding first, so I am afraid that I must drag you away from the charms of Miss Hildred.'

The squire's dry voice robbed the compliment of any grace, but Fanny responded with a warm smile.

'This is your fault, miss,' Bragg remarked, then he followed Jerrard to the pavilion. While he was hanging up his coat, a middle-aged man approached him.

'I am Dr Lys,' he said, holding out his hand. 'Your people asked me to keep an eye on your arm, if need be. Perhaps I ought to have a quick look.'

Bragg pushed up the sleeve of his shirt.

'Hmn . . . That is coming on nicely. I will just put a bandage round it, to support the muscles.'

He went to the back of the room and rummaged in a small Gladstone bag.

'You come prepared, then, doctor.'

'Oh yes. Like you people, we are always on duty . . . There, that should do the trick. Be careful not to let the ball hit the wound, or it will make you sing!'

Bragg followed Lys on to the field, where the squire was busy marshalling his forces. The gentlemen's team was somewhat long in the tooth, Bragg thought, and distinctly unathletic. With the exception of one fair-haired young man, everyone was on the wrong side of thirty-five; and some of them were distinctly corpulent. Bragg snorted to himself; but for his illness, he would have looked as bad as any of them.

There was a scatter of applause as the opening batsmen came out. Bragg unfolded the piece of paper that had been thrust into his hand; it gave the names of the teams. These must be Freeman and Dancer. They were both youngish alert men, not big, but wiry. As Freeman took guard, Bragg was sent to field on the boundary behind the batsman. He smiled as he realised that the vicar was in a similar position of unimportance, at the opposite end of the field.

The bowling was opened by a red-faced auctioneer, named Savage. He tore up to the crease and sent the ball fizzing down the pitch. For the first over, Freeman was content to defend his wicket, and Savage took his sweater with a broad grin. The bowler at the other end was Medlycot, a solicitor living in the village. He was not much younger than Bragg, with a balding head and pallid face. He trundled up to the crease and bowled at no great pace, but straight at the wicket. Dancer merely played the first three balls back to him. The fourth he forced away towards the boundary, and they ran two. For Bragg the game was unexacting. Between the long walks to the other side of the ground, at the end of an over, he had little to do. The two batsmen accumulated runs steadily and the bowlers began to tire. Then Freeman misjudged a ball from Savage, and the fair young man took a diving catch at slip. The next batsman was Wilton, the blacksmith. He came to the wicket with his shirt sleeves rolled up his knotted arms, and stood with his bat raised. Savage, rejuvenated by his success, ran up to the crease and bowled one that squirted along the ground. It missed the stumps by inches. An 'Ooh!' ran round the ground, but Wilton just grinned. The next ball he swung at, and hit it out of the field. There was a pause, while it was retrieved by a small boy. Over. Again the long trek. Bragg bent down and picked a daisy. When had he done that last? So dainty and fresh . . . He heard a shout and saw the ball plummeting down towards him. He ran forwards and, as it bounced, got his boot to it. The batsman turned for a second run as he stopped and hurled the ball to the wicket-keeper. By the merest fluke, it hit the stumps while Wilton was out of his ground. There was some cheering from the boundary and Bragg could see Fanny clapping vigorously.

After that, the game went to sleep for Bragg. The slower bowlers came on, and most of the runs were scored by prods and pushes in the middle of the pitch. The lower-order batsmen were as lacking in technique as Bragg, and tended to lash out at every ball. They either scored runs or gave catches, so that, from forty for three wickets, the players team was all out for sixty-two runs. As Bragg trailed after the others towards the pavilion, he saw Fanny waving to him. Well, he had not disgraced her so far.

He went up the steps into the pavilion, and the fair-haired young man came over to him.

'I am Stephen Bennett,' he said. 'That was a splendid run-out. We badly needed his wicket. I wish I could throw like that.'

Bragg preened himself. 'It must be infectious,' he said. 'One of my constables is Jim Morton; he can hit a beer bottle at thirty yards.'

'Not *the* Jim Morton, of Kent and England?' Bennett asked, wide-eyed.

Bragg nodded.

'Pater! This gentleman is a colleague of Jim Morton.' Bennett beckoned to a man who had been fielding in the slips with him.

'Morton is in rare form, this season,' the newcomer remarked. 'By all accounts, his century in the Oval test, on Thursday, was a real cracker—better even than the one he scored at Lord's.'

'With one match drawn and one in our favour, do you think that we can win the series?' Stephen asked deferentially.

'We must have a good chance,' Bragg replied sagely. 'The last match is in Manchester; it is generally the weather that wins there.'

'Yes,' Stephen said. 'Well, I do hope so.'

'So, Morton is in the police force?' remarked the father. 'I thought there was something odd about him. He comes from a good family, though, does he not?'

'One of the best,' said Bragg expansively. 'Well, I think I'll have a cup of tea, before it is all gone.'

It was ironic, he thought, to be basking in Morton's reflected glory. He did nothing but complain when he took time off to play cricket.

A few minutes later, the players team took the field. Then Stephen's father and Fairhurst, the Congregational minister, went out to open the gentlemen's innings. Confident that he would not be called on to bat, Bragg put his coat on and went to sit with Fanny again.

'I think that you were being unduly modest,' she greeted him. 'You played splendidly!'

'Ah, well,' Bragg smiled. 'Some have gentility thrust upon them, as the MC at the Empire would say.'

Fanny looked intrigued for a moment, then gestured towards the field. 'This is what I meant, about a tournament,' she said.

A tall, well-built young man, with bushy hair and a black beard was approaching the crease. He was taking a run that was longer than the pitch itself. As his arm swept over, the ball rocketed into the ground and bounced head high.

'That is Dick Cleall, the carpenter.'

'I think I will go home,' Bragg said jocularly.

'Oh, no! You are the hero of the hour.'

'I have used up whatever quota of heroism I ever had.'

The bowler at the other end was not a great deal slower than Cleall. Fortunately for the gentlemen, however, the wicket-keeper was far from agile, and several deliveries went through to the boundary, for byes. The first wicket fell when the Congregational minister misjudged the pitch of a ball, and Dancer snapped up a catch at gully.

'This is Dr Lys coming out,' Fanny said. 'He always bats early in the innings, so that he can get away.'

'What happens if the gentlemen bat first, miss?'

'They never do. We have a lively sense of what is important in Bere Regis, sergeant.'

'Do you know, you are the first person who has called me that.'

'Sergeant? . . . Do you mind? I would have thought that it was something to be proud of.'

'Oh, I am. I suppose that I am feeling a bit prickly, because PC Bugby kept me at arm's length over the Ollerton affair.'

'No doubt he feels overshadowed while you are here. Poor Bugby.'

The bowlers had noticeably reduced their speed when

bowling to Dr Lys; but, even so, it was not long before he hit a simple catch to mid-off. He walked in to the pavilion with bat raised, smiling broadly.

'Seventeen for two,' said Bragg. 'They should manage it nicely.'

The squire walked to the wicket, amid polite applause.

'He seems a very shy sort of man, for someone so important,' Bragg remarked.

'I suppose he is rather diffident,' Fanny said thoughtfully. 'But I think that he is respected.'

'You do not know the Jerrards well, then?'

'No,' she said shortly, then turned her attention back to the cricket as a gasp of dismay went round the ground.

'Dancer is the Jerrards' coachman. He probably felt it politic to drop that catch from his employer!'

Fate was not to be trifled with, however. Jerrard played over the next ball, and was bowled. Twenty for three wickets. Stephen Bennett joined his father at the wicket, and together they began to push the score along with drives and deflections.

'A pleasant young man, that,' Bragg remarked. 'And a good cricketer by the looks of him.'

'He is Charles Jerrard's nephew. Both he and his father went to the same school. I suspect that they set more store on sport, there, than on academic work.'

'Are you against sport, then?'

'By no means. I bicycle and play croquet and tennis myself. Do you play tennis, by any chance, Mr Bragg?'

'I am afraid not, miss. In the normal course, I take as little exercise as I can . . . and I think my luck is going to hold, this afternoon.'

He had no sooner spoken, however, when George Bennett's off stump went cartwheeling out of the ground. Thirty for four.

'This is Mr Penfold coming in,' said Fanny. 'He is a surveyor from Dorchester.'

'They are not all locals, then?' Bragg remarked.

'Oh, no. The gentry are thin on the ground here.'

Was there a tart edge to her tone? Bragg wondered. If there was, she was still smiling happily enough.

Penfold survived two balls from a spin bowler, then hit the next on to his boot and was caught at short leg. Savage was the next batsman. He was evidently out of the same mold as the blacksmith. He hit out wildly at every ball and was spectacularly caught on the boundary, for seven. Dear God! Bragg thought. If these people did not concentrate better, he was going to find himself in the firing line!

The schoolmaster walked to the wicket and took guard in an assured manner. He flicked away a few loose pieces of earth and settled to receive his first ball. Bragg's heart leapt, as it snicked the edge of his bat and almost carried to Dancer. It was the last ball of the over, however. Stephen Bennett scored eight from the next, and the score was looking healthy again. The schoolmaster hit the first ball of the next over for a straight six but was out, three balls later, trying to repeat the stroke. Fifty-two for seven.

'I think that you will be called on to don your armour,' Fanny said with a smile. 'The vicar is scarcely a doughty warrior.'

'I can hardly bind your glove to my helm.' Bragg said, as he got to his feet. 'But thank you for sharing the afternoon with me, I enjoyed it.'

He went to the pavilion, where someone helped him to strap on a pair of pads and found him a bat. He swung it several times, to get the feel of it. His arm was all right, so long as he didn't overdo it; but when he really lashed out, pain jabbed in the wound. He went out and sat on the steps, looking sardonically at the incongruous white pads on the dark grey check of his best trousers. What on earth had come over him, to get into this kind of scrape? Then he noticed the vicar, lounging on the pavilion railing.

'I thought you were batting,' he said.

'Alas, no! I fear that Mr Cleall got under my guard after three balls. Mr Fairhurst has to uphold the honour of the cloth, when it comes to playing cricket.'

'But that means there is only me left!'

'True. But young Stephen Bennett is scoring very confidently, and Mr Medlycot is a man of great experience in these campaigns.'

'So you think it is a war, too?'

'Your metaphor could certainly apply to some of the matches in recent years. This one has been comparatively temperate . . . At least so far.'

There was a sudden shout. Medlycot stood stupefied, the wicket shattered. Fifty-six for nine. Bragg felt his mouth go dry. He gripped his bat and, in a daze, walked to the crease. Stephen Bennett came to meet him.

'Only three balls left in this over,' he said encouragingly. 'I think that we all shall manage it.'

Bragg took his stance, conscious of his vulnerable arm. It was idiotic to risk it, he thought. He should have cried off. Why was it that people took a stupid game so seriously? Cleall was glaring at him from the distance, menace in every line. Bragg crouched over his bat as he began to run. Nearer and nearer he pounded, faster and faster. With a choking grunt, he brought his arm over and the ball flew past Bragg's elbow. Dear God! He had not even seen it! If it hit your head at that speed, you would drop like a poleaxed bullock.

Cleall turned again and began to run, his teeth bared in a snarl. Bragg saw a blur, as the ball whistled off the pitch, struck his bat and ran harmlessly to mid-on. He looked up and saw Stephen's smile of encouragement. One more ball from this hairy lunatic. If only he survived it, he vowed he would never disparage cricketers again. Cleall was running up, straining every sinew, hate in his eyes. He felt the impact twisting the bat in his hands. The ball was racing away over the grass. The blacksmith dived for it, but it eluded him and shot under the boundary rope. There was some applause and a brief cheer. Sixty for nine. Only three needed to win. His partner should manage that all right.

The field changed and Stephen settled over his bat. He only had to face Herring, who took two steps, a wild sort of leap and tossed the ball gently at you. Nevertheless,

Stephen treated him with exaggerated respect, watching the
ball intently and merely stopping it with his bat. Four balls
gone, without a score. Bragg's heart began to thump. Surely
he wouldn't have to face that maniac again? The next ball
from Herring was pitched a little shorter. In a flash, Stephen
stepped down the wicket and cracked it for six. He
continued to trot down the wicket and grasped Bragg's
hand.

'Jim Morton infected you to some purpose,' he said with
a grin. 'Thank you for helping out. We have not beaten
them for years.'

'It was a pleasure,' Bragg said smugly, as they walked
towards the pavilion. Perhaps there was something in this
cricket business, after all.

Just before eleven o'clock on the following Monday, Bragg
made his way to the village hall, in North Street, for the
inquest on Ollerton. He joined Ernie Toop, who was
shuffling his way along. It was evidently a red-letter day for
him; he was freshly shaved, his tousled hair had been
combed and his distorted boots gleamed under the film of
dust. They went up the steps into a lobby, where PC Bugby
was chatting to a man who looked like an auctioneer.

'Where shall we sit?' Bragg asked.

'At the back,' Ernie said decisively. 'You always see
more from the back.'

'If, like you, one's interest is at least as much in the
audience as in the performance, I expect you are right.'

They sat on the back row of benches, Ernie on the centre
aisle. The hall was almost full. There was a good sprinkling
of farm workers, despite the harvest. The people were
whispering in suppressed excitement; obviously free enter-
tainment of this kind was a novelty to be seized on. At the
end of the long room was a dais, with a table and chair on
it. A gavel and a carafe of water were the necessary symbols
of authority. Below the dais was a trestle table, on which
had been placed a double-barrelled shotgun and two cartridges. To the left was a carved oak prayer-desk, with a

Bible on it. It had been imported from the church, by the looks of it, to serve as a witness stand. Surprisingly, there were no benches for a jury. The coroner must have decided that he could dispense with one, for this case.

Promptly on eleven o'clock, PC Bugby walked portentously down the hall and through a door at the back. Moments later, he reappeared and bawled: 'Stand!' The villagers shuffled to their feet, as Bugby ushered the coroner to his dais. There was no: 'Oyez! Oyez!' as there would have been in the City coroner's court. To Bragg, it seemed to diminish the whole affair, to turn it into little more than a parish meeting. The coroner was sorting out his papers. He was about sixty, with the air of a prosperous country gentleman. He had a round florid face and thinning hair.

At a signal from Bugby, the villagers resumed their seats. Then their murmurings were stilled by the coroner's gavel.

'We are here,' he began in a forthright tone, 'to enquire into the death of George Ollerton of this parish.' He turned towards Bugby. 'Can I take evidence of identity?' he asked.

'I shall give that, sir,' the constable said. 'His widow is not well enough to come today.'

The coroner looked up sharply, as if wondering whether to challenge this slight to the dignity of his office.

'You knew the deceased personally, officer?' he asked.

'Oh, yes sir. He was one of the most prominent residents of Bere Regis.'

'I see . . . And are you satisfied that the deceased is, in fact, George Ollerton?'

'Without a shadow of doubt.'

'Very well, officer.'

The coroner dipped his pen in the inkwell and wrote for some moments in a large bound book. He carefully blotted his entry, then looked up.

'And who found the body?' he asked.

'Alfred Dyer, from Doddings, your honour.'

'Is he here? Or is he sick, also?'

'He is here.'

'Right, constable, you had better swear him.'

Dyer reluctantly got to his feet and crossed over to the prayer-desk. He was a big raw-boned man, graceless and sullen.

'Take the Bible in your right hand, and say the words printed on the card,' Bugby directed.

Dyer dropped his head. 'I can't read,' he mumbled.

Bugby took him through the oath, a smug look of superiority on his face.

The coroner glanced down at a closely written page in front of him.

'According to the statement you made to the police,' he said, 'you were the first person to discover the body of Mr Ollerton. What were the events leading up to the discovery?'

'I do not understand,' Dyer said.

The coroner sighed irritably. 'How came it that you found the body?'

'We was opening out, at the top of the field,' he began.

'Who is we?' the coroner interrupted.

'Me and my two sons.'

'And what does "opening out" mean?'

'Clearing away the weedy part along the hedge, so the reapers can get a proper start.'

'I see.' The coroner wrote a couple of lines in his book.

'Could you see the stile from where you were working?' he asked.

'No, sir. There's not that much of a slope, and it is a good way off.'

'Then, what led you to go to the stile?'

A dogged look settled on Dyer's face. 'I was not feeling well and I walked down the side of the field.'

'Why?' asked the coroner sharply.

'My bowels . . .'

'You were showing unwonted fastidiousness, for a labourer,' the corner remarked brusquely. 'Why did you need to go anywhere near the stile, for that purpose?'

'I'd walked round the field before I took on the job. I remembered there was some thick grass down there.'

The coroner regarded Dyer sceptically. 'Go on,' he said.

'I was crouched down, when I heard a shot . . . After I'd finished, I went down to the stile. I found Mr Ollerton lying dead.'

'Is a gunshot an uncommon event, in the fields around the village?'

'No.'

'Then, why did you decide to investigate on that occasion?'

'Sometimes the gentry hit a bird and, if it falls in brambles or a thicket, they don't bother to pick it up.'

'So you hoped to find something for the pot?'

'Yes, sir.'

'How would you know where to look?'

'If they don't want it, they will often tell you.'

'But when you came to the corner of the field, you found the deceased's body?'

'Yes, sir.'

'Did you see anyone else?'

'Not then, sir. Tabitha Gosney came up soon after.'

The coroner looked across at Bugby. 'I take it that she will be giving evidence,' he said.

'Yes, sir.'

'Did you touch the body?' the coroner asked Dyer.

'No, sir. I could see he was dead . . . and the man from London came and said I was to leave it alone.'

The coroner looked momentarily perplexed, then told Dyer to stand down. He wrote at length in his book, then looked up.

'Who is the next witness, officer?'

'Tabitha Gosney, your honour.'

'Let her be sworn.'

Bugby beckoned and Tabitha walked slowly from the back of the hall. Her black coat was open, revealing a grey skirt and a dingy white blouse. A shabby black hat surmounted her bedraggled grey hair. Her face was plump, the flesh sagging around her jowls. Round her neck was a pendant which looked suspiciously like a pentagram. She

approached the prayer-desk hesitantly. Bugby impatiently
pushed the Bible at her; she put out her hand and it dropped
from her grasp, hitting the top of the desk and skidding over
the floor. A gasp of apprehension went round the hall.
Bugby retrieved the Bible and placed it firmly in her hands.
He then held the card in front of her. She screwed up her
eyes, and read the oath in a curious sing-song voice that
made it sound like an incantation. Then she thrust the Bible
from her and, standing erect, looked stonily in front of her.

'You are Tabitha Gosney?' the coroner began.

'Yes.'

'We have heard evidence, from Mr Dyer, that you came
to where Mr Ollerton's body was lying.

Tabitha remained silent.

'How was that?' the coroner asked.

'I was walking down the footpath.'

'Were you going down the path for a particular reason?'

'Yes.'

A shadow of irritation crossed the coroner's face, then he
smiled at the old woman.

'And what was your reason for being on the footpath, at
that particular time?' he asked blandly.

'I was going to Doddings.'

There was a nervous titter from the hall. The coroner
frowned. 'Please keep silent,' he said sternly, then turned
back to Tabitha.

'Had you come straight from the village, Miss Gosney?'
he asked.

'Yes.'

'Did you, at any time, hear the sound of a gunshot?'

'Yes.'

'Where were you at that time?'

'I was on the road, near the bridge in South Street.'

'Do you know this footpath well?'

'Yes. I go and gather . . . things down there.'

'Can you tell me how long a time elapsed, between your
hearing the shot and your arriving at the stile?'

'No,' she said shortly. 'I took no particular notice.'

'But you know where you were when you heard the firearm discharged?'

'I know that all right.'

'Can you say how long it would normally take you to walk from that spot, along the footpath, to the stile in what, I believe, is known as the seven-acre field?'

'About five or six minutes.'

'I see.' The coroner made some notes, then looked up. 'What did you see, when you came up to the stile?'

'I saw Mr Ollerton lying on the ground and Mr Dyer bending over him.'

'What was Mr Dyer doing?'

'He was looking frightened.'

'Looking is hardly doing, Miss Gosney. Please try to answer my questions. What was Mr Dyer doing?'

'Nothing,' she snapped.

'What happened then?'

'I got over the stile.'

The coroner glared at the public benches, to quell any sniggers.

'Yes, of course. Did Mr Dyer say anything to you?'

'No.'

'Did you say anything to Mr Dyer?'

'I said I was going to his house.'

The coroner raised his eyebrows in exasperation. 'Did you not remark on the condition of Mr Ollerton?'

'What need was there? I could see he was gone.'

'Did anything else occur while you were in the vicinity?'

'His two sons came running down the edge of the field. I heard him tell one of them to go for the policeman . . . Then I went on to Doddings.'

'Did you see anyone else in the area?'

'No.'

'Very well, you may stand down.' The coroner added a few lines to his record of the proceedings, then looked across at Bugby. 'I will hear your evidence now, constable,' he said.

Bugby strode to the prayer-desk and recited the oath in a ringing voice.

'At what time were you summoned, constable?'

'About ten minutes past two, your honour.'

'Will you describe what you found when you arrived at the scene?'

'Well, your honour, Alfred Dyer and his younger son Ezra were standing between the body and the stream. Another man, whom I know as Joseph Bragg, was bending over the body, peering at the side of the head.'

'Who is this Bragg fellow?'

'He is a visitor from London, your honour.'

'Will he be giving evidence?'

'No, your honour,' Bugby said stolidly.

The coroner's gaze passed over the crowded benches. 'Is Mr Bragg present?' he asked.

Bragg rose to his feet. 'Yes, your honour,' he said.

'Thank you. I may call you, if I feel that it is necessary. I would be grateful if you would stay till the end of the proceedings.'

Bragg received a baleful glare from Bugby, as he sat down.

'Now constable,' the coroner resumed, 'what was the position of the body?'

'It was lying almost at right-angles to the footpath, your honour. The head was pointing into the field. His feet were about six feet from the stile. He had fallen on his left side. His hand was still grasping the barrels of his twelve-bore shotgun.'

'You have established that the gun was his, I take it, constable?'

'Yes, sir. Mrs Ollerton confirmed it was her husband's gun, all right.'

'You say that the hand of the deceased was not near the triggers of the gun?'

'That is correct, your honour. It was nearer the middle of the barrels.'

'Did you examine the gun, constable?'

'I did. It is a hammerless model and its action was closed. The safety-catch was in the off position. When I opened the gun, I extracted two cartridges. The right-hand barrel appeared to have recently been discharged.'

'When you say that the gun's action was closed, are you saying that the gun was cocked and ready to fire?'

'Yes, sir.'

'It is exceedingly dangerous to carry a weapon in that condition.'

'I've said as much to the deceased, your honour, but he would do it.'

'In my young days,' the coroner observed, 'the first thing you were taught was always to carry a gun broken.'

'Yes, sir. I do not think that the deceased was an experienced shot. I think he was just aping his betters.'

The coroner shot a questioning glance at Bugby, then wrote a note in his book.

'In your opinion, constable, could a shotgun being carried at the point where the deceased was holding it, and being in a state where the action was cocked and the safety-catch off, could it be discharged if one of the triggers were to come into contact with, say a twig in the hedgerow?'

'Very easily, your honour.'

'May I examine the weapon, constable?'

Bugby crossed over and, taking the shotgun from the table, handed it to the coroner. He twisted his chair sideways and tried the action in an expert manner.

'These are the two cartridges I extracted from the gun at the scene, sir.'

The coroner examined them both, sniffed at the one that had been discharged and handed them back to Bugby. While the coroner wrote a lengthy note, the constable replaced the exhibits on the table.

'Now I will take the medical evidence,' the coroner said.

The police surgeon turned out to be the man who had been chatting to Bugby in the lobby. He took the stand and hurried through the oath.

'Well now, Dr Shakerley, I gather that you carried out a post mortem examination on the deceased.'

'Yes, sir, on the morning of Friday the fifteenth of August.'

'And what were your findings?'

'There was a severe wound in the right temple, your honour. The cheek bones had been shattered and driven into the cranium by a considerable force. Apart from that, the general health of the deceased was good.'

'Are you saying that the wound was the direct cause of death, doctor?'

'There can be no doubt about it, sir.'

'And, from what you have observed, did he suffer from any medical condition which might have caused, say, a momentary spell of dizziness?'

'No, sir.'

'Is the wound, in your opinion, consistent with the discharge of a shotgun at close range?'

Shakerley squared his shoulders importantly. 'During my examination, I removed a quantity of lead shot from the cranium. I later obtained a twelve-bore cartridge of the same make and type as those exhibited, and broke it open. In my opinion, those pellets were identical to the ones removed during the post mortem examination.'

'Thank you, doctor . . . I know that you are a busy man, so I am happy to release you now.' The coroner smiled warmly at Shakerley, then turned to his record book.

'Is there any other evidence?' he asked at length.

Bugby crossed to the prayer-desk. 'Your honour,' he said firmly, 'there is a matter that I feel I should bring to your attention.'

'What is that, constable?'

'About a week ago, Alfred Dyer's small daughter was badly hurt by a cart belonging to the deceased. Dyer was very angry. He was heard to say, in the public house, that the day his little maid stopped breathing would be Ollerton's last day on earth. Your honour, Anna Dyer died early in the morning of Thursday the fourteenth.'

A shocked murmur ran through the hall. The coroner looked flabbergasted.

'What are you suggesting?' he asked coldly.

'I am not suggesting anything, sir. I thought it was something you ought to know about.'

'You should have told me before Mr Dyer took the stand. Recall him.'

But Dyer was no longer in the hall, and a messenger sent to the two pubs, failed to locate him. The coroner sat drumming with his fingers on the table, while Bugby stood stolidly at his side, oblivious of his annoyance. When it was finally established that Dyer was no longer in the village, the coroner brought the meeting to order with his gavel and began his summing up.

'This is an inquest into the sudden death of George Ollerton, of Ninety-one, West Street, Bere Regis,' he began. 'Death occurred on Thursday the fourteenth of August 1893, in a field belonging to Court Farm, at a stile on the footpath to Doddings.

'A shotgun, one barrel of which had been discharged, was found by the body. The police surgeon gave it as his opinion that the wound in the head of the deceased could have been inflicted by the discharge of that gun. He recovered a quantity of lead shot during his post mortem examination, which was identical to shot obtained from a cartridge of the same make as those exhibited. It has been said that the deceased was a prominent resident of the parish and, to judge by his gun, a prosperous one also. There has been no suggestion of any circumstances tending to indicate that he might have taken his own life. It has, however, been said that he was not experienced in firearms, and that he was habituated to carry his gun with the action closed—and the safety-catch off. From the account of the position of the body, it appears that the deceased was carrying the gun by grasping the middle of the barrel, at the moment that he met his death. Had he attempted to cross the stile, as it appears he did, there was a very real danger that a twig from the hedgerow could catch on one of the triggers and discharge the gun. It is, of course, a not uncommon occurrence, particularly amongst those people who have not been properly trained in the use of firearms. I cannot stress too strongly the dangers attendant on the handling of guns by the inexperienced.

'I have also to deal with the evidence given concerning the alleged threat against the life of the deceased by Mr Alfred Dyer. I am inclined to feel that if my child had been injured unto death, I, also, might have been so distraught as to utter wild threats against the person I considered responsible. It is apparently true that the deceased met his end on the same day as Anna Dyer died. Yet we must not conclude that there was a causative link between the two. It is fortunately rare for the threat of violence to be translated into violence itself. We have heard from Mr Dyer's own mouth of the events leading up to his discovery of the body. Some aspects of his evidence might appear unsatisfactory; yet it is beyond doubt that, having discovered the body, he stayed by it and sent his son to bring the police constable. In my view, that is not the action of an unsophisticated person, who has just carried into effect his threats of vengeance against the person he held responsible for the death of his daughter. Having weighed this evidence I have, therefore, disregarded it. In my judgement, the only possible verdict on the evidence before me, is one of accidental death. And I so find.'

The coroner rose, gathered his papers together and, with measured tread, walked out of the hall. From the chattering of the villagers, it appeared that they agreed with the verdict.

'I am surprised, Ernie, that you had not heard of Dyer's threat to murder Ollerton,' Bragg remarked.

'If I'd told you, you would have known as much as me,' Ernie retorted peevishly.

Bragg laughed and walked over to the table that held the exhibits. The coroner had been impressed with the gun. Bragg stooped down and found the maker's name engraved on the lock. It meant nothing to him, but he made a note of it and of the serial number. The ammunition was a common make of black-powder cartridge.

'Not happy with the verdict, then?' Bugby was standing at his elbow, a sneer on his face.

'I would not remotely question it, on the evidence.'

'You should be glad,' Bugby said truculently. 'Had it been homicide, the first man I'd have come looking for would be Ted Sharman. I can't think of anybody who will gain more, now Ollerton be out of the way.'

'As I understand it, Mrs Ollerton is going to continue the business, with Harry Green as foreman.'

Bugby snorted contemptuously. 'If she be pinning her hopes on him, she'll be wasting her time.'

'From your evidence, constable, you clearly thought that Alfred Dyer could have murdered Ollerton,' Bragg said mildly.

'What I be thinking, or what I be not thinking at any particular time, be no concern of yours . . . sir.' Bugby turned and strode officiously out of the hall.

CHAPTER ———————
——————— FOUR

On the afternoon of the inquest day Bragg was persuaded by
the vicar to go in search of the lost section of the ancient
trackway. Ryder set off up Butt Lane at a great rate,
chattering enthusiastically about Bere Regis and its history.
Soon Bragg was breathless and had to call a halt.

'I am so sorry,' the vicar said solicitously, 'I keep
forgetting that you have been unwell . . . What a splendid
view there is from here!' He turned and looked back
towards the village. 'And how sinister Black Hill looks,
even on the sunniest of days. If one gives one's fancy a little
play, one can imagine that it is another world, held in sway
by primordial forces.' He laughed uncertainly. 'It is only
the darkness of the heathland, of course, in contrast to the
fields around it.'

'I don't know,' Bragg said. 'I used to come over Black
Hill on my way to school. There is a big slab of rock
standing by the path. They called it the Devil's Stone, in my
day. It was a lot of nonsense, of course, but I never lingered
there, all the same.'

'It is a pagan sarsen,' the vicar said eagerly, as they resumed their trek along the lane. 'Undoubtedly, it was an important place of heathen worship. This area is particularly rich in relics of the ancient Britons. Look at the top of Bere Down, just beyond the Roman Road. There are literally scores of round barrows.' He waved his arm vaguely to the north. Bragg could not distinguish the Roman road, let alone the barrows, but there was no point in mentioning it. He was here for the exercise, after all.

'Unfortunately, the barrows were all excavated forty years ago, when the mediaeval fields were first being enclosed. And, if I may be uncharitable, it was done very badly. I know that there was pressure to unearth their treasures, in case the mounds were levelled by the plough, but that is no excuse for the haphazard methods used. The records of the excavations are lamentably meagre, indeed they are sometimes downright inaccurate.' The vicar's face was quite flushed with indignation.

'Did they find much?' asked Bragg.

'Oh, yes! Amongst other things, there were some magnificent urns, which have now been acquired by the British Museum. I must confess that their existence was a powerful influence in leading me to press for this living . . . Recently I did considerable research on the work that had been carried out. I found that one barrow, on Bere Down, was not mentioned in the records at all. This, I thought, was the perfect opportunity to make my reputation as an antiquary. I was determined to excavate it myself, last summer. I was scrupulous with my measurements and took great pains with my records, but all to no avail.'

'Was there nothing there?'

'I decided to dig a trench across the middle of the mound,' Ryder went on, disregarding Bragg. 'There was no great labour involved, since the barrow was, by then, a mere three feet high. For weeks I laboured joyfully. You can imagine my delight when, near the centre of the mound, I found a piece of pottery that was clearly a fragment of a burial urn. I redoubled my efforts, and I did succeed in unearthing further fragments . . . But I also discovered a broken, clay tobacco pipe!' Ryder pulled a rueful face. 'So much for my dreams of worldly recognition.'

'Did you find anything else?' Bragg asked.

'Nothing I felt able to write a paper about . . . I have suggested to my wife that the Lord might call me to a parish in Wiltshire, where there are barrows as yet unexcavated, but she resolutely closes her ears.'

'Bad luck!'

The vicar brightened. 'Of course, there is always Woodbury Hill. The British camp there has, thus far, remained undisturbed. I have a mind to do a trial dig, before the onset of winter. Would you be interested in assisting me?'

'I am back on duty on the eighth of next month.'

'But we could make a beginning and, who knows, you might become as fascinated by the sublime science as I am myself.'

Bragg laughed. 'I doubt that, but I will give you a hand.'

'Good! Now, you will have realised that the path we are following has been well below the level of the surrounding fields—in a cutting, as it were. That is an infallible indicator of an ancient pathway . . . It is humbling, is it not, to feel that we tread where our forebears have trod for thousands of years . . . But here, as we descend the northern slope the weather has scoured away the land, and our pathway peters out. I feel sure that it must have run along the line of the hedgerow, there. Although the hedge itself is comparatively recent, there are a few trees scattered along it, which seem to suggest a more ancient boundary. Shall we walk along it . . . ?"

Next morning, Bragg felt almost his old self again. After his hike with the vicar, he had expected to be stiff and lethargic. Full of his new wellbeing, he decided to walk over to Briantspuddle. It would be a kind of pilgrimage. His wife had been brought up in that village and, indeed, his sister had married a carpenter there. When his father died, it was

to her that his mother had gone. It would be good to see
them again.

He followed one of the vicar's ancient trackways, over
Black Hill and down into the valley of the river Piddle. It
was scarcely more imposing than the Bere Stream at this
point, with rivulets separating and reforming in the marshy
ground. To Bragg's city eye, Turner's Puddle seemed a
nothing of a place. A few houses and a couple of farms, that
was all—and a chapel in the Gothic style, built by a
well-to-do lady. Goodness knows where she thought the
people would come from to fill it! The Briantspuddle people
had always gone to Affpuddle church. It saved crossing the
river. Still, it was no doubt her passport to heaven, he
thought sardonically. He walked past the house where he
had been born. In his youth, the yard would have been full
of carts and wagons, with great shire horses shaking their
heads at the flies. Now it had been taken over by a builder.
Pyramids of timber were seasoning on one side; along the
house wall were piles of bricks and stone. In the middle of
the yard was an accumulation of rubbish—old window
frames, rusty paint tins, rubble from a demolished building.
And there was no one about. It seemed lifeless . . . He
hurried away, crossed the river by the rickety footbridge and
struck out briskly for his sister's house. So much for
romantic pilgrimages, he thought. They were always a
let-down. It was people, in the end, that mattered, not
places.

His sister was in the garden, feeding the hens. She flung
her arms around him and hugged him.

'You might have let me know,' she said chidingly. 'We
have only a bit of boiled bacon for lunch.'

'That will do fine,' he said, holding her at arm's length.
'You have put on weight, since I last saw you.'

'Well, you should come more often, then you wouldn't
notice! I wish I'd known. Ma would have wanted to dress
herself up a bit, for you.'

'Then, I'll tell you what. I will pop down to the shop for
some more tobacco. Is twenty minutes enough for you?'

'Lovely . . . It's still kept by Mrs Webb.'

Bragg sauntered down the dusty street, past thatched farmhouses and cob cottages; beyond the cross-roads, where a few imposing residences for the gentry stood, and down to where the valley was framed by low rounded hills. One of the pleasantest spots in the kingdom, he reflected. Not like a Landseer painting, maybe, but he liked his countryside domesticated. After sitting for a time on an old tree stump, he retraced his steps and called in at the village shop for his tobacco. Mrs Webb seemed to have shrunk into a little old woman, but her eyes were as bright as ever.

'I thought it was you,' she said. 'Your mother told me you would be coming. You've been in the wars, they say.'

'Just a scratch, Mrs Webb. These doctors make a great fuss about things.' He asked after her health, then excused himself and tramped back up the lane.

His mother was wearing her best frock, with a little lace cap on her head and a string of beads around her neck. She greeted him tremulously.

'What have they been doing to you?' she asked.

'It was just a slash on the arm. Look.' He took off his coat and pushed up his shirt sleeve.

His mother drew in her breath. 'Does it hurt?' she asked.

'Not any longer. I am just malingering, to get the chance to see you all.'

'Why don't you give it up?' she asked. 'Surely you could retire? Albert Clark, who was the policeman at Wool, he retired and he was only forty-five.'

'I am barely forty-three, mother, as you should know! Anyway, in the City police, retirement is not as cut and dried as all that.'

'There's no sense going on till you get yourself killed.'

'I promise that I won't do that.' He turned to his sister. 'Is John around?'

'No. He's over at Throop, putting a new roof on a barn. He'll be working until the light goes. It's got to be finished by the end of the week. Now, make yourself useful, and carve . . .'

After the meal, Bragg brought them up to date with the news from Bere Regis. His mother was perturbed to hear that Ted's business was in a poor way. But, of course, Ted had absorbed his father's customers, when he died. So Ted's loss was hers also, in a way. She soon forgot about it, however, and began to tell him of the doings of people he no longer remembered or, perhaps, had never known. He would have preferred to talk about the past, of his father, of his boyhood. But his mother had her feet firmly planted in the present. It was good: he ought to welcome it. But, if he were honest, they had precious little in common any more. When she mentioned that there was a little cottage down by the Farmer's Arms, that would be just right for his retirement, he began to think of excuses to get away. Then there came a knock at the back door and a small boy came in.

'Is Mr Bragg here?' he asked shyly.

'I'm Bragg.'

'Mr Colegrave said I was to present his com . . . compri . . . Anyway, he wants you to pop in to his house, before you go.'

Bragg flipped the lad a penny. 'Tell him I will be glad to.' The boy grinned and disappeared.

'Who is this Colegrave man?' he asked.

'He's a big shot,' his sister said proudly. 'He was a colonel in some cavalry regiment or other. When he retired, they made him Chief Constable of Dorset.'

'Did they now? I wonder why he wants to see me.'

'Why wouldn't he?' his mother said sharply. 'I made sure that he saw that cutting from the London paper, where they praised you to the sky.'

'Mother! I wish you wouldn't do that kind of thing.'

'I'm proud of you, son.'

Bragg crossed over and kissed her cheek. 'Well,' he said, 'since I am bidden, I had better go and see him. I will pop over again, before I go back to London.'

He walked down to the cross-roads and was directed to a large stone house, with a semi-circular carriage drive in front. The door was opened by a manservant, wearing a green apron.

'My name is Bragg. The colonel asked me to pop in.'

'Yes, sir,' the man said in a clipped, soldierly voice. 'Will you come this way?'

Bragg was taken down an oak-panelled passage, to a room at the back of the house. A tall, spare man with a military moustache and weathered face, rose from a desk in the window bay.

'Richard Colegrave,' he said briskly, holding out his hand. 'Glad to meet such a distinguished fellow-police-man.'

'That is over-generous, sir, as you well know.'

'Nonsense! I was at a meeting, earlier this year at the Home Office, and I got talking to your Commissioner. Sir William was exultant—no other word for it—over that counterfeiting case.'

'Without his support, in the face of the Bank of England, we would never have pulled it off.'

'I do not doubt it. It is my belief that the best service we amateurs can render is to decide whom we can trust, then let them get on with it. Sir William gave all the credit to you and your young constable . . . Morton, is it not?'

'That's right, sir.'

'His father used to be colonel of my old regiment. He ended up a general, of course.'

'It's a small world.'

'Yes.' Colegrave took a chair by the fireplace and motioned Bragg to one opposite. 'I believe that you have had a bit of trouble in Bere Regis,' he said amiably.

Bragg smiled. 'I am afraid that I have rather raised the hackles of the local policeman. I heard someone calling: "Help! Police!" so I instinctively dashed off to the scene. When your Constable Bugby arrived, he very soon put me in my place. He was right, of course, in a way.'

'We are spread very thinly in the country areas.' The colonel reached over for a tobacco jar from his desk, and put it on a table between them. 'My personal mixture, from

Grunebaum's, of Bond Street,' he said, gesturing to Bragg to take a fill.

'One of our most worrying limitations,' he went on, 'is that the man on the spot is unlikely to have experience of detective work. We have to rely on his assessment of an incident, before we commit trained men to it—and you are well aware of the calibre of the man on the beat.'

'I suppose that we are lucky in the Square Mile,' Bragg said. 'Though perhaps we overdo it. In the case of violent death, for instance, the police surgeon is there almost as soon as the detective. It is not unusual for the coroner to come to the scene, as well. We can integrate the post mortem examination and the police investigation in a way which is obviously not possible in the country. The great advantage is that nothing is disturbed, until all the information that can be gleaned at the scene has been recorded.'

Colegrave smiled. 'Do I gather, from your emphatic tone, that we fell far short of those standards in the Ollerton business?'

'I . . . No. I'm sorry, sir. I'm out of order.'

'Come now, Bragg. This is a privileged occasion. I shall take any remarks you make, not as criticism but as accumulated professional wisdom.'

Bragg pondered for a moment. 'I suppose all I am thinking is, that there is no reason why a village bobby should not carry out basic scene-of-crime procedures. Take last Thursday as an example. A man was found shot in the head, on a footpath, near a stile. However lacking in experience, the policeman should have examined the area thoroughly.'

'And that did not happen?'

'Constable Bugby had a perfunctory look round. He took no measurements, made no sketch, did not even take notes on the spot. He examined the gun, apparently decided that it was a shooting accident, and had Ollerton's body carted off as if it was a dead donkey.'

'It does sound rather precipitate, put like that.'

'I imagine that he regretted it later. Between then and the

inquest, he seems to have been told that the man who found the body had threatened to kill Ollerton.'

'I gathered from the coroner, last night—we were playing whist together—that he disregarded that particular evidence.'

'That is true. As you know, he brought in a verdict of accidental death.'

'And you, having made what was perforce a limited examination of the scene, are not happy with that verdict?' Bragg could detect no irony in the colonel's tone.

'Let's say that I am uneasy, sir. I have had a lot of experience with violent deaths, and a good number of them involved firearms. They were mostly revolvers, I grant you, but there cannot be much procedural difference between a hand gun and a shotgun. For instance, I examined the area round the wound for scorch marks. There weren't any. The discharged cartridge in the gun was an ordinary black-powder type, but there were no powder marks around the wound. If the gun had been accidentally discharged, as the coroner assumed, I would have expected to find both . . . Can you tell me how far shotgun pellets travel, before they begin to spread, sir?'

'Which barrel was fired, Bragg?'

'The right one.'

'That would be the barrel with less choke. I am afraid that any expertise I might claim is concerned with military rifles; so you should check with an expert. However, I would say that, for three feet, the effect would be as of a single projectile.'

'When I examined the body, there was a spray of shot marks over the neck and head, although the great bulk of the shot had still been bunched together . . . There was another ridiculous thing about the inquest. The police surgeon had extracted shot from the cranium. He then broke open an identical cartridge to the one in the gun, and gave evidence that the shot from it was similar to the pellets he had found in his post mortem examination. What does that prove?'

'So you think the verdict was wrong?' Colegrave said thoughtfully.

'I do not think that the coroner had enough evidence to support the decision he came to. Take the place where Ollerton was holding the gun—around the barrels, above the fore-end. He would hardly have been carrying it like that, so far from the point of balance.'

'The coroner felt that he had been pulling it across the top rail of the stile. After all, it would be the front trigger that a twig would touch first, and fire the right-hand barrel. To that extent, the theory hangs together. But I can see that, if it were so, the end of the barrel would have been much closer than three feet from the head.'

'And that top rail is not much more than three feet from the ground,' Bragg said. 'Ollerton was six foot and over. If the coroner were right, you would have expected the shot to have been travelling upwards, from below the head, not straight at the side of it.'

'So you think it was murder?'

'Well, I don't think it was an accident.'

'At this time of year,' the colonel said musingly, 'there are a great many itinerant labourers about: rootless, masterless men, some little better than criminals. Do you think that one of them might have attacked him and shot him with his own gun?'

'There was no sign of a struggle, sir. Though with the ground as hard as it is, you would not expect it. But his pocket-book was untouched, if that is any guide. And people who were in the vicinity claim that they saw no one else around.'

Colegrave knocked out his pipe in the empty grate. 'Anyway,' he said, 'if someone had wrested Ollerton's gun from him, he would hardly have stood still and waited to be shot.'

'Perhaps you can clear up another point that is worrying me,' said Bragg.

'What is that?'

'The gun was lying against the body and Ollerton's right

hand was round the middle of the barrels—as Bugby told the coroner. It was as if he had rested it against him, while he had a nap. Now, if it had happened as the coroner believed, I would have thought he would instinctively drop the gun.'

'Not necessarily, Bragg. Odd things can happen in the moment of death. I have seen artillerymen with their heads blown off, still clutching their ramrods.'

'Oh, then I can forget that one!'

'So, where are we now?' The Chief Constable gave a wry smile. 'You have convinced me that the coroner's verdict may not be correct; but, because of that verdict, there is no obligation on the police to investigate further. Indeed, it would be injudicious to be seen to do so. Yet, since we appear to be thrown back on the staple of motive and opportunity, my only course would be to send detectives to the village . . . How long are you going to be there, Bragg?'

'I go back on the seventh of September, sir.'

'Well, till then, I would be grateful if you could rummage around discreetly. The miscreant we postulate is likely to be someone from the area, if not from the village itself. Would you do that? . . . You could report to me here.'

'Why not?' Bragg said with a smile. 'It would be better than loafing around outside the pub.'

Bragg strolled home contentedly. It was half-past four on a glorious summer evening. The breeze had fallen away and, if anything, it was hotter than ever. They had finished reaping the oats, down here, and were beginning to cut the wheat—a smooth gold blanket spattered with blood-red poppies. He reached over and pulled an ear; it was nice and compact, though not as fat as he had known. But the early summer had been too dry for a heavy crop. He rubbed the grains between his palms, to get rid of the husks, then chewed them. They were hard and sweet, as he remembered them.

He stood for a while, watching the reapers. There were five of them in a slanting line, the right-hand one the most

advanced. In that way, the point of a blade could not injure
the next man, should it slip. The scythes swung in a steady
rhythm, cutting what seemed only a moderate amount of
corn at each stroke, but progressing steadily, inexorably, in
a pattern of overlapping half-moons. From time to time a
reaper would pause and upend his scythe, to sharpen it. The
rough whetstone, grating on the steel, made a sound like a
demented corn-crake. Then the soft, crackling swish would
start again. Behind them, was a dozen or so of women and
children, whose job it was to gather the cut wheat. Children
would collect armfuls into neat bundles on the ground. Then
their mother, acting as bandster, would take a good handful
of the stiff, dry stalks and divide it into two. With a dextrous
twist of her hands, she would tie the two halves together,
making a long band of straw, then secure the rest of the
bundle round the middle. Two men went behind the
women, stooking the sheaves. They would set four upright,
in a cluster, then spread two more, upended, over the top to
keep out the rain. It was all back-breaking work, Bragg
thought. Then, after ten days or so, they would be properly
dried and ready to stack. He could almost feel the ache in
his shoulders, as he recalled the relentless pressure to get
the corn in, before it got rained on . . . tossing the
sheaves higher and higher, till the load towered up above
you; then sprawling in the stubble for a moment's rest, as
the horses came stamping into the field with another cart to
load. Dear God! He couldn't tackle it now, to save his life.
Yet there were a couple of men, over there, who were
fifteen years older than he was . . . or maybe it was just
that they looked it! He strolled on.

Down by the river, a herd of cows had been let into a lush
water-meadow. They were tearing greedily at the grass,
their udders distended with milk. As he watched, a boy and
a dog appeared at the far corner of the field and began to
round them up. You could see why artists would want to
paint it all. It would be pretty and quaint to their towny,
middle-class eyes; having little or no connection with the
milk they drank and the beef they ate.

He crossed the river and walked through Turner's Puddle again. A cart, loaded high with sheaves of oats, was turning into a farmyard, the two horses straining up the slight incline. They must have finished their reaping here, and were wasting no time in bringing the dried corn home. He turned, to resume his stroll, then saw a figure on a bicycle coming towards him. She waved, and he realised that it was Fanny Hildred. He stepped to one side to let her pass but instead she stopped and slipped off the saddle.

'Good afternoon, Mr Bragg,' she said with a warm smile. 'It was such a lovely day, that I decided to go for a spin.' She was wearing a demure skirt and bodice, and a small hat was perched on her upswept hair. She looked very stylish and lively.

'I have been visiting the haunts of my boyhood,' Bragg said cheerfully. 'I am just on my way back.'

'Then I will walk with you, if I may.'

'That would be very agreeable, miss. At least for me! Let me push your bicycle for you.'

She gave him a charming smile and surrendered her machine. It was one of the new patent bicycles but, to Bragg, it still seemed heavy for a young woman. Perhaps she was stronger and sturdier than she appeared. She was certainly attractive; and there was no side to her, for all that she lived in a big house.

'You do not strike me as a sentimental man, Mr Bragg,' she said lightly.

'You mean, wandering off around here? I don't think that I am. But, occasionally, I get a spasm of wanting to belong somewhere.'

'Do you not belong in London?'

'More than anywhere, I suppose. But it is only because my job is there. Part of the trouble is that I have not got a home of my own. I live in lodgings; and, however used to it you become, it is not the same as having your own things about you.'

'Your wife died soon after you were married, I believe . . . I am sorry.'

Bragg smiled at her. 'It was twenty years ago, miss. In another life . . . Now, I was going to take the footpath, over Black Hill. Can you manage it?'

'Of course!' she said with a tolerant smile. She set off up the steep path, Bragg toiling behind her with the bicycle. As they reached the crest, by the Devil's Stone, there was a flurry in the heather and a black figure went scurrying down the hill.

Fanny turned and smiled. 'That will be poor Tabitha Gosney,' she said. She had nice white teeth, Bragg noticed. When she smiled, her face was transformed.

'Why "poor"?' he asked.

'She has become a little strange over the last few years. Her mother was very skilled in the use of herbs for healing, and she passed her knowledge on to Tabitha.'

'I hear that she is the poor folk's doctor.'

'That is certainly true. Most of the people she helps cannot afford to pay her. We try to see that she wants for nothing, but she is a curiously distant person. She will go to all kinds of lengths to prevent anyone from going into her cottage. Mamma says that it is because she is too proud to want people to see how poor she is.'

'But you think it is something else?'

Fanny smiled. 'I would hate to have to hide anything from you, sergeant,' she said lightly. 'It is my belief that she has got hold of some old books—she is one of the few working people who can read—and has steeped herself in the lore of two centuries ago.'

'I do not suppose that Bere Regis was all that different then.'

'No indeed!' Fanny pulled a wry face.

'And, why should that turn her queer?'

She hesitated. 'I think that she looks on herself as a witch.'

'I noticed that she was wearing a pentagram at the inquest,' Bragg remarked.

'That does not surprise me. I do not mean that she thinks she can fly around on a broomstick, or anything like that!

But she has taken to gathering her simples at certain phases of the moon . . . and they say that she sells love-potions.' Fanny coloured and looked away.

'So she is a white witch? I don't suppose that will do anyone any harm.'

'She seems to haunt this spot.' Fanny gestured towards the stone. 'It is said to be an ancient place of magical significance . . . Poor old Tabitha.' She began to walk slowly down the hill, Bragg following with the bicycle.

'Do you regard yourself as belonging in Dorset, Mr Bragg?' she asked, over her shoulder.

'If I am honest, miss, no. I come down here wanting to belong, and every time I go back disappointed. The trouble is, you grow out of a place.'

'Indeed! You are fortunate, in that you can return to your busy metropolitan life. My only escape is to retreat into a novel.'

'I cannot get on with novels,' Bragg said. 'They seem to spend an inordinate amount of time getting nowhere. If you ask me, they are written for people who have more time on their hands than they know what to do with.'

'*Touché,*' Fanny said with a smile. 'But have you not read Hardy's novels?'

'I can't say I have ever heard of him.'

'But he writes about Dorset, about the towns and villages around here. In *Tess of the D'Urbervilles*, his Kingsbere is Bere Regis!'

'Is it, now. Perhaps I'll try him, one day. The novels I do like are Rider Haggard's—full of action, with none of this endless mooning about.'

Fanny laughed. 'I can imagine that, of you. What other books do you read?'

'Travel books, history books, books about long-gone civilisations. I suppose that I am trying to make up for the education I never got.'

'You make me feel ashamed. I am afraid that I wallow in sentimental novels. It is pure self-indulgence, but I could not get through the winter without *Jane Eyre* and *Northanger Abbey*.'

'A fine young woman like you should not be having to talk about getting through the winter,' Bragg said roundly.

Fanny smiled mischievously. 'You are right, sergeant. Self-pity is an unappealing vice, particularly on a lovely day like this. And now, since we are back at the road, I feel that I should go on ahead. It would scarcely be proper for us to be seen emerging from the heath together!'

'I'm sorry, miss. I was enjoying our conversation so much, I never thought . . .'

'Perhaps we can continue it on another occasion? I do not possess a Rider Haggard, but I could lend you a volume of modern poems, to while away the time. Would you like that?'

'Yes, miss,' Bragg said warmly. 'I would indeed!'

CHAPTER ————————
————————— FIVE

Next morning, Bragg begged some paper from Emma and began to make notes of the circumstances surrounding Ollerton's death. If it were murder then, according to Colegrave, someone from the area would be involved. Well, it would have to be a person with a powerful grudge against him. Nevertheless, it need not be an open enemy. A seeming friend might have cajoled Ollerton into parting with his gun—perhaps by pretending to admire it. That theory got over all the difficulties he had listed. Except that no one had seen a second person. Still, it was worth following up. Wondering how he would set about it, Bragg realised that, handled properly, Ernie Toop could be a mine of information about the goings-on in the village. He spent most of his time lurking in doorways or sitting on walls. He was of no importance, so people ignored him. They probably thought of him as half-witted. In return, he seemed to take a perverse delight in hugging to himself scraps of information about other people. Possessing them gave him—not an advantage, for he was not seeking power

over them—but added importance, stature in his own eyes.
If Bragg could persuade him to share his knowledge, he
might get nearer to a solution. And no one could possibly
suspect the cripple of committing the crime.

Accordingly, at eleven o'clock, Bragg went up to the
Cross and beckoned Ernie to join him. By the time that
Bragg had come from the pub, with the customary beer,
Ernie was perched on the wall. He drank greedily, then
wiped his mouth on his sleeve.

'Enjoy that, do you?' he asked with a smirk.

'What is that?'

'Fumblin' about in your trouser pocket!'

Bragg laughed. 'It's a rubber ball,' he said, bringing it
out. 'I have to keep squeezing it to strengthen my arm
muscles.'

'Both my balls are rubber,' Ernie observed sourly. Then
his eyes gleamed. 'I'd have thought you'd found better
things to squeeze,' he said.

'I don't understand you.'

'Come on! I saw you and her ladyship having a roll on the
heath, yesterday.'

'You are a wicked devil,' Bragg said evenly. 'I have
never known anyone who got as much pleasure out of
making trouble as you do.'

Ernie chuckled. 'I saw her come up the road on her
bicycle, and you walkin' after. You'll be all right in her bed.
My God! I wish she'd let me crawl in . . . She's the same
age as me, d'you know?—thirty-four.'

Bragg fought down the urge to clip him round the ear.
'We did happen to meet, as I was walking from Briantspuddle, and we did walk part of the way back together. But
it was pure chance.'

'Oh yes? Then she just chanced to ask me where you'd
gone, that's what . . . Her bicycle has not been out of the
shed for two years. It was lucky I chanced to know where
you'd gone, wasn't it?'

'I am much too old for her to be interested in me. Still,
it is surprising that she is not married.'

'Perhaps she was meant for me, only I came out like this.' There was a bottomless resentment in his mirthless grin.

'I do not remember their house being there, when I was a lad,' Bragg remarked.

'Her father had it built, soon after I left school.'

With a start, Bragg realised that he had not expected Ernie to have attended school. In a city slum, he would have spent his life in the gutter, abandoned. Here he had, at least, been brought up in some semblance of a normal life.

'He owned Hildred's brewery in Dorchester,' Ernie went on. 'He had this house built for his retirement.'

'He must have been many years older than his wife.'

'He was—but he was a nice chap. D'you know, her ladyship used to go to Miss Scutt's school, in North Street, when they first came. Then she went to a boardin' school in Dorchester . . . Mrs Hildred still owns most of the shares in the brewery, they say. You want to get your feet under the table, there.'

'Is that the brewery up by the station?'

'Yes . . . That's the trouble with her ladyship.'

'I don't follow you.'

'She's always been too good for the farmers and trades-men, but not good enough for the gentry.'

'Well, I will bear your advice in mind,' Bragg said lightly. 'When is Ollerton's funeral?'

'Friday. You want to go to that. She'll be puttin' him away proper.'

'No, thank you. I am not partial to funerals.'

Ernie cocked his head. 'Have you found out who killed him, yet?' he asked.

Bragg looked at Ernie steadily. 'Some day, you will stir things up to your own detriment,' he said.

'Come on! Everybody saw you lookin' at the gun, and old Bugby chewing your balls off.'

'Well, you were at the inquest, what do you think?'

Ernie became thoughtful. 'I don't know,' he said finally.

'Maybe not, but you have a sharp mind. And you know more about this village than anyone else.'

'I don't let on what I know,' he said emphatically.

'But I bet you could work it out . . . It was Constable Bugby's evidence that led to the verdict of accidental death.'

Ernie gave a sneering laugh. 'Bugby! Fat lot of good he is . . . There were plenty who'd fallen out with Mr Big Boots.'

'The constable sees Ted Sharman as a likely candidate.'

'Bugby's not the only one,' Ernie said with an unpleasant smile.

'What about Alf Dyer?'

'He has it in for them, all right. Alf and the two lads are always brawlin'. They are a rough family, given to poachin' and worse. Not much better than gypsies. Still, as the coroner said, he would hardly hang about and send for the police, if he'd done it.'

'But it might not have happened like that. Tabitha Gosney appeared on the scene and saw him. There would have been no point in his running away then. And, although we know that the two boys appeared soon after, we have no independent evidence that he shouted for them to come. Dyer might have found himself compelled to summon the constable, because he knew he would have to brazen it out.'

Ernie's eyes sparkled. 'If those two had heard their father and Ollerton arguin', they'd have come runnin' to help, for sure.'

'There is just one flaw in that theory,' Bragg said. 'When Tabitha heard the shot, she was still in the road, near the bridge. She had to get over the first stile and walk three hundred yards to the second, before she saw Alf Dyer. Surely, if he had done it, he would have escaped in that time?'

'What have you been goin' on for, then?' Ernie exclaimed crossly.

'You have to test every theory: turn it over and over in your mind and try to break it. The one you cannot break is probably the truth . . . Tell me Ernie, can you remember anyone in the past, who has had a real up-and-downer with George Ollerton, then become friendly with him again?'

Ernie appeared to have lost interest. 'It don't do to scratch the surface too deep in Bere Regis,' he said tartly.

'If it was a murder, it is the duty of everyone to help bring the culprit to justice.'

'In London, maybe; down here it's different.'

'No. It is no different throughout the length and breadth of the kingdom.'

Ernie looked up at Bragg craftily. 'Then you ought to go and see Jim Hodge, the travellin' thatcher.'

'Why is that?'

'He told me he was thatchin' a hayrick, just the other side of the Poole road. He says he saw two men down by the stile. Then he heard a shot. When he looked up, there was nobody there.'

'We will make a detective of you yet!' Bragg exclaimed. 'Where will I find him?'

'He's lodgin' with Mrs Tucker, but you'd be sure to find him in the Drax Arms, around seven.' Ernie looked up the street and began to chuckle to himself as Tabitha Gosney came towards them.

'Hurry up, you old crow! You'll be late!' he shouted. This time she did not answer his gibe, but scurried on, head down.

'She must be goin' soft in the head,' muttered Ernie, baulked. 'Do you know, they say she wouldn't lay George Ollerton out? Mrs Priddy and her daughter had to do it—and made a poor job of it, I'm told—I can't remember anybody that old Tabby hasn't laid out before. She'd get up from her deathbed to lay someone out, would the Old Crow.'

'He was a rather gruesome sight. Perhaps that was the reason.'

'Tommy Green was worse.'

Bragg diverted the conversation from this lugubrious channel. 'You were an adult when the Ollertons came to live here, weren't you Ernie?'

'Yes.'

'And you live next door to them. You must know more about them than anyone.'

'Not much. They always were a close lot. I told you they were from Yorkshire.'

'But you must have noticed a great deal, nevertheless,' Bragg persisted. 'I am interested in how he managed to build up such a prosperous business in as short a time as fourteen years.'

Ernie looked up sharply. 'He worked hard, that's what. Harder than Ted Sharman ever would. He kept a tight rein on his drivers, and he cut a few corners . . .' His face darkened. 'It's the little maid's funeral on Friday, too. She is bein' buried in the mornin', to keep the families apart.'

'How do you reckon Ollerton managed to get all the coal haulage for himself?'

'I don't know, Mr Ball Crusher.' Ernie twisted himself off the wall. 'But it looks as if Ted Sharman has the chance to get them back, now he's out of the way, doesn't it?'

At seven o'clock that evening, Bragg pushed into the smoke-filled public bar of the Drax Arms. He managed to catch the eye of the landlady, Lily Applin. If she was a lily, he thought, it wasn't a madonna lily. She was full-breasted, with a generous, smiling mouth and plump arms. As she served him, she leaned across the counter to display her charms. No wonder this pub was better patronised than the Royal Oak!

'Is Jim Hodge here?' Bragg asked.

She glanced around the bar. 'I can't see him, love . . . Dicky, have you seen the thatcher?' she called.

'He be gone,' a man replied from the table by the door.

'There you are,' Lily said, then smiled warmly towards a new customer.

Bragg took his pint and pushed his way to Dicky's table. 'Where did he go to?' he asked.

'Dunno. He just up and went this morning. Farmer Sturdy weren't too pleased, neither. He left a rick half-thatched.'

'I wonder why he went.'

'What d'you expect from they travellers? Nothin' better than tinkers, they be. Like I said to Farmer Sturdy, if he'd kept his money till the job were finished, he'd still be here.'

Suddenly impatient of wasting time, Bragg guzzled his beer and went out into the fresh air. Why would Hodge leave so precipitately? So far as Bragg knew, he had told no one but Ernie of what he had seen. And this was precisely the kind of information that the little cripple would hug to himself . . . Hodge had not been involved personally, since he had been up the haystack. Did he think he was in danger? Certainly, if he had been able to see men at the stile, he was also in their range of vision. The killer would easily have been able to find out who was thatching that rick. Mind you, a man at the stile would have had precious little to see—only Hodge's head over the ridge of the stack. It was very unlikely. But that was hardly the point. If Hodge thought he might suffer Ollerton's fate, he would be off—and who could blame him?

Bragg hurried down South Street, in the evening sun, and struck off along the Doddings footpath. He should have come back before, to have a proper look round. Blast Hodge for running away! He might have been able to recall things like age, stature, dress. Bragg wondered how he could track him down. The trouble was that, at this time of year, there would be work for him on any farm in four counties, without his travelling more than a day. It would need a big police operation to find him. Even then it could fail if he were intent on lying low.

As Bragg approached the stile into the cornfield, he could see the hayrick that Hodge had been thatching. It was a few hundred yards away, in the corner of a meadow. Anyone on the top of it would have a good view of the stile—indeed of the footpath in both directions. Bragg climbed into the cornfield and stood where the body had lain. He could now appreciate why Dyer and his sons would not have seen the incident from the top edge of the field. It did not slope evenly. In outline, it began level, like a ledge, then the lower half sloped gradually down to the stream. With the standing corn in front of them, the stile would have been screened from view.

Bragg crouched down and examined the ground minutely. There was a black patch of dried blood, where Ollerton's head had been. Here the grass was tussocky, the permanent margin of the path. The earth was hard beneath it and would not have taken the imprint of a boot. On the other side of the path, there was a stretch of long grass and cow parsley, mingling with the water-cress that bordered the edge of the bank. Running between the stile and the stream was a short length of hedge. In front of it, the grass had been trampled. It might not be significant. The stream divided at that point, leaving a small island, and on the far side of the island was a luxuriant growth of water-cress. People going down by the hedge could easily hop on to the island and pick it. Nevertheless, someone on the trampled grass would have been about six feet from where Ollerton was probably standing. Allowing for the length of the gun, a shot fired from there might well have produced the impact pattern he had seen on Ollerton's head. Bragg searched the flattened grass carefully. All he found was a screwed up toffee paper and an empty matchbox, faded by the weather.

He went to the edge of the stream and looked at the little island. The ground was softer there, and the surface was covered by the indentations of feet. There were many small holes, made by the heels of women's shoes. So his surmise had been correct. He jumped across the narrow channel and looked for the imprint of a man's boot. There were marks that could be interpreted that way but, equally, they could have been made by youths fishing for trout. Bragg sighed irritably. It was all inconclusive. One thing was certain, if you wanted to get from the island to the far bank, you would have to be prepared to get your feet wet. The stream widened to about three feet beyond it, and the bank was steep on the other side. Nevertheless, there were well-marked footholds and, once you had scrambled up it, you would be out of sight from the footpath. The hedge there did not follow in a straight line from the one on this side. Instead, it cut back to the south-west, towards the middle of Rye Hill. In five minutes you could be up on Black Hill, with roads leading to Bovington and Wool, Turner's Puddle and Dorchester. Bragg jumped back on to the bank and walked the length of the field. The wall of stiff wheat stalks was unbroken. No one had dived in there, for cover.

He turned back pensively. What had he discovered? If he were honest, nothing very conclusive. Alf Dyer's evidence was more valid than it had sounded at the inquest. And, certainly, if Hodge had been up on that rick, he would have been able to see two men at the stile. Again, if another man had been there, he could have expected to get away without too much risk of being seen. Furthermore, unless the attack he postulated was totally unpremeditated, it argued that the murderer was either someone who was close enough to Ollerton to know his movements, or had actually made an appointment to meet him at the stile. But why should Ollerton agree to such an appointment? Unless it concerned something that he wanted to keep very confidential . . . Of course, there could be another explanation. Suppose that, after he had told Ernie what he had seen, Hodge had discovered that the assailant was one of his friends, an itinerant like himself. Would he not want to protect him? And would that not be an equally convincing reason for his flight?

Bragg got back to the Old Brewery in a thoroughly disgruntled mood. As he entered the yard, Ted came out of the harness room.

'Ted, I want to talk to you,' Bragg said firmly.

Ted looked at him coldly. 'Can't it wait?' he asked.

'No, it can't. You know full well that people in the village are saying you killed George Ollerton.'

'They had better not say it in my hearing,' Ted said grimly.

'I know you didn't do it, and I want to help you. I realise that you were only letting off steam, the other night, when you wished him dead.'

'Thank you for that much,' Ted said sarcastically.

'But you have got to help yourself.'

'I take no heed of gossip.'

'It is not just gossip, Ted. After the inquest, Constable Bugby came across to me. He said that if the verdict had been homicide, you were the first one he would have come looking for.'

'Just let him come!' Ted said truculently.

'That kind of attitude will only make tongues wag the more. You have to realise that the verdict of accidental death is not a protection for you. If there is enough of an outcry in the village, or if evidence turns up which strongly suggests that it was not an accident, then it would all be opened up again.'

'So?'

'So you would be an obvious candidate for having done away with him.'

'Just because I said that I would like to shoot him?' Ted said with a sneer.

'Not just that. They would be looking for someone who had a motive, and also the opportunity to commit the crime.'

'Suppose I didn't try to get back my customers. Suppose I packed it all in. What then?'

'It would make no difference. Any jury would accept that you could have expected to get them back, once Ollerton was quietly out of the way.'

Ted gave a grim smile. 'I suppose so,' he said. 'But then, I was out on a job when he was killed. Robert will tell you what time I came in. He was waiting to put the horse in the van, to go out himself.'

'I know. He told me that you only got back at half-past two—he is as worried about the rumours as anyone.'

'So you have been having a good snoop?' Ted said bitterly.

'It won't do, Ted. You were due to pick up a half-load of flour at the West Mill, at ten o'clock. Were you, by any chance, late?'

Ted's lip curled. 'No. I wouldn't dispute it. There were plenty of people who saw me.'

'You were taking it to the baker at Puddletown, which is a bit more than six miles. You would be there and unloaded, by half-past eleven; so you could easily be back here by one o'clock. Ollerton didn't die till just before two.'

Ted said nothing.

'Did you have another delivery to make, or go anywhere else?'

'No . . . Surely I am allowed a bite to eat?'

'I expect that Emma packed you some food,' Bragg said quietly.

'I can eat it in a field gate, if I want to, can't I?'

'That's fine, if you can prove it. Did you see anyone who can testify that you were on the road, away from Bere Regis, after two o'clock?'

'No.'

'Think carefully, Ted. You are very well known in the district, and it's a busy road. Surely there was someone?'

'I tell you there was no one!'

Bragg looked steadily at his cousin. 'It would be bad for you, if there were someone who could say that you did come back to Bere Regis, around one o'clock.'

'For Christ's sake, Joe, leave me alone!' Ted burst out angrily. 'Why don't you just mind your own bloody business!' He turned and stamped off towards the house.

CHAPTER ———— ———— SIX

On the Thursday morning Bragg stayed in his room until he saw his cousin emerge from the kitchen door. Robert had gone off with the cart, some twenty minutes earlier, while Ted seemed to be pottering about aimlessly. He began to sweep the yard, then left it and went into the harness room, which seemed to be the place where he went to ground. Taking his chance, Bragg went down to the kitchen. Emma was bustling about, her usual cheerful self. So Ted had not told her of their near-quarrel, the previous night. She cooked him a great plate of ham and eggs, and, while he was eating it, kept up a stream of chatter. Rose had been in, on the Wednesday afternoon, and there was endless gossip about the goings-on in the big house to retail. Bragg found himself wondering whether or not he ought to cut short his visit. The way things were going, it would not be long before Ted was ordering him out of his house. And, since Emma seemed oblivious of the strained relationship between them, that would send her up in arms. But perhaps he ought not to initiate his departure. He and Ted had not quite come to an open breach and, if they were as hard up as it seemed, his money would come in handy.

Bragg walked up to the Cross, wondering how long he could continue to believe in Ted's innocence while he maintained his present attitude. He was uneasily aware that, last night, he had come near to conspiring with him to concoct an abibi . . . But, blast it, Ted was his cousin! As Bugby had made plain, he was not an officer in the Dorset police. Bragg looked for Ernie, but he was nowhere to be seen. For once, he was glad. His thoughts were turbulent enough, without having the peevish little cripple provoking him. He turned and began to walk slowly along West Street . . . It would not do. He was a policeman wherever he was. He could not enforce the law in the City of London, then bend it elsewhere. Moreover, in accepting Colegrave's invitation to keep a discreet eye open, he had been enrolled as a kind of irregular in the Dorset force. He heard light steps behind him.

'Good morning, Mr Bragg.'

He turned and raised his hat. 'Good morning, Miss Hildred. Another lovely day.'

'I saw you pass the house, so I took the opportunity of bringing you the book of poems I promised you.'

'I am grateful to you.'

She was wearing a slim skirt and white cotton blouse that set off her willowy figure. Her straw hat was decorated with a perky tuft of coloured feathers. She seemed brimming over with wellbeing. In her hand she held a small blue volume, but made no attempt to pass it to Bragg. Instead, she fell into step with him.

'Did you enjoy your childhood here, Mr Bragg?' she asked.

'To be honest, miss, I've not thought much about it. I suppose I must have done. I was something of a scapegrace, and we had a lot of fun . . . Strange that I should have spent my early years flouting authority, and my manhood upholding it.'

'No doubt the one was excellent training for the other,'

Fanny said happily. 'I used to love a summer's day like this when I was a girl. I would lie in the grass and watch a wisp of cloud drift from one horizon to the other. In those days the sky seemed so vast.'

'I expect it still is, miss. Not that I get much chance to look at it, in London. There is something of a vista along the Thames but everywhere else the buildings crowd in on you.'

'I have not visited London for over five years,' Fanny said wistfully. 'And that was only to attend a family wedding. I would love to spend a few weeks there, in May or June.'

'There is plenty going on then, and no mistake: parties and balls, theatre and opera.'

'I do not mean that I hanker to be part of society, Mr Bragg,' she said hastily. 'But it would be such a change to be in an environment vibrant with vitality.'

'Then, why don't you go?'

'I could hardly go on my own! If I did, propriety would not allow me to participate in social life. And we no longer have any acquaintance in London.'

'Could you not persuade your mother to go with you?'

'Alas! My mother regards the brewery in Dorchester as a personal trust, encapsulating my father's lifetime of achievement. I am sure that she feels it would melt away, if she turned her back on it for a moment!'

'That is a pity.'

They walked some way in silence, then Fanny looked at him with a smile. 'Where do you live in London, Mr Bragg?' she asked.

'In a little street called Tan House Lane, near the eastern border of the City. It is not all that far from Aldgate, really.'

'And is the family you lodge with, congenial?'

Bragg laughed. 'Well, miss, I don't think I could call Mrs Jenks a family in her own right!'

'Is she the only other occupant of the house?' Fanny asked, momentarily crestfallen.

'That's right, miss. I have a bedroom and a sitting-room

on the top floor, and she has all the rest. Though I must admit, I have most of my meals in the basement kitchen. It's always warm, down there.'

'But there are servants?'

'Bless you, no! Mrs Jenks is the widow of a dustman and used to hard work. She can get round the house in no time.'

'I see.' Fanny was pensive for a moment, then said lightly: 'Tell me what you would be doing now, if you were back in London.'

'A Thursday morning? Well, I might be kicking my heels in a magistrate's court, waiting to give evidence; or I could be knocking on doors, looking for a suspect—or my boss could be chewing my ear off, for not solving my cases quickly enough. It is nine parts drudgery to one part of excitement.'

Fanny touched his arm gently. 'If this is the result of the excitement, I could wish, for your sake, that it was all drudgery.'

Bragg smiled. 'It would be insupportable then, miss. I might as well be a parish clerk.'

A cloud crossed her face. 'Of course, we are not immune from unpleasantness here,' she said. 'First, poor little Anna Dyer, then Mr Ollerton . . . One of his twin daughters has worked for us, for some years. She is such a sweet child, I feel very sorry for her. She has hardly stopped weeping since it happened.'

'It is a bad business,' Bragg said quietly.

'We would like to help, but Mrs Ollerton is such an independent person.'

'I doubt if she needs money, miss; and it is good that she has the business to worry about, it will take her mind off other things.'

'I suppose so.' Fanny stopped and turned to face Bragg. 'I must leave you now and buy some postage stamps. Here is the book of poems. You must tell me what you think of them.'

Bragg returned her smile. 'I will, miss,' he said.

He continued his walk in a high good humour. She was

a pleasant young woman. In any part of the country she would rate as upper middle class, and yet she was not at all standoffish. An intriguing mixture, too. Athletic, for a woman, yet given to reading sentimental novels; fond of the countryside, but hankering after the high life of London. Self-consciously, he slipped the book of poems into his pocket and strolled back. It wouldn't do if he were to catch her up. It would look bad.

He got back home to find that he was eating alone. Ada and Kittie had gone stooking with Mrs Toms, the saddler's wife. Robert was not yet back from Wimborne, and Ted was out somewhere. Emma vowed that she was much too fat already, so she left him in the kitchen with a plate full of roast beef and mounds of potato and cabbage. He felt guilty that she should have spent hours preparing this spread for him, when he could easily have bought a piece of a stand-pie in the pub. As a result, he ate far too much and got up from the table feeling thoroughly bloated. He decided that he would have to walk it off. In five hours, he would be expected to demolish a substantial supper. A brisk walk, up to Gallows Hill, would be just the ticket. Five miles, there and back, and a good view of the Purbeck Hills over the valley. As he strode down South Street, he overtook two small boys with jam jars and long bamboo canes.

'Going fishing?' he asked, good-humouredly.

'Yes,' the elder said, looking at Bragg distrustfully.

'What are you after?'

'There be a rainbow trout, what we saw yesterday,' the younger said eagerly.

'And where is it lying?'

'In a pool, up the stream.'

'The one with the big willow tree?'

'Yes.' The boys looked at him with wondering eyes.

'I've fished there, many a day, when I was young. But I never caught anything as grand as a trout. What are you using for bait? Worms?'

'Maggots.'

Bragg smiled indulgently. Real fishermen would be

horrified at the thought of anyone attempting to take a trout on anything but a minute wisp of feather! 'Well, I hope you catch it,' he said.

They reached the bridge and the boys crossed the road to get to their footpath. Bragg casually glanced downstream. Oh God! He ran to the parapet for a better look. Not another!

'Boys,' he called, 'come here, will you?'

Arrested by the urgency of his tone, the children reappeared.

'I want you to run to the police station and tell Constable Bugby to come down here. Tell him Mr Bragg said so . . . And, if you get him in ten minutes, there is a sixpence for you.'

At that, the boys dropped their fishing tackle and took to their heels, the elder soon outstripping the other.

Bragg climbed over the stile and ran down the bank of the stream. The edge of the black coat stirred gently with the current; the hat was tugging to float away, held in the sodden grey hair by a hatpin. Bragg stepped into the shallow water and, grabbing one of Tabitha's arms, dragged her on to the bank. Her flesh was still warm. He felt for a pulse, then ripped open her bodice to see if there was a heartbeat. There was none.

'I thought you was all for leaving things as they are,' Bugby said in a disgruntled voice, as he dropped down from the stile.

'Give me a hand to drain her out,' Bragg directed. 'She's not been in the water long.'

They took a leg each and held her upside down. Bugby caught sight of the two boys, gaping at the proceedings from the bridge.

'Hey, you two!' he shouted. 'Go and get Dr Shakerley. His trap is outside the butcher's.' The boys hared off up the road again.

'I'll try and get her breathing,' Bugby said. 'Lay her down.' They lowered her prone on the bank, and Bragg could see that, over the buttocks, her coat was still dry.

Bugby tilted her head to the right then, bestriding her, began to press her ribs rhythmically. On the right side of her forehead, there was a lacerated area. It was roughly oval, an inch and a half across, by two inches high. It was recent, no doubt about that. Bragg looked in the bed of the stream to see if there was a stone that could have caused the wound, when she fell. There was none. On the grass, by the arch of the bridge, was a small mound of newly picked water-cress.

There came the crisp clip-clop of a horse's hooves, then Dr Shakerley appeared, clutching his bag. Bugby abandoned his efforts and helped Sharkeley to turn Tabitha on her back. The doctor listened briefly for a heartbeat with his stethoscope, then stood up.

'Dead,' he pronounced flatly.

'It cannot have been long,' Bragg said.

Shakerley turned to face him. 'When you are dead, you are dead,' he said coldly. 'When it happened is of little account to you.'

'But it is the second death in a week! Surely that counts for something?' Bragg protested. 'You see the contusion on the forehead?'

'If the coroner orders an autopsy, I shall carry it out.' Shakerley snapped his bag shut. 'Until then, I have more urgent things to do.'

'If there is a post-mortem, would you let me be present?' Bragg asked. 'I did find her,' he ended lamely.

'Certainly not! Good day to you.' Shakerley turned on his heel and strode away.

Bugby was grinning unpleasantly. 'If you want to help . . . sir,' he said, 'you could get someone to come for the body—while I examine the area!'

Bragg trudged up the road in his wet boots. So his conversation with the Chief Constable had leaked out? No doubt his visit to Colegrave's house would soon have become public knowledge, but it went beyond that. It sounded as if he had been issuing instructions on new procedures, and Bugby had put two and two together. That would not make life any easier. Damnation! Why did he

have to get involved? He borrowed a handcart from a
painter's yard, and trundled back to the bridge.

That night, Bragg found it difficult to sleep. Another sudden
death; two, seven days apart, in a community of a thousand
people. Another violent death, moreover. Chance was a
queer thing, but this seemed to be stretching coincidence
beyond credence. Suppose that they were connected? But
what could possibly link the deaths of a prosperous carrier
and a half-mad white witch? Certainly, she had seen Alf
Dyer standing by Ollerton's body. But everyone accepted
that if he had been the killer he would not have hung about
the place. Round and round Bragg's mind went, sifting the
same evidence, testing the same theories. It was a totally
profitless exercise, but he could not stop. He dismissed the
notion of getting up and going for a walk. It would wake
everyone in the house—and they had to work next day, even
if he had not. Then he remembered Fanny Hildred's book of
poems, in his pocket. He had to look at it sometime, it
might as well be now. It would at least turn his thoughts into
a different channel. He lit his candle and took the book back
to bed with him.

   It had a good feel to it. The paper was thick and
silky-smooth to the touch. He riffled through the pages.
Most of the poems were short, and saved from insignifi-
cance by the elaborately decorated initial capitals. It was all
a bit arty for him. He skipped through a couple. Not his cup
of tea at all! But he had promised he would tell her what he
thought of them . . . Perhaps he would only give the book
back to her just before he left. She would not have time to
quiz him about them, then. Suddenly he noticed that a
pencil line had been drawn down the margin by one verse.
He turned the pages . . . here was another . . . and
another. She did not look like the type of woman who would
vandalise a book—particularly one of this quality. He
turned to the fly-leaf.

To Fanny, from Mamma.
On her birthday,
12th September, 1889.

Well, she had not been a callow girl, four years ago. He found the first marked verse.

> *Give me instead of beauty's bust,*
> *A tender heart, a loyal mind,*
> *Which with temptation I could trust,*
> *Yet never linked with error find.*

Hardly remarkable, he thought. In fact, a bit stodgy. Ah! The next one was a bit of Browning. That should be better; he was partial to Browning.

> *The bee's kiss now!*
> *Kiss me as if you entered gay*
> *My heart at some noonday,*
> *A bud that dares not disallow*
> *The claim, so all is rendered up,*
> *And passively its shattered cup*
> *Over your head to sleep I bow.*

Bragg felt strangely disturbed. It was direct, all right. Not the sort of poem you would expect a well-brought-up young woman to note. After the playful moth-kissing of the first verse, she wanted his tongue down her throat; and other things stuck elsewhere, no doubt. Dear God! Was Browning's wife one of them? He'd always thought of her as an invalid . . . Where was the third poem that Fanny had marked?

Like mine own dear harp is this my heart,
Dumb without the hand that sweeps its strings;
Tho' the hand be careless or be cruel,
When it comes my heart breaks forth and sings.

Bragg put the book down and stared into the shadows. He
was not sure that he wanted this glimpse into a young
woman's mind, or to hear what she seemed to be telling
him . . . He was worldly-wise enough to be free of the
notion that women were tepid, artless creatures, without a
carnal impulse in their body. But usually it was hot-blooded
married women that ran off the rails . . . Not that Fanny
Hildred was likely to have done that. It would just
be in her mind—an innocent longing. Well, not exactly
innocent . . . He had always been sorry for these middle-
class spinsters, trapped in a system that neither gave them
independence, nor allowed them to marry outside their
class. Not that Fanny fitted the stereotype. She was energetic, wholesome, good company . . . Too good for the
tradesmen, not good enough for the gentry—that was what
Ernie had said. Now, somebody like Catherine Marsden
would say: 'To hell with marriage. I am going to have a
career of my own, not moulder away because there is
nobody suitable.' But Fanny was of a different generation,
and stuck in the depths of the country. What would become
of her, for all her liveliness? No doubt, in time, she would
inherit the brewery. But she was not of the same mettle as
her mother. Or else her mother had dominated her for too
long. Either way, he could not see her running the business.
She would rely on someone else to do it . . . He thought
of the poems again. Was it just a cry from the heart? he
wondered. A crystallisation of unfulfilled longings? . . .
But suppose it were something more—focused on him, Joe
Bragg? What on earth could he say? Nonplussed, he
reached over and nipped out the candle, then pulled the
sheet over his head.

CHAPTER ———————
——————— SEVEN

There was a good handful of villagers in Church Lane, next morning, when Bragg went up. They were not in their best clothes, though most of them were soberly dressed. In the main, they were women. However the Dyer clan was regarded by the community, it was a little girl that was being buried. Some of them would be there out of sympathy; some, no doubt, from a superstitious desire to ward off a similar happening in their own family.

At half-past ten the vicar came to the churchyard gate. He was wearing a newly laundered white surplice over his black cassock—the victory of life over death. From his lack of composure, he was none too sure of it himself. He shifted restlessly from one foot to the other, evidently embarrassed to be waiting alone by the gate, yet unwilling to join the group of villagers in the lane. Perhaps, thought Bragg, he regarded himself as a kind of janitor, ushering the discarded clay into the keeping of the church. There was a murmur from the onlookers. The vicar glanced quickly at his prayer-book to see that his finger was in the right place, then he pushed open the iron gate and advanced with measured tread to meet the funeral procession.

Even when this representative of St Peter had taken up his position at the head of the cortège, and begun to drone appropriate scripture, the occasion would not rise above pathos. The little group contained no mourners other than members of the family. Behind the vicar, Dyer and his elder son carried the coffin between them. It was made of plain unvarnished deal, with the simplest of fittings. It seemed so small that it was hard to believe a human being could be contained therein. The family wore threadbare garments, well brushed, but looking like a job lot from a jumble-sale. Dyer's face was hard and angry, and tears trickled down his cheeks. His wife walked behind them, with her younger son. She was beyond tears, and looked numb and exhausted. They had gone past the onlookers now, the gap of indifference widening between them. On an impulse, Bragg stepped forward and joined the procession; then several women followed his example. The vicar led them to a remote corner of the churchyard, where a small grave had been scooped out of the ground. It was next to a rotting heap of discarded flowers; beyond it was a rampant growth of nettles and brambles. It was like a pauper's funeral, Bragg thought angrily. A little girl, playing happily with her friends a short time ago; now being put in a hole and covered over, to be forgotten. Life was hard, but it need not be unfeeling. Why should the shiftlessness and ill-repute of her menfolk be visited on her? She had been part of the community, too. Bragg took in little of the service and, when it was over, walked quickly away. He strode along North Street until he had come to the end of the village and his anger had cooled. Then he turned back.

He pulled out his watch. A quarter to twelve. Somehow it seemed disrespectful to go into the Royal Oak for a beer, so he continued on home. His cousin was on the stable roof, replacing the loose slate. He stood in the kitchen doorway watching, till Ted slithered down the roof and got his footing on the ladder. If he were of a mind, he could easily come over and make some remark that showed he wanted to heal the rift. Instead, Ted stayed on the ladder and began to clean out the gutter. So be it, thought Bragg. He might as well get some dry newspaper from Emma, to stuff his other boots; they were still very damp from the day before. He was about to go inside, when a man came into the yard. Seeing Ted up the ladder, he crossed over to him.

'I am Detective Inspector Milward, from Dorchester,' he announced.

Ted's face went white, and he clutched at the ladder.

'I understand that you have a Mr Bragg staying with you.'

Ted muttered something inaudible and gestured towards the doorway. Milward came over. He was clean shaven, with a long face and jutting jaw.

'Mr Bragg?' he asked.

'That's me.'

'I would like to have a word with you.'

'Then let us go into the parlour.' Bragg led the way to the cosy room at the front of the house. 'Will you have a beer?' he asked.

'I am on duty, sir.'

'Very well, please sit down.'

Milward looked at Bragg distastefully. 'I don't know about you,' he began, 'but I find these new telephones a nuisance I could do without.'

'Oh, yes?'

'They bring the guv'nor much too close, for my liking.'

'Our area is so small, you cannot get away even if you try,' Bragg replied amiably.

'My Chief Constable thinks that two sudden deaths in one village, in the space of a week, are a bit suspicious,' he said. 'I believe that you know him.'

'I met him once, socially.'

'Yes.' Milward gave him a cold stare. 'He has suggested that I should come and talk to you. For some reason, he thinks that you, with your experience in the big city, might have noticed something we missed.'

He was just as hostile as Bugby, thought Bragg, but with a bit more polish. 'I doubt that very much,' he said deprecatingly.

Milward was not to be mollified. 'Constable Bugby tells me that you are not satisfied with the coroner's verdict in the Ollerton case,' he said truculently.

'That is an interpretation that Bugby has chosen to put on it,' Bragg said. 'However, since the inquest, I have been told that someone saw two men at the stile, immediately before the shot.'

'Bugby did not say anything about that.'

'I have not yet told him.'

'So, now we have a policeman withholding information from the police,' Milward said sarcastically.

'It was not information, just gossip that I could not confirm.'

'It is our function to make enquiries, Mr Bragg, not yours.'

'I have made no enquiries. The man concerned was an itinerant thatcher. He left the village the following morning.'

'So it is worth nothing?'

'Possibly not.'

'The coroner's verdict was accidental death,' Milward said didactically. 'And, from what I have heard, there is no evidence inconsistent with that. There was one gun, one shot, one body.'

'It need not be so simple,' Bragg said cautiously.

'We are simple folk, down here,' Milward said with a sneer. 'We have not got time to complicate things and dramatise things.'

'There are other possibilities . . .'

'Yes. One of them Ted Sharman. Is that him, up the ladder?'

'Yes.'

'I shouldn't think he would thank you for stirring it up . . . for getting him a short walk and a shorter drop.'

'Ted is no murderer.'

'Oh?' Milward's lip curled scornfully. 'Have you got to be a particular type, to be a murderer? Is that your experience in the big city? . . . I tell you, Bragg, I don't like being ordered to waste my time conferring about an incident on my patch, with somebody from another force— and a sergeant, to boot.'

'I can understand that.'

'What about the Gosney woman?' Milward said abruptly.

'One is bound to wonder if the two deaths are connected . . . Has there been a post-mortem?'

'I believe so,' Milward said grudgingly.

'There was an abrasion on her forehead that could not have been caused by anything on the bed of the stream. She could have been knocked down and her head held under the water till she drowned. In that case, there might be bruises on the back of her head, caused by the pressure.'

'Your imagination is running away with you! Who would want to murder a mad old biddy like her?'

'I don't know.'

'What possible motive could there be?'

'It could be connected in some way with Ollerton's death,' Bragg said quietly.

'You are getting fanciful, man!'

'Do you know what the police surgeon found?'

'No, I do not.' The sarcasm was back. 'You will have to wait till the inquest, won't you?'

'Presumably so.'

Milward got to his feet. 'And, if you see your friend Colonel Colegrave again,' he said unpleasantly, 'you will let him know I called, won't you?'

'So you was at the little maid's funeral?' Ernie looked up challengingly.

'That's right,' Bragg replied.

'Still after Alf Dyer, are you?'

'I am not after anyone. I am on holiday.'

Ernie gave a lopsided grin. 'Oh yes?'

'In any case, it seems unlikely that Dyer was involved in Ollerton's death. I think the coroner got it right, there.'

A smart brougham came down the road from Poole and stopped outside the Royal Oak. A man and a woman, in deep mourning, got out and crossed the road to the Ollerton's house.

'It's as bad as a Woodbury Hill fair day,' Ernie said peevishly. 'We won't be able to move, soon, with all these carriages and traps.'

'It seems that he was well thought of—by his business acquaintances, anyway.'

Ernie merely snorted in reply.

They were sitting on the wall, waiting for Ollerton's funeral to start. But the house remained silent, its blinds drawn against the outside world.

'Are you goin'?' Ernie asked.

'No.' Bragg smiled. 'I told you, I am not partial to funerals.'

'It will be a good do, afterwards. They say there'll be cold poached salmon and baked ham.'

'We can manage without that.'

A bell began to toll as, with due solemnity, a shining black hearse approached up South Street. It was pulled by two jet-black horses, with black harness and tossing black plumes. The sides of the hearse were gleaming bevelled glass. It was empty. On the box were two black-clad figures, as grim as the old reaper himself. Two mutes walked behind the hearse, their faces composed in the extremity of grief. The little procession turned into the yard behind Ollerton's house and disappeared from sight.

'All the way from Wareham,' Ernie said approvingly. 'Didn't I say she would put him away proper?'

'It is a big contrast to this morning's funeral,' Bragg remarked.

Ernie shifted impatiently on the wall. Then, suddenly, he turned to Bragg. 'Geroge's watch was missin',' he said. 'Did you know?' His eyes were gleaming mischievously.

'Ollerton's?'

'Yes. When Mary got his clothes from the mortuary, there was everything there, except his watch. It was silver . . . made in Leeds, she says.'

'Is she sure that he had it with him, that afternoon?'

'Not what you would call sure. But he generally kept it on a chain, in his waistcoat.'

'Perhaps Constable Bugby put it somewhere safe.'

'That's what Mary Ollerton says. I expect we'll know tomorrow.'

Mourners were beginning to collect at the end of Church Lane now. There was to be a service in the church, before the burial. All Ollerton's employees and their families were there. They would have been invited to the house afterwards, of course. On the fringe were ordinary village people, conversing animatedly, savouring the spectacle.

Ernie dug Bragg in the ribs to gain his attention. 'I hear the police came for Ted Sharman—only he got away,' he said slyly.

Bragg forced a smile. 'As usual, you are only half right. Inspector Milward came to see me.'

'What about?'

'It was just a social chat—as between fellow policemen.'

'Go on!' Ernie said scornfully. 'He would never come from Dorchester, for that!'

'I took it that he was already in the village.'

'Ah! . . . They don't think they was accidents, then.'

At that moment, there was a scrabbling of hooves and the hearse began to emerge from Ollerton's yard. One of the men who had been on the box was now walking gravely in front, carrying a wreath draped with black crape. Ollerton's coffin was of rich polished oak, embellished with elaborate brass fittings. On top of the hearse was a mound of wreaths and flowers. With great solemnity, the cortège turned into the street. Mrs Ollerton walked alone, behind the mutes, her face sad but composed. Then came the two girls: one brown-haired and stocky, like her mother, the other fair and slender. They were red-eyed and walked hand in hand, for comfort. It was always the children, Bragg thought, that

excited one's compassion; though they would get over it
soonest. The hearse travelled a mere twenty yards up the
street, and pulled up by the end of Church Lane. The driver
got down and, with no sign that he comprehended the
absurdity of the proceedings, opened the rear door. The
undertaker's men took the coffin on to their shoulders, then
transferred it to six men of the village. They shuffled off
uncertainly towards the church, the attendants discreetly
following with arms full of funeral flowers.

'I'll tell you one man who will be glad Ollerton's out of
the way,' Ernie said darkly.

'Who is that?'

'Bill Applin.'

'The landlord of the Drax?' Bragg asked in surprise.

Ernie gave a smirk. 'Ollerton's been shaggin' his wife . . .
Not that he was the only one. I reckon anyone could have it up
her—except me.'

'Did Applin know, do you think?'

'Maybe. Lily hasn't got much to say for herself at the
moment!'

Bragg thought back to the evening he had enquired about
Hodge. She had been free with the men then, all right, but
her husband had not been in the bar. Perhaps she would
have been more circumspect if he had been there . . . Was
it possible that Applin had been provoked into murder? He
would know Ollerton well enough to have arranged to meet
him by the stile, or he could have followed him there. He
was of medium build and could never have overpowered
Ollerton, but he could fit the theory of the friend asking to
examine the shotgun.

'If he did for George, then who killed the Old Crow?'
Ernie asked waspishly.

'We shall have to wait and see what the inquest finds,'
Bragg replied non-committally.

'Come on! You found her.'

'It could have been an accident.'

'But you don't think so.'

'Who could have possibly wanted to kill her?'

'Me!' Ernie exclaimed with a scowl. 'She didn't make much of a job of deliverin' me, did she?' Then he spat. 'No. It were my da did for me, randy old goat. Always tuppin' my ma, wouldn't leave her alone. Stands to reason . . . I'll kill the old devil, one day.'

Bragg found himself unable to respond to this flash of bitter self-disgust. If ever there was resentment that could boil over into murder, it was in that grotesque, contorted body. Was it possible? he wondered. One would ordinarily dismiss the thought out of hand. And yet, within the limitations of movement imposed by his twisted limbs, Ernie was mobile. He could easily shuffle down to the bridge and back. What if he had done so when Tabitha was there? What if she had ignored his gibes again, and he had flung a stone at her? There had not been a stone in the stream, true, but it might have lodged in the grass. She could have staggered, missed her footing and fallen, unconscious, into the water . . . But it all seemed too far-fetched and, anyway, according to Ernie, he had been with Robert that morning. It should be easy enough to confirm.

'I reckon she had foreseen her death in her crystal ball,' Ernie said pensively. 'They say she went queer after George died.'

'There was nothing magical or infernal about Tabitha's death,' Bragg said firmly. 'For my money, she simply drowned.'

'Or was drowned.'

'Very well, if you want to explore that theory. But there does not seem to be anyone with a motive for killing her—apart from you, that is.'

'Unless it was the same one that did George in.'

'In that case, we have to establish opportunity for both.'

Ernie gave a malicious leer. 'What about Ted Sharman?' he asked.

'I cannot conceive of any reason why he should want Tabitha dead.'

'Maybe. But what was he doin', sneakin' home round the back of Black Hill, that Thursday?'

'Who says he was?'

'I do. I saw him come over the bridge. Me and Robert had just got back from Wimborne. It was nearly half-past two.'

'Rubbish!' Bragg exclaimed. 'We were still down by the stream then. It would have been folly for him to have come back that way, if he had done it.'

'I tell you, he was sneakin'! You didn't see him.'

'I would swear that he knew nothing about it when I told him that night.'

Ernie squirmed off the wall crossly. 'You are like all the others,' he said. 'You will only believe what you want to believe.'

CHAPTER _____

_____ EIGHT

Saturday morning found Bragg pushing a hand-cart up the lane leading to Woodbury Hill, with the vicar prancing joyfully ahead. It was one of his ancient pathways, below the level of the surrounding fields, and, with a hedge on either side, it was impossible to see anything. One thing was certain, the hill had suddenly become steeper. Bragg wondered if he should stop, to rest his aching arm. Then the lane levelled off and, to the left, he could see a track leading into a grassy arena.

'Here we are,' the vicar said proprietorially. 'Our very own Iron Age fort. Not so impressive as Maiden Castle, perhaps, but every bit as interesting.'

'Nothing like as big,' Bragg remarked.

'No. But it encloses over twelve acres. That would have protected a substantial community. Of course, there would have been a double bank of gravel round the whole site. Most of the earthworks have disappeared, but the general plan is clear enough.'

'More erosion?'

Ryder smiled. 'I imagine that our Saxon forebears found it a convenient source of building materials for their new village, down in the valley. Now, if you will follow me with the equipment, I will endeavour to borrow a wheelbarrow.'

At the far end of the enclosed area was a group of brick cottages, with low, tiled roofs. The vicar bounded off to the nearest one, and returned trundling a rickety wooden barrow.

'By that low mound, there,' he directed. 'Excellent, excellent!' Despite the warmth of the morning, he was clad in clerical broadcloth. But it was shinier than his usual garb, and the bottoms of the trousers were frayed. Well, thought Bragg, he never knew when he would be called on to practise his trade, either; and appearance was the main part of a parson's craft.

'I intend to excavate one corner of the site,' Ryder said. 'That will give me an insight into the problems I might encounter, were I to launch a full-scale operation next year.'

'Surely, you would not try to tackle all this on your own?' Bragg said, gazing round the enclosure.

'No, no! My interest is not in the fort itself, but in a much later building. This mound is said to be the site of a mediaeval anchoret's chapel. In addition to a strong oral tradition, I have seen an eighteenth-century etching which shows the foundations of the chapel to be in this area.'

'How old is it, then?'

'I have been unable to establish a precise date. We know that a certain John Sperhauk was chaplain of Woodbury in fourteen hundred and eight. But presumably the anchoret had long departed this life by then.'

The vicar walked to the corner of the nearest cottage and, taking a small compass from his waistcoat pocket, took a bearing on the mound. He scribbled briefly in a notebook, then began to pace out the distance from the cottage.

'The first peg will be here,' he announced, sticking his pencil into the ground to mark the spot.

While Bragg unloaded buckets and spades, tarpaulin and riddle, the vicar began to hammer pegs into the soft earth, until the site was boxed in. Then he took a spade and skimmed the turf off one corner. It looked hard work, but he swung the spade with fierce energy. When he stopped for breath, some twelve feet square had been exposed. He then got a ball of twine from the cart and stretched it between the pegs, until a grid covered the area.

'I am sorry that we shall not be able to achieve much today, Bragg,' he said. 'I'm afraid that I must be back in time for the flower show.'

'I didn't think that was a church do,' Bragg said.

'It is not. But Mrs Ryder feels it is the more incumbent upon us to attend. However, we can make a start. I shall excavate the soil in each square in turn. I doubt if it will be more than a foot deep, before we encounter the chalk. I will place the soil in the wheelbarrow. What I would ask you to do, Mr Bragg, is to take buckets of the soil and pass it through the sieve. You will find it quite friable. In that way we will recover any objects of interest.'

'That seems straightforward enough.'

The vicar attacked the corner square with his spade. Soon the wheelbarrow was half full of dark soil, threaded through with grass roots. Bragg filled a bucket and, squatting down, began to shake it through the riddle. He was left with a scattering of pebbles at the bottom.

'How will I know what is interesting?' he called.

Ryder came across and poked among the debris. 'There is nothing there,' he said. 'We are looking for anything that shows the imprint of man. For instance, we shall unearth many flints; but only those which appear to have been knapped, to create a tool, would be of significance.'

'I would be no judge,' said Bragg. 'Best if I give you a shout.'

'Very well.'

The vicar went back to his digging, while Bragg processed several more buckets of earth. Then he found a shell in the bottom of his sieve.

'I don't know if this is significant,' he called, but it is certainly unexpected.

Ryder hurried across and turned it over in his fingers. 'It is certainly of archaeological interest,' he said with a smile, 'though it is of comparatively recent date. The Woodbury Hill fair of our times is a comparatively insignificant, and entirely parochial, affair; but in the Middle Ages, it was the most important fair in the south of England. Can you imagine the whole of this arena crammed with stalls and booths? Along the central concourse, was a row of permanent wooden buildings. They would be occupied, for the period of the fair, by the officials whose duty it was to collect the tolls and so on. No doubt they housed the more prosperous traders, also . . . Here is something that will interest you.' He pointed towards the cottages. 'You see the lean-to, on the end building? Tradition has it that it was used as a lock-up for thieves and vagabonds during fair time.'

'I did not realise that it went back so far.'

'Indeed! There are records which show that the servants of King Edward the First purchased four great locks here, for Corfe Castle, in 1282. So it was much more than a purely agricultural fair.'

'And where does this shell fit in?' Bragg asked.

'In olden times, it used to last five days and the second was Gentlefolk's Day. There would be mummers and tumblers—all kinds of entertainments—and, traditionally, large numbers of oysters were consumed. So the last person to hold that shell could have been a gentleman in doublet and hose, or a grand dame with a wimple!'

'What a queer place to hold a fair,' Bragg said. 'You would wonder that people would ever come so far.'

'It is said that the fair was attracted by the crowds of people who came to the anchoret's chapel. According to legend, a sacred relic made of gold, which had been placed in the anchoret's well, gave its water extraordinary healing power. On the anniversary of its dedication, the twenty-first of September, vast throngs of people came here to worship and to drink the water.'

'And the traders and jugglers came where the crowds were? It's a nice story, anyway.'

'There is generally some truth behind our oral traditions,' Ryder said with conviction, then pulled out his watch. 'Great Heavens! I shall be late for the flower show. Give me a hand to cover the excavation with the tarpaulin; then we had better be off.'

When Bragg got back home, he was feeling ravenous. The fresh air must be doing him a power of good, he thought. What with Emma's cooking and the beer, he would be getting a corporation again, if he wasn't careful. He went into the kitchen, to find Emma and the girls finishing a snack lunch of sandwiches.

'I thought you wouldn't mind, Joe,' Emma said apologetically. 'I will give you a proper meal tonight, only, we are going to the flower show.'

'That's all right, love. I shall enjoy some bread and cheese for a change.'

'Can we get ready now?' asked an excited Ada.

Emma smiled indulgently. 'Yes, run along. I have put your things out on the bed . . . And see that Kittie puts clean socks on!'

'Young scamps,' Bragg remarked with a smile. 'Is Ted around?'

'He has gone off somewhere. He knows I would drag him to the show, else.'

'Emma,' Bragg began hesitantly, 'I have been thinking that I might cut my visit a bit short.'

Emma bridled immediately. 'Are you not being looked after well enough?' she asked sharply.

'It is certainly not that! It's just that I am not sure Ted wants me here. We have only had a couple of real conversations, all the time I have been here. I am getting to feel that I am keeping him out of his own home.'

Emma's face clouded. 'Take no notice of him,' she said firmly. 'He was like this before you came. He is worried about the business, that's all.'

'If it were only that, I would have expected him to be feeling more optimistic. He must be hoping to get some of his customers back now.'

'We will see, won't we?' Emma said flatly.

'We were so close as boys . . . perhaps I was expecting too much. It is not surprising that we should have grown apart. I just feel that he resents my being here.'

'Take no notice, Joe. He'll come round. Now, why don't you come to see the show too? You will enjoy it and it will be a nice change to have someone squiring me around.'

'Put like that, I can hardly refuse!'

Bragg brought his best boots down to the kitchen and found a tin of blacking. They were dry now, but a wavy white tide-mark had formed above the welts. Blast it! He had only just broken them in. He had paid over the odds for them, too; nice supple leather and they had shined up a treat. Now look at them! He covered them liberally with polish and set them in the sun to dry. When he brushed them off, the white line had disappeared, but you could see where it had been. There was a weal along the upper, like a half-healed scar. They would never be the same again. Disgruntled, Bragg went upstairs to change. He'd better put a clean shirt on, too . . .

When he came down, Emma was waiting for him. She was wearing a light floral print dress and a wide-brimmed straw hat, decorated with artificial flowers and cherries. For the first time that he could remember, she was wearing gloves.

'You look a real treat!' he said admiringly.

She smiled and bobbed a curtsy. 'Thank you, sir! . . . I've sent the girls on. They couldn't abide in their skins any longer.'

She put her hand on his proffered arm and they walked with some ceremony to the Cross, then along North Street. As they neared the recreation ground, Ada and Kittie came scampering towards them.

'Ma! Ma! You've won a prize!' they chanted.

'Goodness me! How do you know?'

'We crawled under the side of the big tent. There was a card saying "First" by your gooseberry pie!'

'I am not a bit surprised, either,' said Bragg.

Emma looked anxiously at their dresses. 'If you have messed yourselves up,' she said, 'I'll scalp you!'

'We haven't!' The girls swirled round and took to their heels.

'You are lucky,' Bragg said pensively.

'With the children, you mean?'

'Yes. It is something I shall never know.'

'I will wrap them up in brown paper, and you can take them back with you!' Emma said with a chuckle.

Bragg paid their entrance fees and they went into the ground. The cricket square had been carefully roped off. The marquee that had served as the beer tent on the previous Saturday now housed the exhibits. By the entrance was a low platform, with a few chairs on it. A couple of side panels had been looped back to allow a draught of air into the tent, and Bragg glanced inside. Two men were going along the trestle tables, peering at the floral exhibits and discussing them intently.

'Who are the judges?' he asked.

'The little tubby one is the secretary of Wareham Horticultural Society,' Emma said. 'The other is the head gardener at Shitterton Manor. 'Tis good that he is judging, or the squire would walk off with all the prizes!'

Down at the bottom of the field, an area had been roped off for children's races, and Bragg could see a pile of flour sacks by the hedge. No doubt the fathers would make fools of themselves in a sack race, later on. Near the cricket pitch, there was a semi-circle of chairs, and a brass band was busy setting up music stands and unpacking instruments.

'There'll be a dance, tonight,' Emma said in a rallying tone. 'You'll come and do the lancers, won't you?'

'Now, that is one thing the doctor expressly forbade,' Bragg said with a grin. ' "No capering around with strange women," he said.'

'Joe!' exclaimed Emma chidingly, as if it were the most *risqué* remark ever made. Five children, and still coy. She ought to hear how Marie Lloyd went on, at the Empire!

One of a group of men standing by the platform suddenly came to life and marched importantly in the direction of the gate. Bragg could see the squire and his wife advancing towards the marquee. He was wearing a grey frock-coat and a top hat. Mrs Jerrard was tall and slim, with an austerely beautiful face. She wore a pink silk gown with a fitted waist and frilled train. Her straw hat was trimmed with black ribbon, flowers and white plumes. As a couple, they would not have been out of place in Hyde Park, Bragg thought. She was certainly playing the part of the lady of the manor for all it was worth. The little man had taken off his hat and was greeting them obsequiously. The squire looked embarrassed, but Mrs Jerrard acknowledged him with a disdainful half-smile, then swept by him. He hopped and bounded along beside her, like an ineffectual sheep-dog, until they came to the platform. The other members of the committee then mumbled their greetings, and the Jerrards seated themselves. By now, a substantial crowd had gathered around them.

'Doesn't she look lovely?' Emma whispered.

'Yes. But I wouldn't like to have to pay her dressmaker's bills,' Bragg grunted.

'Ladies and gentlemen.' The little man was holding up his hand for silence . . . 'Ladies and gentlemen, welcome to the fifth flower show of the Bere Regis Horticultural Society. Let me, once again, say how much we owe to the generosity of Mr and Mrs Jerrard, of Shitterton Manor, whose unfailing encouragement and support has enabled this happy occasion to take place . . . I now call upon Mrs Jerrard to open the show.'

There was a polite ripple of applause, as she advanced to the front of the platform.

'Ladies and gentlemen,' she began tentatively, as if she had never before thought to associate the words with the faces before her. 'Unlike last year, we have been blessed with a glorious day.' Her voice was clear, if a bit on the sharp side, Bragg thought. Her enunciation was scrupulously pure, without a trace of west-country accent. All in all, she seemed to have a deal more character than her diffident husband.

'I am told that the exhibits are of a very high standard,' she went on, 'and I am looking forward to seeing them for myself. I hope that you all have a very enjoyable afternoon. I now declare the 1893 flower show open.'

There was more applause, the band struck up a jaunty tune and, surrounded by the fawning committee members, Mrs Jerrard entered the marquee for her tour of inspection. After a discreet interval, the village people poured after them. As Bragg and Emma drifted towards the entrance, they came up with Fanny Hildred and her mother. On Bragg's greeting them, Emma excused herself on the grounds that she ought to find the children, and disappeared.

'You are becoming quite addicted to our village occasions, Mr Bragg,' Fanny said with a warm smile.

'I don't aim to get myself roped in for anything dangerous, this time, miss!'

'By the way, sergeant,' Amy cut in crisply, 'I have been meaning to have a word with you. I fully realise that your cousin is going through a difficult time—in more ways than one. If he wanted to apply for a temporary beerseller's licence, for the period of the Woodbury Hill fair, I am sure that I could get him one.'

'Thank you ma'am,' Bragg said. 'I will mention it to him.'

'Indeed, if he wished to apply to have his premises licenced as an ale-house, I would use my influence on his behalf.'

'That wouldn't suit the Royal Oak and the Drax!'

'No matter. It is time that we had an outlet for Hildred's beer in the village.'

Bragg laughed. 'It seems strange,' he said, 'to find an

upright church-going lady, like you, encouraging men to drink to excess.'

'They will drink to excess anyway,' Amy said blandly. 'They deserve to have the best beer in the country to fuddle themselves on.'

'Ted did say, the other night, that he had been thinking of starting the brewing again.'

'In that case, I withdraw my offer of support!'

'But he decided that the bank would not allow it.'

'Mr Bragg,' Amy said sharply, 'I suspect that you are amusing yourself at my expense. It is quite unseemly in a grown man. Come along, let us look at the exhibits.' She swept into the marquee.

Giving a conspiratorial smile, Fanny followed, with Bragg close behind. On a table, at one end of the tent, was a magnificent floral display that dominated the whole show. Fanny gave a cry of delight and hurried over to it. Surely, Bragg thought, that must have won the highest award? He picked up a card from one end of the table.

'It is not in the competition,' he said.

'But it is exquisite!' Fanny exclaimed.

Amy looked at a card beside the arrangement and sniffed. 'I thought as much. "From the gardens of Shitterton Manor". Ruby Jerrard cannot compete, since her head gardener is one of the judges—indeed, I do not suppose that she would deign to compete with the people of the village, anyway. But she cannot resist demonstrating that the produce of her gardens is infinitely superior to anything we could aspire to.'

'Do I gather that you regard yourself as one of the village people?' Bragg asked in surprise.

'Of course I am, sergeant. We have lived here for over twenty years. I own most of it. How could we not be?'

'The sentiment does you credit, ma'am,' he said and turned down the aisle between the trestle tables. Was it jealousy that had produced the comment? he wondered; resentment at knowing that she could never be top dog here?

The floral exhibits were dominated by dahlias; but there

were plenty of roses, delphiniums and daisies of various kinds. Suddenly Fanny gave an excited gasp.

'Mamma! I have won first prize for my rose!' she exclaimed. It was a creamy-white rosebud, flushed with pink on the tips of its petals. Bragg was oddly gratified that she was prepared to take part in the ordinary activities of the village.

'That is a most beautiful flower, miss,' he said. 'It deserves its first prize.'

'Thank you, Mr Bragg,' she said, colouring with pleasure.

At the end of the marquee, the Jerrards were chatting to the vicar and his wife. Then they began to make their way to the exit, the little secretary still dancing attendance.

'Hardly worth getting dolled up for such a short time,' Bragg remarked.

'In a small community, sergeant, the *noblesse* are obliged to take such pains, if unwanted familiarity is to be avoided,' Amy said acidly. 'Come along, Fanny. We have monopolised quite enough of Mr Bragg's time for one day.'

'Very well, mamma.' Fanny gave a regretful smile and followed in her mother's wake.

It was right enough, Bragg thought. There were plenty of tongues wagging in Bere Regis, already. But how damned stupid, that you could not spend an afternoon in the company of a personable young woman, without people thinking there was a further fetch to it.

He turned into the vegetable section. Here the tables were covered with precisely conical carrots, displays of full-podded peas and enormous striped marrows. Fanny had taken second prize for a bundle of asparagus—utility as well as beauty! At the far end were the preserves and baking sections. Looking at the exhibits, Bragg wondered how they could be judged without being sampled. Indeed, how could the public appreciate them, without being able to stick a finger in the jam or break a corner off the cake? He was amused to hear the disparaging remarks of the villagers on some of the prize-winning entries. This section lay much nearer to the hearts of the women. In her own kitchen, every housewife was an expert. Emma had seen his approach, and was hovering in the pastry section, with a look of excited modesty on her face. Yes, there was the coveted red card, propped against her entry. And this time, the judging had been thorough. Emma's pie had been violated by the removal of a narrow wedge of the pastry to reveal the densely packed fruit within.

'That looks good,' Bragg said. 'Are we going to have it for supper?'

'No,' Emma whispered in embarrassment. 'After the show they are given to the poor of the parish.'

'Oh, I see . . . Well, I hope there is another like it.'

At least, Emma did not see herself in that category.

'Why don't we have some tea?' Emma suggested. 'I'm parched.'

'A good idea. I notice that, although beer is provided at the cricket match, tea is the strongest beverage allowed at the flower show!'

'That's Mrs Jerrard. She doesn't hold with it. I suppose she is right, in a way. Men never know when to stop. But plenty will come up from the Oak for the dance.'

To Bragg's mild irritation, Emma insisted on paying for the tea. Had she been stung by her own remark about the poor? Or was it that, having received his allowance, she refused to take more from him? Whatever the reason, Bragg felt diminished. He was pettishly looking away from her, when he noticed that one of the women serving the tea was Mrs Ollerton. She was hollow-eyed and pale, but she was working as hard as any of them. Like Martha Dyer, she had to carry on. Men could posture and fret, but the women had to keep things going. With a sudden access of compassion, he went across to her.

'Mrs Ollerton, my name is Bragg. I want to offer my condolences over your husband's death.'

A flicker of pain crossed the drawn face. 'Oh, yes. You were down there, weren't you?'

'Yes. I shall be in Bere Regis for a couple of weeks yet.

If there is anything I can do for you, please let me. Time is weighing heavily on my hands.'

She looked at him wearily. 'The men are working all right,' she said. 'It's the books that worry me. George used to keep them and nobody else knows how to do them. I've got bills coming in, and I don't know whether I have the money to pay them or not.'

'Well, at least I can help you there,' Bragg said reassuringly. 'My father ran a carrier's business, so I know what to expect. And I was a bookkeeper in shipping offices, for six years, as a youth. I will gladly write up the books for you.'

'I would be that relieved if you would.'

'I had better start well before I am due to leave. Will towards the end of next week suit you?'

'Whenever you are ready. Just come up—I shall not be far away.'

After supper, Bragg smoked a pipe then went into the yard. Ted was leaning on the gate, gazing out over the fields. There was a listlessness about him, an air of defeat. Bragg strolled up and leaned on the gate beside him. Ted moved over, to make room, but otherwise did not acknowledge his presence. Bragg said nothing, deciding to let him make the running. He had tried to force himself on Ted in the past, and had only provoked exasperation. Perhaps he would not be able to help him. Perhaps it was something an outsider could never get to the bottom of. The silence prolonged itself into minutes. It was not antagonistic or resentful; rather it was inert, spent. Bragg was about to move away again, when Ten spoke.

'What did Milward want?' he asked in a dead voice.

'He was canvassing my views on the two deaths—as a fellow policeman, you understand . . . The Chief Constable had sent him.'

'Oh?'

'They are not happy,' Bragg added, trying to build a conversation.

'And I am top of their list?'

'You are on it, certainly.'

'Bloody gossip! Just because Ollerton pinched my customers.'

'I imagine that you had made unwise remarks to others, as well as me—remarks that sounded like threats.'

Ted did not reply and seemed to be sinking into despondency again.

'Where were you on Thursday, when Tabitha Gosney died?' Bragg asked abruptly. 'You were not at home for lunch, but you had not taken a load out. Where were you?'

Ted swung round angrily. 'What the bloody hell has it got to do with you?' he cried.

'It is no use flying off the handle. I want to protect you from the likes of Milward and Bugby, but I must know the truth.'

'I was out.'

'I know that. But you were seen coming back, over the bridge, at half-past two.'

'Who by?'

'Ernie Toop. He said you were sneaking home.'

'He had just come back from Wimborne with Robert. I am sure your son would be able to confirm or deny it, he had just brought the cart into the yard.'

Ted was silent for a moment, then: 'Would I have walked back, bold as brass, if I'd just drowned the old cow?' he asked harshly.

'You might.'

'Well, I didn't.'

'What I cannot understand is that we were still down there at that time. The doctor's trap was stopped on the bridge—you must have seen it, and wondered what was going on. Yet when I told you about Tabitha's death, that evening, you made out that you knew nothing about it.'

'All right,' Ted said irritably, 'I did come over the bridge. I did see the trap, but I thought nothing of it. I was in a hurry. I had to take the dog cart into Dorchester, for some parcels, and I was late—Sunlight soap and biscuits, that is all I'm good for, nowadays . . . And I did not sneak home!'

'Where had you been, that lunchtime?' Bragg asked quietly.

'Up on Black Hill.'

'Did you meet anyone?'

'No, I did not!' Ted shouted defiantly.

Bragg waited for his anger to subside. 'You know, Ted,' he said in a conversational tone, 'if I were Milward or Bugby, and had all the facts that I know, I would be asking for an arrest warrant, just in case you slipped away.'

Ted's lip curled in contempt. 'That would just suit you, Joe. You would be able to make out you'd done better than any of us, then, wouldn't you?'

Bragg was taken aback. 'That is a bloody stupid thing to say!' he exclaimed. 'Though it shows how warped your mind has got. I am just a flat-footed copper, and I shall never be anything better. But I do care about my flesh and blood—and that includes you. Your worries over the business seem to have got you down to such an extent, that you feel you are finished. Because of that, you are not trying to defend yourself. But, before long, it might not be just village gossip you have to worry about. Believe me, Milward and Bugby will have no interest in proving your innocence. You will have to help yourself.'

Ted looked at him dully, without speaking.

'I accept that you did not kill Tabitha Gosney,' Bragg said. 'But it is possible that someone did. Just think back. Did you see anyone, that day, as you were coming down from Black Hill?'

Ted looked away, across the fields. 'I saw a man . . . walking along the field bottom, on the other side of the hill,' he said reluctantly.

'Who was it?'

'I couldn't see him properly. He was in the shadow of the hedge.'

'Was he trying to conceal himself?'

'No, he was walking as normal.'

'In what direction was he going?'

'How do I know? Turner's Puddle, Briantspuddle . . .
anywhere.'

Ted turned and went into the harness room, leaving
Bragg to wonder whether he had been telling the truth, or
not.

CHAPTER ————

————— NINE

Just before eleven o'clock on the following Monday morning, Bragg went up to the village hall again. This time, the inquest was on Tabitha Gosney. The coroner had gone up in his estimation. Her death had not been spectacular, like Ollerton's, and yet he had ordered a post-mortem and an inquest. Probably it was the one death closely following the other; but some country coroners would have been tempted to cut corners, and give a burial certificate on the witness statement alone. He pushed through the doors into the lobby and saw Dr Shakerley standing in the corner, smoking a cigarette. Bragg nodded, then crossed over to him.

'Good morning, sir.'

'Good morning.'

'I was wondering if I might ask you a question.'

'Not about this case, you can't,' Shakerley said curtly.

'No, no. It is a general question in your field.'

'Very well.'

'I learned, the other day, that corpses are sometimes

found clutching tightly on to things. The example I was given was a dead artilleryman still grasping a ramrod.'

Shakerley nodded. 'The dead man's grip, yes. So far as I know, it is found only in cases of violent death. The technical name for it is cadaveric spasm.'

'How firm is the grasp?'

'Very tight indeed. I have only encountered one instance of it, myself, but there have been many cases described in the medical journals. It is an extraordinary phenomenon.'

'How long does it take to wear off?'

'It is not easy to be precise. Generally, the mortuary attendants have to break the grip in the course of their duties. Where that has not happened, it has been known to persist for some days. There is a reported case of a woman's body being recovered from the sea, three days after falling—or jumping—from the harbour wall. She was still firmly clutching some small coins in her hand. The spasm occurs at the instant of death, you understand. It has nothing to do with rigor mortis, if that is what you are thinking.'

'I see. So it would not have gone in twenty minutes?'

Shakerley looked at Bragg suspiciously. 'No,' he said shortly.

'Thank you, sir.'

Bragg passed into the hall and saw Ernie beckoning to a place beside him.

'I thought you wasn't comin',' he said, his eyes bright with excitement.

'I could hardly miss this,' Bragg said genially. 'After all, I found her.'

'Hey! Have you heard?'

'What?'

'Alf Dyer has made a run for it.'

'Dyer?' Bragg repeated incredulously.

'Yes. They say he skipped straight after the little maid's funeral. He went home and changed into his workin' clothes, then walked out. Nobody has seen him since.'

'Good God! Where has he gone?'

'Nobody knows.'

'I expect his wife has a good idea.'

'If she has, she's not for tellin' . . . So it wasn't Ted Sharman, after all!' Ernie gave a twisted smirk.

'It was never going to be Ted.'

'Stand!' Bugby appeared at the rear door, to call the assembly to order.

The coroner walked purposefully to the dais and took his seat. Once again, Bragg noted, he did not regard the case as of sufficient importance to merit a jury. He banged with his gavel to still the murmurings.

'This is an inquest into the death of Tabitha Gosney, a spinster of this parish,' he said, then turned to Bugby. 'Who gives evidence of identity?' he asked.

'I do, sir. She lived alone and had no known relatives.'

'I see. And did you know the deceased personally?'

'I knew her very well, sir,' Bugby said firmly.

The coroner looked up quizzically. 'I have a persistent conviction that I know the name of the deceased, yet I cannot recall why.'

'She appeared before you last Monday, your honour, as a witness at the inquest on George Ollerton.'

'So she did.' A frown crossed the coroner's brow, then he dipped his pen in the inkwell and made a note.

'Who is to give evidence of discovery, officer?'

'I am sir.' Bugby took the Bible from the prayer-desk and recited the oath. Then he glanced at his notebook.

'At approximately two o'clock in the afternoon of Thursday the twenty-first of August,' he began, 'I was summoned by two small boys, who requested me to accompany them to the bank of the Bere Stream, near South Street.'

'These boys would appear to have made the actual discovery,' the coroner interrupted. 'Are they known to you?'

'Yes, sir. They are Joshua Russell's boys.'

'Then, why are they not here to give evidence?'

'They be but six and eight years old, your honour.'

'Are you saying that they are too young to give an account of what they saw?'

Bugby hesitated. 'Yes, sir.'

'Very well. Proceed.'

'I arrived at the footpath, downstream of the bridge. There is a pool about eighteen inches to two feet deep, under the bridge. Then the stream spreads out and becomes shallow again.'

The coroner held up his hand and scratched away in his book for some moments.

'And where was the body lying, when you first saw it?' he asked.

Bugby's face reddened. 'It was on the bank, sir.'

'That is not what you said in your witness statement, is it?' The coroner took up one of his papers and began to peruse it.

'No, sir.'

'Then, what is the truth of the matter, constable?'

'The body had already been pulled from the water.'

'By the two small boys?'

'No, sir. By a man called Mr Bragg. He was visiting the village at the time.'

'Is that not another name I recall from last week?'

'Quite possibly, sir.'

'Has Mr Bragg now returned home?'

'No, your honour.'

'Why was he not called to give evidence?' the coroner asked sharply. 'Where is he staying?'

'At the Old Brewery, sir.'

'Then send someone for him.'

Bragg got to his feet. 'I am here, sir.'

'Good. Please take the stand, Mr Bragg.'

Bugby glowered as he got Bragg to repeat the oath.

'Since you are not resident in the parish,' the coroner said, 'I must ask you to give me your full name.'

'Joseph Bragg, your honour.'

'Your address?'

'Eleven, Tan House Lane, London EC.'

'And your occupation?'

'Sergeant of police, City of London police force.'

The coroner lifted his head and looked searchingly from Bugby to Bragg.

'I see,' he said slowly. 'Well now, Mr Bragg, since we are so fortunate as to have you present, despite your not having been summoned, please be so good as to tell me how you came to discover the body of the deceased.'

'I was walking down South Street, your honour. As I got to the bridge, I happened to glance downstream and saw a woman lying in the water. I sent the two small boys for Constable Bugby, then got over the stile and down to the stream.'

'To what part of the stream?'

'As the constable has said, the stream becomes shallow again about three feet from the bridge. Miss Gosney was lying at right-angles to the bank, some three feet further on.'

'So, she was six feet from the stonework, is that it?'

'Yes, sir.'

'Where was she, precisely, in relation to the bank?'

'Her feet were some eight inches into the water.'

'Did you see anything which might indicate that she had slipped into the stream, sergeant?'

'No, your honour. The bank is grassy there and the ground is, of course, very dry.'

'Would it be possible for someone to slip on the grass, and thus into the water?'

'I suppose it would be possible.'

The coroner wrote a brief note. 'Now, how was the body lying?'

'She was prone, with both her her arms straight down by her sides. Her face was on the bed of the stream. By that, I mean that it was not inclined to right or left.'

'I understood you perfectly,' the coroner said acidly. 'What else did you observe?'

'The back of her coat was dry.'

'Suggesting that she had not rolled over, or struggled to get out of the stream.'

'That is correct, sir.'

'How deep is the water at that place?'

'Not more than six inches.'

'Then any struggles would have been unlikely to saturate her back.'

'True, sir, but her arms were by her sides.'

'The inference had not escaped me, sergeant. Anything else?'

'There was an abrasion on her forehead. I looked in the stream, but I could find no object which might have caused it, if she had fallen there.'

'Now, perhaps you would explain why you removed the body from the water.'

'She was still warm, sir. Constable Bugby helped me to hold her up, to drain her. Then he tried to get her breathing again, until Dr Shakerley came and pronounced her dead.'

'I see. Thank you. You may stand down, sergeant.'

Bragg returned to his seat, irritated that he had not been allowed to express his opinions more fully.

'Now, Constable Bugby, perhaps you would take the stand again.' The coroner's tone was verging on the sardonic. 'What have you to add to Mr Bragg's testimony?'

Bugby shot a malevolent look at Bragg, then returned to the prayer-desk.

'I examined the immediate area, your honour,' he said. 'There was a bunch of water-cress, about eighteen inches from the stonework of the bridge. It was loose, as if it had been dropped . . . There were no drag marks visible.'

'What do you mean by that?'

'On the ground, your honour.'

'Does that add anything to the observations made by Sergeant Bragg, in answer to my earlier question?'

'I suppose not, sir,' Bugby mumbled.

'You say that you knew the deceased well. Can you give me your opinion as to her probable state of mind?'

'Well, sir, she was a bit odd—but no odder than usual. She went in for folk-medicine. She used to gather herbs and such, and make potions when people were ill. She would deliver babies, too.'

'So, she led an active and useful life in the community?'

'I suppose you could say that, your honour.'

'You do not think that she might have been in a mental state which would lead her to take her own life?'

Bugby smiled. 'No, sir. Anyway, you would hardly try to commit suicide in six inches of water!'

The coroner looked at him coldly. 'You may stand down, constable,' he said. 'I will now take the medical evidence.'

Shakerley was called and rehearsed the oath mechanically.

'I performed a post mortem examination on the deceased, on the day after her death,' he reported. 'There was some fatty degeneration of the heart but, otherwise, her health was good for a person of her age.'

'Which was sixty-two,' the coroner murmured, looking at his papers.

'The lungs were distended with water. There was also a quantity of sand in the nostrils and mouth, similar to that on the bed of the stream. In my opinion, the cause of death was asphyxia by drowning.'

The coroner wrote busily for some moments. 'Did you examine the abrasion on her forehead?' he asked.

'I did, your honour. I concluded that it had been caused by a moderately severe impact, shortly before death. The tissues had been lacerated, but the skull was intact.'

'How long before death, would you say?'

'Oh, not more than a few minutes.'

'Have you any observations on the probable cause of this injury?'

'Well, sir, the bridge was close by. If she had stood up incautiously, she could have easily struck her head on the stonework. The blow was certainly severe enough to cause her to faint.'

'I see . . . Thank you, Dr Shakerley.'

The coroner completed his record of the evidence, then surveyed the assembled villagers.

'This is an inquest into the sudden death of Tabitha Gosney, of Seven, North Street, Bere Regis,' he began.

'Death occurred on Thursday the twenty-first of August, some six feet downstream of the bridge in South Street. We have heard that Miss Gosney was a practitioner of folk-medicine, and used to gather herbs for this purpose. It has been said that a bunch of water-cress lay on the bank, within eighteen inches of the bridge. The deceased's body was in the stream, face down. She had drowned. There was an abrasion on her forehead, which had occurred shortly before her death, but which had not been caused by anything lying on the bed of the stream. We were told that the bank thereabouts is grassy. On the evidence before me, I have concluded that the deceased, in the course of gathering water-cress, struck her head on the stonework of the bridge. She staggered a few steps along the bank, swooned and fell into the stream. My verdict is that her death was accidental, and I commend the two police officers for their efforts to resuscitate her.'

The coroner gathered his papers together, bobbed his head to the people in the hall and went out.

Ernie dug Bragg in the ribs. 'We have a mortal lot of accidents in Bere Regis, all of a sudden,' he said.

'You take care of yourself, lad,' Bragg said seriously. 'You know too much for your own good. You could be the next.'

When Bragg got back home, he found lunch waiting for him. Emma was still off her food, but the two girls sat down with him to an enormous steak and kidney pie. He tried his best to make conversation. At fifteen, Ada was at an awkward age, one minute wanting to play, the next solemnly aping her mother. If Ted's business had been anything like successful, she would have been busy all day, preparing food for the drivers and washing up. What an existence for a bright young girl! Never to get away from the village, never broaden her experience. If she were lucky, she would marry a farmer; exchange her mother's kitchen for one of her own—still cooking and skivvying for the rest of her life. Some would say there was nothing wrong in that. His own sister had done much the same thing, and he fancied she would claim to be happy with her lot. But, if he had had a daughter, would he have wanted that for her? Kittie was coming eight, determined and unruly. What would happen to her? She would not be able to work at home, too, not even if the business recovered. Perhaps Ted would let her stay on at school. She seemed to have more about her than Rose and Ada. With a bit more education, she might better herself. But what chance did she really have in Bere Regis? He caught himself speculating on her being able to find work in London, living with him in Tan House Lane. It was ridiculous! Mrs Jenks would have a fit if he so much as mentioned it. She had some queer notions of his sexual appetites, already. To turn up with a young girl, claiming that she was his cousin once removed, would be the last straw! Anyway, Emma wouldn't thank him. She was broody enough because Peter had had to leave home, and go to work in Poole. Yet what a waste . . .

After the meal, he sat by himself in the parlour, filling his pipe. Then he decided that the day was too fine to waste indoors, and went to see if he could find Robert or Ted. He popped his head into the stable and the cart-shed, without success. Perhaps Ted had gone to ground in the harness room? Bragg pushed open the door, but it was empty. He went inside, the smell of sweat and leather sweet to his nostrils. He had spent many happy hours of his youth in just such a place; polishing the horse-brasses till they shone like gold. He put his pipe in his mouth and struck a match—but it broke off, leaving a short piece in his fingers. He bent down to retrieve the match and there, tucked well under the bench, was a pair of working boots . . . with a white tide-mark round the uppers. He took them out. They were still a bit damp—and it had not rained, all the time he had been here . . . He suddenly got a picture of the stile, Ollerton's body, the stream that would have to be crossed to get to the hedgerow and concealment. Bragg grimly replaced the boots, his mind once more in tumult.

That night he slept but fitfully; passing the evidence through his mind like a rosary, but gaining no enlightenment. When he went down for breakfast, Ted had already gone outside. Today, he seemed to be knocking about the yard, occasionally glancing towards the kitchen door. It was almost as if he would welcome an approach. But Bragg was not ready for that. His expressed belief in Ted's innocence had derived from his knowledge of him as a youthful companion, coupled with the fact that there was only circumstantial evidence against him—not evidence even, merely conjecture. The boots had changed all that. They shouted aloud that he had something to hide. Otherwise, he would have had them drying in the sun, have been rubbing neat's-foot oil into them to restore their suppleness. So, when Ted went into the stable with some hay, Bragg slipped out of the house.

He strolled up to the Cross, hoping that Ernie might have some gossip for him; some reaction to the previous day's inquest, perhaps. But he was nowhere in sight. Now that they were bringing the dried sheaves to the farms, he had probably begged a lift to the fields. Bragg turned down Church Lane, half hoping that he would meet Fanny Hildred, but it was deserted. He went into the churchyard . . . and there she was, arranging some flowers on little Anna Dyer's grave. He stood and watched her for some moments, taking in her lissomness, her unselfconscious grace. He crossed over to her.

'You know, miss, you are one of the few really good people I have ever met,' he said feelingly.

'Why, Mr Bragg!' She stood up in confusion.

'There are not many women would bother to do that.'

'But she was, so recently, a lovely happy child. The whole village feels the loss of her.'

'It was a bad business.'

She moved away from the grave to the path. 'I do not know if it is proper for me to mention this, Mr Bragg,' she said hesitantly, 'but it is rumoured that you are making enquiries into the death of Mr Ollerton.'

'Now, where did you get that from?' Bragg asked with a smile.

'His daughter, Lucy. She works for us, if you remember.'

'Ah, yes. Well, miss, the young lady has got it wrong. As a policeman I am interested, naturally. And maybe I have my own ideas about some things, but that is as far as it goes.'

Fanny looked disappointed. 'Perhaps it would be better if you were involved. The village is rife with gossip, even to the extent of naming certain individuals as possible murderers.'

'One of whom is my own cousin, Ted Sharman, no doubt.'

She rested her hand briefly on his arm. 'I am sorry,' she said. 'That is, of course, absurd. What concerns me, is that the harmony of the village is being destroyed. It could take a generation to heal, if this is not checked.'

'That would not make it a very pleasant place to live in.'

'Is there anything that you can do?' Fanny asked pleadingly.

'Well, it is not that I am disinclined. Indeed, it is my duty as a police officer to uphold the law, wherever I may be. The trouble is that the local constabulary are not at all that keen on having me involved. Not unnaturally, they have accepted the coroner's verdict that Ollerton's death was an accident. So they look on me as someone who wants to muddy their nice clear pool.'

'Constable Bugby is a dullard,' Fanny said spiritedly. 'We can hardly expect better in a village of this size, I know. But for him to obstruct someone of your experience and calibre is insupportable!'

Bragg laughed. 'Steady on, miss,' he said. 'I have to go back to London by the seventh of September. I can hardly stir things up here, then walk out on it. That would be worse than doing nothing.'

Fanny stopped and turned to face him. 'I am sure that you know best, Mr Bragg. I am equally sure that you will not close your mind to our situation. If, therefore, you wished to make enquires outside the village, I would be happy to drive you . . . You could rely on my total discretion,' she said lightly, then resumed her walk.

'You might find out I would take up your offer, just for the pleasure of your company!'

'Why, that is a risk I shall have to take, is it not?' She smiled teasingly. 'Now, what did you think of the poems?'

'I have not read them all yet, miss. To be honest, the poems I like best have more of a story in them.'

' "Half a league, half a league, half a league onward!" ' Fanny declaimed.

'Right enough! But some of Browning's are good, too. There's that one about the Italian painter . . . Lippo Lippi. I like his poetry, it's abrasive, sinewy. I suppose that it's a man's poetry.'

'As opposed to sentimental verse, fit only for women?'

'I didn't mean that.'

'Oh, but I am sure that you are right, to some extent. Poetry, for me, must express emotion.'

'I expect it is a shortcoming in me,' Bragg said slowly. 'I was finished with emotion, by the time I was twenty-four.'

A momentary shadow crossed her face, then she smiled warmly. 'There is a Browning poem in the book I lent you, is there not?'

'Yes, the one about the kisses . . . To tell you the truth, I found that a bit near the knuckle, for my liking.'

'But it is so vivid! One can really believe in the intensity of her passion.'

'I don't know, miss. It is something I have never experienced.'

'Nor have I, sergeant. Yet I cannot read it, but that it makes me tingle. That, for me, is poetry!'

When Bragg got back home, he found a message from Colonel Colegrave, asking him to supper on the following evening. In the circumstances, he could hardly refuse. He had been asked to report back to him, but had not really had

anything to tell him . . . Or was it that the evidence had
been building up against Ted? He certainly would not want
to point the finger at him. Blast it! Why had he got himself
into this mess? He was doing undercover work for the Chief
Constable of Dorset, against the members of his own force.
That was what it amounted to and, what's more, they were
aware of it. So he had to endure the sarcasm and distrust of
a bunch of country bumpkins, whose world was made up of
the odd burglary, a bit of poaching and the regular Saturday-
night brawl. He should have ignored the whole business, let
them get on with it. And now Fanny was expecting great
things of him. If he had been really in charge of the
investigation, he would have shaken the buggers until the
truth dropped out. As it was, he could only pick up crumbs
of information from people like Ernie Toop. So, it looked as
if Fanny would be disappointed. He found the idea irksome
and, as a result, spent that afternoon and the following
morning examining the scenes of death again. The wheat-
field had been cut now, so he was able to search a wide area
for clues. But despite this, he added nothing to his knowledge.

There was one advantage in having to go over to
Briantspuddle, he thought. If he called on his mother, he
would not need to go again before returning to London.
Accordingly, he set off in mid-afternoon. He had to confess
that he enjoyed the walk—not so much for itself, or for its
youthful associations, but because of his returning vigour.
He was practically as good as new. Before long, he would
be itching to get back to work.

He made a fuss of his mother and of his ten-year-old
nephew. He even managed a brief chat with his brother-
in-law, when he returned from work. At half-past six he
made his farewells and walked down to Colegrave's house.
His manservant was without his apron this time. Spare and
erect, he was every inch an old soldier—Colegrave's
batman, probably. Bragg was shown into the study, where
the Chief Constable was reading some papers. He rose and
shook Bragg's hand.

'Good to see you again,' he said, waving him to a chair. 'Are you fully recovered from your wound?'

'Yes, thank you, sir, I feel fine now.'

'Good! I thought it might be useful to have a chat, before supper.' He went over to a tantalus on a side table. 'Whisky?'

'Thank you, sir.'

Colegrave poured a generous measure into the glasses and brought them over to the hearth. He handed one to Bragg, then stood with his back to the empty fireplace, legs a-straddle.

'Since we last met,' he said, 'you have had another death and, indeed, another inquest. Are you happy about that one?'

'I cannot say that I am, sir.'

'Why is that?'

'You know the basis of the verdict, I assume.'

'Yes.'

'Take the bunch of water-cress, for a start. She could not have picked it by the bridge, because there is none growing there. Everybody cheerfully assumed it was Tabitha's, but it might not have anything to do with her at all. Then, there is the wound on her forehead. It was accepted by the coroner that she had hit her head on the bridge, though I cannot see why she ever had any reason to be near it. Now, the police surgeon said that it was a moderately severe impact, enough to cause her to faint—by which, I imagine, he meant that it could have rendered her unconscious. I suppose it is just possible that she might have walked six feet, before "swooning", as the coroner expressed it, but I have my doubts. If she did, I cannot see her ending up stretched out across the stream, with her arms by her sides, can you?'

'Perhaps not,' Colegrave murmured, pushing over the tobacco jar.

'The sand in the mouth and nostrils, leads me to think that her head was held under the water till she drowned,' Bragg said. 'To my mind, Dr Shakerley should have looked for bruises on the back of the head. I suggested as much to

Inspector Milward, but it didn't happen.' He pulled his pipe from his pocket and began to fill it.

'I have to concede,' Colegrave said thoughtfully, 'that it is statistically improbable for there to be two unnatural deaths within eight days, in a village of that size. Three, if we include the little girl—though her injury occurred some days before Ollerton's death. By the same token, it would seem even less likely that there should be two murders in that space of time.'

'Unless they were linked in some way.'

'Have you any evidence of that?'

'No, sir.'

'I suppose it is always possible that there is a connection which falls short of a linkage . . . I am thinking of a case where the occurrence of a murder puts the idea of murder into the head of someone who is quite unrelated to the first situation.'

'I am sure it happens,' Bragg said. 'The trouble is that I cannot find the shadow of a motive for anyone wanting to kill Tabitha Gosney—and, of course, your people are not looking for one.'

Colegrave ignored the implied criticism. 'Do you think it is purely fortuitous, that both death occurred on the bank of that stream?' he asked.

'I have wondered about that. But, unless we are dealing with a madman or a fetishist, I cannot see any significance there. Mind you, some people would not be surprised to hear that satanism was involved. Tabitha Gosney was reported to be a bit of a witch!'

'God forbid!' the Chief Constable said, with a sceptical smile. 'Perhaps there is a more rational significance in the fact that both deaths took place on a Thursday, between one and two o'clock in the afternoon.'

'I suppose they did,' Bragg said thoughtfully.

'Do you think that the man we are looking for might not be a resident of the village, but rather someone who visits it regularly—say, every Thursday, around lunchtime?'

'You mean, like a commercial traveller? It would fit the

pattern, wouldn't it? I think your people would be better placed to follow up that idea than I am.'

'Yes, I will put it in hand . . . Have there been any further developments regarding Ollerton's death?'

'I had a chat, at the second inquest, about dead men clutching ramrods. Dr Shakerley gave it a fancy name and said that it is well known. The interesting thing was that he said it would not wear off for some days. So I am back with my feeling that Ollerton's shotgun was put in his hand, after he was shot.'

'Hmn . . . Anything else?'

'Well, as I told Inspector Milward, there was an itinerant thatcher, called Hodge. He claimed that he saw two men at the stile, just before the shot.'

Colegrave frowned. 'That has not been reported to me,' he said.

'I expect that is because he could not confirm it,' Bragg said diplomatically. 'Hodge up and went, the next day.'

'If there is any substance in the story, we should be looking into it.' Colegrave took a pad from his desk and scribbled a note.

'We have someone else with a motive, as well,' said Bragg. 'One of the local publicans, William Applin, has a rather frisky wife. It appears that one of her lovers was George Ollerton.'

'A classic scenario for murder. Is Milward following that up?'

'I would not know, sir.'

Colegrave scribbled another note. At this rate, Bragg thought, Bugby would be trying to get him behind bars, instead! He drew a deep breath and took the plunge.

'My cousin, Ted Sharman, is also a suspect,' he said. 'He had a motive for the murder of Ollerton, because his business in on the rocks. Now that Ollerton is dead, he may well see a turn in his fortunes. So far as I can discover, there is no independent confirmation of his alibi for that day. The difficulty, as I see it, is that his motive was so obvious, he would have been mad to do it.'

'People do act irrationally, in such situations.'

'Indeed they do, sir . . . He appears to have no confirmation of his whereabouts for the day that Miss Gosney died, either. Though he has no apparent motive for killing her.'

'You seem to have selected rather uncomfortable lodgings for your convalescence,' Colegrave remarked with a smile.

'There is also the suggestion that Ollerton's silver watch was missing, when the body got to the mortuary.'

'I can confirm that, sergeant.'

'Then it would support your theory that he was robbed by an itinerant, sir.'

'Having become familiar with your analytical methods, Bragg, I take it that you will now demolish that proposition!'

'Well, sir, it could be that Alfred Dyer killed Ollerton, ran off and then came back to plunder the body. When he was disturbed by Tabitha Gosney, he would have had no choice but to stay there, and pretend that he had just discovered it.'

Colegrave pondered. 'It would certainly explain why the watch was taken, while the pocket-book was not,' he said. 'It would also give us the first smell of a motive for the old lady's death.'

'Yes, sir. In addition, it would explain why Dyer fled immediately after his little girl's funeral. I gather that the loss of the watch was first rumored that morning.'

'Excellent, sergeant!' Colegrave said with a broad smile. 'My reason for asking you to call was not, as you might have supposed, to ask for information, but to impart it. Immediately the loss of the watch was discovered, Milward sent detectives round the local towns. It had been manufactured in Leeds, and was a distinctively engraved half-hunter. It was discovered in a pawn shop, in Wimborne. By great good fortune, the proprietor of the shop remembered the person who had pledged it. The name in the book was George Ollerton, but the date of the transaction was two days after his death. The description of the customer was that of Alfred Dyer. Bugby is looking for him at this moment.'

'So, to your mind, it is all sewn up?'

'You sound disappointed, sergeant.'

'Well, it is not conclusive, is it? Dyer need not have killed him. He could just have found the body and purloined the watch.'

'I respect your determination to keep an open mind,' Colegrave said. 'Particularly as your cousin is a suspect.'

Bragg smiled wryly. 'Sometimes I think policemen should not have relatives. They should be taken from a box, and wound up like clockwork toys.'

CHAPTER ——————
—————————— TEN

Bragg shook the riddle vigorously and watched the fine soil stream through on to the heap. Another harvest of roots and pebbles! He began to think that the gravel ramparts had been scattered within the fort, not carted away by the villagers. The vicar was swinging his spade with manic energy, bringing bucket after bucket of earth to the wheelbarrow. It was as much as Bragg could do to keep up with him. Even so, little impression had been made on the mound which covered the foundations of the chapel. Even given Ryder's limited objective, it was hard to see how he could hope to finish before the bad weather. In addition, there was the Woodbury Hill fair in a little over three weeks. Altogether, it was a crazy enterprise. Far from becoming fascinated by the sublime science, as the vicar had called it, Bragg was beginning to find it irksome. He picked a brass button out of the bottom of his sieve and read the manufacturer's name, stamped on it. He wondered whether he should show it to Ryder. *Artefact No 2: brass; Mancunian c. 1885*. Irritably, he flipped it away into the grass and refilled his riddle. Once more, he went though the routine of shaking out the soil, poking about in the residue and throwing it on to the heap, as of no importance. A farm labourer came out of one of the cottages, with his dog at his heels. He came over to them and stood watching Ryder's unco-ordinated efforts with amusement.

'At it again, then vicar?' he remarked.

The vicar looked embarrassed. 'Now, if I could call on you for assistance, John, it would take but a fraction of the time,' he said.

The man grinned. 'Not I, sir. It be too hard work for the likes of I.' He walked away chuckling.

Ryder came over to Bragg. 'Have you found anything of interest this morning?' he asked.

'Only a modern brass button, from somebody's overalls,' Bragg said sourly.

'It is fortunate that the gratification of discovery is so intense,' Ryder said. 'Otherwise, the effort of excavation would become dispiriting.'

'I suppose that every job has its drudgery,' Bragg said. 'Not least my own . . . Which reminds me, I want to be back in the village by twelve o'clock.'

The vicar looked surprised, then his face clouded. 'You are not expecting another death, are you?' he asked.

'Not expecting, no. But there may be some significance about Thursday lunchtime that no one has looked into.'

Ryder sighed. 'I suppose it is too much to hope that one could escape from the dreadful events that have plagued us recently. Indeed, I am probably failing in my duty, by even allowing the wish to form in my mind. Yet there is a kind of primitive excitement, an anticipation, among the people of the village which, however much it interests me as a scholar, revolts me to the depths of my soul. Sometimes even I long to be in a sophisticated town parish. I am afraid that my predecessor was a preacher of the hell and damnation school. Consequently, fire and brimstone are never far below the surface in Bere Regis. It is widely believed that the devil had a hand in at least one of the recent deaths.'

'You mean Tabitha Gosney, I suppose.'

'Yes. I have been placed in a most invidious position. The churchwardens have represented to me that Miss Gosney believed herself to be, and was indeed, a witch.'

'The worst I ever heard of her was that she sold love potions,' Bragg said with a smile. 'I reckon that most of them must have been drunk in the Drax Arms!'

Ryder coloured. 'The Applins are Methodists,' he said dismissively. 'But Tabitha was one of my flock and I cannot reconcile with my pastoral duty a refusal to bury her in consecrated ground.'

'Is that what the wardens want you to do?' asked Bragg in astonishment.

'Indeed it is. To my mind, it smacks of the worst excesses of the seventeenth century; but they have pressed their request most strongly.'

'It's obscene!'

'On the other hand, my wife maintains that Miss Gosney could hardly have been an enthusiastic member of the Women's Union, yet in communion with Satan at the same time. She is emphatic that the interment should be in her family grave, in the churchyard.'

'I should think so!'

'You think that it is my Christian duty?' Ryder asked doubtfully.

'I cannot say that I am strong on religion, vicar. But when Christianity starts running counter to plain humanity, then it's time to throw it overboard.'

'It is easy for worldly-wise city dwellers to accept that as a self-evident truth,' the vicar said dolefully. 'But, down here, I fear that there will be endless repercussions. I fully intend to bury her in the graveyard; but, in doing so, I shall be defying the wishes of the whole parochial church council . . . I might even find myself having to dig her grave, so strong is the feeling.'

'Then, you can count on me to help you . . . Bloody nonsense!'

The vicar disregarded the oath. 'I feel sure that someone will write to the bishop,' he went on. Then his face brightened. 'But it may yet prove that the hand of the Lord is in it. Perhaps it is His way of reinforcing the promptings that I should move to a parish in Wiltshire!'

Cheered by the thought, he resumed his excavating with renewed vigour. Almost immediately, his spade grated on a rock. With a whoop of excitement, he dropped on his knees and began to slice away the earth with a trowel. Before long, he had uncovered a large piece of dressed stone. He made careful measurements, by reference to the twine grid, then eased it out of its position. Without doubt, there was a slight curve to the face of it. Bragg watched as, with infinite patience, the vicar removed slivers of earth to reveal a similar stone on either side of the first.

'I do believe that we have uncovered the remains of the anchoret's well,' he cried jubilantly. 'If you would assist me, we might be able to confirm it before ceasing work for the day.'

So Bragg took a trowel and together they began to scrape away the earth. After an hour they had exposed a wide square of chalk and, within it, a circular depression filled with soil.

'It must be the well!' said Ryder, bubbling with excitement. 'Look! There is clearly another course of dressed stones beneath.'

'How deep will it be?' Bragg asked.

'Fifty feet, at the very least.'

'Could you excavate it?'

'Since it must have been wholly cut through chalk, it should present no great problems—assuming that one could acquire a sufficient supply of children.'

'Children?'

Ryder looked abashed. 'I am being facetious, of course,' he said. 'Though neither you nor I would find it easy to work to any great depth in the shaft itself! On the other hand, to excavate the well pit would involve removing the back-filling behind the stone lining. That would be a very considerable enterprise.'

'It could be worth it!' Bragg said with a grin. 'You might find the anchoret's golden relic at the bottom!'

'If it ever existed,' Ryder said seriously, 'it is much more likely to have been incorporated into the courses of masonry forming the well-head. It might even have been visible to the pilgrims, through an aperture or a piece of glass.'

'You could find it yet, then!'

'Have a care, Mr Bragg. You are becoming dangerously infected by enthusiasm!'

'Not me, sir. But I would like you to find something worthwhile, after all your years of digging.'

'Thank you, sergeant. However, noon approaches and the cares of the present obtrude upon us.'

They pegged a tarpaulin over the site, then walked down the hill to the village in almost unbroken silence.

At the Cross, the vicar shambled off home, leaving Bragg to take up his watch by the Royal Oak. The village was unusually quiet. A few women bustled along with their shopping baskets; at twenty past twelve, one of Ollerton's carts came languidly down the road and turned into the yard. A fortnight ago he would have been out on the road, tapping his leggings with impatience. For another ten minutes Bragg watched the fitful breeze swirling the dust and piling up little drifts of stray corn stalks. Then he abandoned his vantage point and strolled up to the Drax Arms. When he went into the public bar, Lily Applin was serving a customer. She seemed subdued and, somehow, looked different. Of course! Last time he had seen her, she had been wearing her hair piled up on her head. Now it was hanging loose about her face. As he watched, she shook her head and he glimpsed the unmistakable, yellowing remains of a bruise on her cheek. One thing was certain, her husband must be aware of it. Most likely he had inflicted it. But it could hardly have resulted from a quarrel that pre-dated Ollerton's death. Bruises didn't take a fortnight to fade. Still, it could have been occasioned by a quarrel after his death—perhaps a sharp word from Lily, an accusation . . . She glanced around the bar and caught him staring at her. Immediately, she swung on her heel and went through the archway into the parlour. Moments later, a young barman appeared.

'What can I get you?' he asked.

'A pint of bitter, please . . . Is Lily avoiding me today?' Bragg asked with a grin.

'I wouldn't think so. Why? Should she?' There was a gleam of amusement in his eyes.

'Not me, no! Is the landlord in?'

'No, he will not be back till four o'clock, today. He goes to the brewery, in Blandford, every Thursday and has his lunch there.'

'Very nice, for some!'

The barman elected to take umbrage. 'Someone has to do the ordering,' he said sharply, then turned away.

Bragg carried his beer to the doorway and leaned against the jamb, observing the street. It was odd, he thought. He had been looking for a stranger who was only in Bere Regis on a Thursday lunchtime, and he had discovered, instead, a villager who was always out of Bere Regis at that time. He drained his glass and sauntered back toward the Cross. To his surprise, Ernie Toop was perched on the wall, looking expectantly towards him. He went into the Royal Oak and brought out a couple of glasses of beer. Ernie drank deeply then, as usual, wiped his mouth on his sleeve.

'They say the police is beatin' Bere Wood for Alf Dyer,' he announced.

'Are they now?' Bragg said in a neutral voice.

'He's been hidin' up in a woodman's hut.'

'I see.'

'So, it were him all the time?' Ernie grinned provocatively.

'That being so, you will still get your rides from Robert Sharman.'

Ernie was visibly disappointed that Bragg had not reacted to his needling, and took another gulp of beer.

'In any case, we would have to rule out one of our favourite suspects,' Bragg said.

'Who's that?' Ernie asked sharply.

'Bill Applin. Apparently, he is in Blandford till four o'clock, every Thursday.'

Ernie cocked his head, in thought. 'Not last Thursday, he wasn't,' he said.

'How do you know?' Bragg asked in surprise.

'Robert took me to Blandford that day. You know that long hill, this side of the town? Well, we were just reachin' the top on the way home, when Bill Applin overtook us in his trap. He was pushin' his horse a mite, as well; seemed to be in a right tizzy. He barely nodded to us.'

'What time was that?'

'We left the market square about a quarter to twelve. So it must have been about ten past.'

'Could he have been in Bere Regis by, say, half past one?'

'Easily, as long as his horse didn't go lame.'

'That was the day Tabitha died.'

'That's right.'

'And if he could do it that day, he could have done it on the Thursday before . . . You are quite sure?'

' 'Course I'm sure!' Ernie said waspishly. 'Ask Robert.'

'But Robert is not independent of all the suspects in the way that you are.'

Ernie smirked with pleasure at the distinction conferred upon him. 'And them wastin' their time, lookin' for Alf Dyer,' he said.

'Tell me, Ernie, are there any commercial travellers who call in Bere Regis, on a Thursday?'

The cripple looked up peevishly. 'One minute you are sayin' it's Bill Applin,' he complained, 'the next you are off on a different scent. I can't keep up with you!'

'Both deaths did occur at about the same time, on consecutive Thursdays.'

Ernie pondered for a moment. 'I don't know,' he said, 'but I will find out.' He squirmed off the wall and shuffled slowly across the road.

Bragg began to patrol the length of West Street again.

Things were looking up. At the very least, Ernie's question would start a new rumour, which should still some of the malicious gossip directed at Ted. And Applin was looking distinctly more promising as a suspect. The premature return that they knew about, related only to the day of Tabitha's death. And, so far, there was no whiff of a motive for Applin to kill her . . . Unless it was the love-potions . . . The idea was absurd! Yet aphrodisiacs un-doubtedly existed and Bill Applin was a taciturn, undemon-strative man. Well, to build a proper case against him, one would need to find someone who had seen him in the village around half-past one. That was a job for Milward—if he could ever be inveigled into doing it . . . The snag about Applin, as a suspect for Tabitha's murder, was that it was all much too untidy. He was unlucky that Robert and Ernie had seen him coming back from Blandford. Otherwise, no one would have questioned his whereabouts at the time of her death. Yet, knowing he had been seen, why did he go through with it? Intolerable emotional pressure? No, not Applin. And, anyway, his wife's infidelity was no new thing, if Ernie was to be believed. Moreover, he would hardly have rushed back early, on the pure offchance of finding Tabitha alone. Where would he have started to look for her? He would not have had much time to find her. Would he really have gone down to the stream first? Of course, he might have made an appointment to meet her by the bridge. But, if he had had murder in mind, he could hardly have chosen a less propitious spot . . . So it boiled down to an impulse killing during a pre-arranged meeting.

'Bragg! Bragg!'

He turned round and saw the squire hurrying across the road.

'Good morning, sir,' he said genially.

'Good morning, Bragg. Beautiful day!'

'At this rate they will have the harvest home in record time.'

'Yes.'

The conversation seemed to have died before it had

properly begun. Yet the squire had clearly wanted to speak to him. They walked slowly along the road for a hundred yards, and Bragg could see a growing look of embarrassment of Jerrard's face. Finally, the squire cleared his throat.

'They say in the village,' he began, 'that you are carrying out enquiries of your own into the two recent deaths.'

'That is no more than gossip, sir. Inspector Milward was courteous enough to talk them over with me, but I was unable to be of assistance to him.'

'From one point of view, it would be a good thing if you were doing so. With your experience, you would be able to teach them something. I am afraid that our policemen are not particularly intelligent or industrious . . . On the other hand, they are all that we have. I would not want the confidence of the villagers in their efficiency undermined for no good reason.'

'I appreciate that, sir. In any case, the whole thing is likely to be resolved when they catch Alfred Dyer.'

'Dyer?'

'I am sorry. I thought they would have told you. Apparently he pawned Ollerton's watch, in Wimborne, on the Saturday after his death.'

'Did he? That seems fairly damning. An unfortunate family, that, I feel sorry for his wife . . . Perhaps we can do something; I will mention it to Mrs Jerrard. When do you go back to London, Bragg?'

'In just over a week.'

'I see. Well, it was good to meet you.' The squire nodded briefly, then followed his dog down Shitterton Lane.

Bragg felt in his pocket for his notebook. Seeing the squire had reminded him that he had taken the number of Ollerton's gun, at the inquest. He had intended to ask Morton to check up on it, then had forgotten. Well, there was still time—if Morton was not too involved with his cricketing. He could not send a telegram from the village, but Fanny Hildred had offered to drive him anywhere he wanted to go. A trip to Dorchester would be very enjoyable, and it would at least appear that he was trying to live up to her expectations. He idly wondered if her mother would come, as well.

Shortly after half-past two, Bragg knocked on the front door of the Ollertons' house. He noticed that, as usual, the window sills had been stoned white, the threshold and pavement washed that morning and the brasswork polished till it gleamed in the sun. No wonder that she wasn't popular with the women of the village! From the length of time they were taking to answer, it seemed likely that this door was seldom used. Perhaps he ought to have gone round to the back door but, in a curious way, it would have seemed presumptuous. Anyway, Mrs Ollerton might not want her employees to know that he was helping her. He was only grateful that Ernie was not around; if the acerbic little cripple had seen him, he would not have been able to avoid explanations. He knocked once more. This time the door was answered by the brown-haired daughter.

'My name is Bragg,' he said. 'I promised your mother that I would call round.'

'Come in,' she said shyly and led him down a dark passage, to the back of the house. He found himself in a large kitchen, where Mary Ollerton was busy icing a cake.

'Is it someone's birthday?' he asked cheerfully.

A brief smile touched her lips. 'The girls'. I am giving them a bit of a party. Mrs Hildred is letting Lucy off, after tea, so they will be having a few friends round.'

Bragg turned to Sarah. 'And how old are you today?'

'Fourteen,' she said and blushed.

'Why, you are quite grown up, now. Do you help your mother in the house?'

'Yes.' The girl picked up a feather duster and escaped upstairs.

'Nice child,' said Bragg warmly. 'I must say that I admire your fortitude, Mrs Ollerton. Not many women could have coped as you have.'

'Where I was brought up, you had to,' she said flatly. 'It was a coal-mining village. Many a time there were pit accidents—roof falls, fire-damp explosions. It was no use being soft, you had to carry on.'

'Well, I hope I shall be able to help a bit with the books. If I bring them up to date, do you think that you will be able to carry on, if I show you how?'

'I could try. All the business papers are in here.'

She led the way into a gloomy little room, off the kitchen, with a scarred table and shelves along one wall.

'Are the old books here, too?' he asked. 'I might have to look back over earlier years.'

'As far as I know, everything is on those shelves. Mr Ollerton never brought anything to do with the business into the house. This was the proper place, he said.'

'Very well. I am sure I shall be able to find my way around. Where are the bills, and so on, that have not been entered?'

Mary pointed to a folder on the table. 'They are all in there. The earliest at the bottom.'

'And would you like me to send out invoices, as well?'

'If you can . . . I think Mr Ollerton used to send them out at the end of the month.'

'Well, today is the twenty-eighth. You will pick up the odd two working days, when you send out the invoices next month.'

Bragg settled down to his task and, shortly afterwards, Sarah brought him a cup of tea. They could hardly be more grateful, he thought. Though whether he would be able to help much, was another matter. Most of the bills in the folder were for fodder and repairs to the wagons. On top was a note, prepared by Mary Ollerton, showing wages due to employees which were still unpaid. She had evidently run out of cash over a week ago.

He took down the books and ledgers from the shelves and began to study them. They appeared to constitute an adequate system of bookkeeping. There was a ledger which showed the amounts invoiced to customers and details of payments made. This was supported by an analysed cash book, which had been written up a few days before

Ollerton's death. Bragg entered the week's wages which Mary had been able to pay, and pencilled in all the amounts owing. Then he examined the day book. It was meticulously kept, and reflected Ollerton's obsession with extracting seventy minutes from every working hour. For each job was shown its date, the name of the customer, details of the load, the price quoted, the name of the driver, the time of departure and the time the cart returned. It was not surprising that he was an unpopular employer! The last entry had been made on the day he died, recording the return of Harry Green from Winterborne Zelston at a quarter to one. Then he had gone out with his gun, aping the gentry, and came back on a hurdle.

Well, his widow's pressing need was cash. So the best thing Bragg could do, was to get some in. He spent the next couple of hours entering the work done in various ledger accounts, and preparing invoices. Ollerton had built up an interesting mix of customers. He clearly had an extensive connection with importers of all kinds at Poole docks. As Ted had complained, he seemed to have a virtual monopoly on carrying coal from there to the towns and villages in the area. This generated a large part of his income. In addition, he had a good connection with importers of timber. It was obvious how he could undercut Ted's prices. He had carts going regularly near any place you cared to mention. A part-load cost him virtually nothing; for Ted, it had to show a profit on its own. But Ted had been in that position, when Ollerton had started his business. And he had sworn that the newcomer was not undercutting him then—how could he be?

With an ear for the clatter from the kitchen, Bragg rummaged through the shelves till he found the books for the early years. The business had started in the autumn of 1879, with one horse and cart. Although he had no employees, Ollerton was, even then, obsessed with efficiency. The day book was kept just as rigorously, and it supported Ernie's assertion that the man had worked like a donkey. After three years, he had bought another cart and

was employing Harry Green. The business had grown
steadily, but not spectacularly; though, by now, it must have
been providing serious competition to Ted's established
trade. Then, quite suddenly, in 1883 he had acquired
several big coal importers as clients; and this was followed
by most of the timber merchants. Bragg remembered the
names well. There was scarcely a business of importance
that Ollerton did not act for. How on earth had he been able
to handle the virtual quadrupling of his business in the space
of eighteen months? Bragg turned to the cash book for that
year. He had hired one or two vehicles, with their drivers,
from carriers in the Poole area; but he had also bought new
ones himself—and quite early in the proceedings. It was
almost as if he knew the additional business was on its way,
that he could rely on keeping it. Strange . . . Perhaps he
was a gambler; though from what little Bragg had seen, he
doubted it. He flipped through the ledger again. The
business had continued to prosper, but never again had there
been comparable growth.

Bragg turned back to the current books, to check that all
the invoices had been sent out. Suddenly, he noticed a
ledger account for a customer whose name he did not
recognise. He scrutinised the day book for the period of that
account. In no case had details of journeys for this customer
been entered. It would have been odd in any business, but
with someone as meticulous as Ollerton, it was astonishing.
Perhaps these were the journeys he had done himself?
Perhaps he no longer felt he needed to keep a check on his
own movements? But no—his name was scattered throughout the day book, on short journeys with parcels. What was
so special about his customer? Invoices had been sent in the
normal way, the receipts debited in the cash book. So why
the reticence about the work done? Assuming the journeys
had a consistent pattern, there seemed to be a seasonal
element to them. Certainly, the invoices for the winter
months were for considerably greater amounts than those
for the summer months. Was it something to do with fuel?
Paraffin, perhaps? Bragg took out his notebook and jotted

down details of the customer. He smiled to himself. Inspector Milward might like to play around with the problem. It would be a pleasant diversion for him, after beating Bere Woods for Dyer!

CHAPTER ——————
—————— ELEVEN

'You drive well, miss,' said Bragg admiringly.

Fanny glanced round with a smile. 'Thank you, Mr Bragg,' she said.

'A Stanhope gig is generally reckoned to be too heavy for a woman to handle—particularly with a horse as mettlesome as this.'

'I find it exhilarating!'

They were bowling down a long hill, Fanny leaning forward, alert and excited. There was never a moment when Bragg thought that she might lose control. She took a tight line round the corner at the bottom, then flicked the reins to urge the horse along the flat. He could hardly have done it better himself—probably wouldn't come near her standard, nowadays. And with the rubber tyres, they'd be going faster than it sounded.

'I wager you are not allowed to drive your mother at such a cracking pace!'

'Indeed not! But we are on police business today, so I can indulge myself.'

Bragg laughed. 'In the City, there is so much traffic that you are lucky if your cab can get up to a trot. I sometimes think it would be quicker if we walked.'

'Then, there are some advantages in being in the country?'

'At the moment, miss, I can think of a great many.'

Fanny gave him a happy smile, then concentrated on guiding the horse through a narrow, winding section of road. After that, they began to encounter other vehicles as they approached the outskirts of Dorchester, and Fanny was content to allow the horse to moderate his pace. She relaxed and became, once again, a demure young woman.

'When is it that you must return to London?' she asked, giving Bragg a sidelong glance.

'A week on Sunday at the latest, I am afraid.'

'Will you be fully recovered by then?'

'To be honest, miss, I am fully recovered now.'

'Then we should be grateful that you are still among us. I would have expected you to be longing to get back to your work.'

'I am not wedded to the job, if that is what you think,' Bragg protested. 'I suppose, being single, I put in a lot of time because I have nothing better to do. And, in the nature of the job, you cannot work regular hours. Mrs Jenks is always complaining about the suppers she cooks and has to throw away.'

'Is she a relative of yours?' Fanny asked.

'Not her!'

'Having been widowed young, it seems surprising that she has not remarried.'

'Why people marry or don't marry, is always something of a mystery. But less so in her case than most. She has a bit of a shrewish nature and a complaining way with her. She wasn't like that when I first went to lodge there. It seemed to come on her gradually, after her husband died.'

'But she looks after you satisfactorily?'

'That's true enough, if treating you like a naughty child counts as satisfactory!'

'I am surprised that you have not remarried, yourself, Mr Bragg,' she said lightly.

'I won't say that I haven't thought of it. But as you get older, it becomes more difficult. It is not so much that you become set in your ways, as that your perceptions change. If I am honest, I do not think that my first marriage would have been particularly happy. My wife was a village girl and, even before I had married her, I had outgrown her. It seems a callous thing to say, but her world was that of a tiny Dorset village. She could not cope with the hurry and bustle of London. It frightened her. And yet she had to put up with it, because it was my world.'

'Such situations must occur frequently, when men gain advancement in their careers.'

'I am sure that they do. But having experienced it is not much help to you, a second time round. Over the years I have changed, become a bit more sophisticated, as your vicar would say. But at bottom, I am still an uneducated, rough sort of man, incapable of the little courtesies that a cultured woman would expect. You can never escape from your upbringing.'

'I fear that you may share a common misconception about what a so-called cultured woman desires,' Fanny said firmly. 'Sometimes I think that the village women are fortunate, for all their privations. They, at least, have an important role in their family. They are demonstrably engaged in something which directly affects other people's lives. In the upper classes, women are too often treated as fragile dependent creatures, who have to be cossetted and protected from the rough world around them.'

'It can be rough, miss, make no mistake.'

'The events of the last few weeks, in our own village, amply confirm that. But it is reality. It is better than being kept in emotional purdah. I know that you distrust emotion, Mr Bragg; but to be cut off from it, to have to elevate trivia into a whole social code, is a total perversion of the meaning of existence.'

'I would not say that I distrust emotion, miss. It is just

that I have not found much use for it. Men—or at least
Englishmen—seem to get on very well without it.'

'Poor benighted creatures! . . . Now we are coming to
the centre of Dorchester. Normally, I would leave the gig at
the Phoenix inn. Would that be convenient?'

'I would think so. I want to go to the main post office,
and then call on Inspector Milward at the police station.'

'May I come with you?'

Bragg smiled. 'I would consider it a great honour,
ma'am. How about that for a compliment?'

Fanny pursed her lips. 'It would be considered passable,'
she said judiciously. 'But it is as nothing, compared to your
allowing me to accompany you!'

'Ah, but I am using you to protect me from the Inspector's wrath!'

They left the gig at the inn and strolled along the street,
Fanny's hand in the crook of Bragg's elbow, until they came
to the post office. There he composed a short telegraph to
Morton, and had it despatched. Then they walked the few
hundred yards to the police station. Bragg was concerned
lest they should bump into the Chief Constable. That would
be doubly embarrassing. Colegrave would hardly wish to
acknowledge their relationship in front of his own men.
Equally, he might be annoyed at Bragg's going direct to
Milward. However, they gained the public counter without
seeing him.

'Is Detective Inspector Milward in please?'

The desk-sergeant glanced at Fanny with interest. 'I will
go and see, sir. What might your name be?'

'Bragg, Joseph Bragg, from Bere Regis.'

'Just one moment.'

Fanny squeezed Bragg's arm. 'This is the first time that
I have been in a police station,' she whispered. 'You are
opening up new worlds to me!'

Milward strode through the doorway behind the counter,
a truculent look on his face. On seeing Fanny, he checked
in surprise.

'Good morning, Inspector,' Bragg greeted him affably.

'What do you want . . . sir?' Milward growled.

'I have discovered two items of evidence, which may have a bearing on the deaths in Bere Regis. I feel it is my duty, as a citizen, to acquaint you with them.'

Milward's face was flushed with suppressed anger. 'I see, sir,' he said. 'I cannot think they would have any bearing on the matter. We already know the man we are looking for.'

'Dyer? Yes, I realise that. But I am sure you will be keeping an open mind on the other possibilities. In my judgement, these are matters you would wish to be aware of.'

'In your judgement . . .' He was only controlling his temper with difficulty.

'Yes, Inspector. Each fact is distinct. One may be related to the deaths of both Miss Gosney and Ollerton. The other, on the face of it at least, is related to Ollerton only.'

For a moment, Bragg thought that he had goaded Milward beyond endurance, then he let out his breath with a snort and took a piece of paper.

'Go on, then,' he said curtly.

'William Applin's alibi for the time of death of both Ollerton and Miss Gosney, rests on the fact that he goes, every Thursday, to Hall & Woodhouse's brewery in Blandford Forum. He habitually goes around ten in the morning, has his lunch in that town and returns to Bere Regis at four o'clock in the afternoon.'

'So?' Milward said irritably.

'On the afternoon that Miss Gosney died, he was seen leaving Blandford at a quarter past twelve. He could easily have been in Bere Regis by half-past one.'

'What has that to do with anything?' Milward burst out angrily.

'For a start, Miss Gosney was still alive at that time. Also, it suggests to me that he could have done precisely the same on the previous Thursday. Since Ollerton was his wife's lover, we have a clear motive and, now, a possible opportunity to kill him. I expect that enquiries in Blandford would be able to prove or disprove the point, but that is a matter for the police.'

'And who saw Applin on the way back home?'

'Ernest Toop and Robert Sharman, both from Bere Regis.'

'Sharman!' Milward sneered. 'It would be very convenient for his father, wouldn't it?'

'No one has yet suggested that Ted Sharman was in any way connected with the death of Tabitha Gosney, Inspector.'

Milward glared at Bragg, then made a few rapid notes. 'And what is the other point?'

'It concerns the books of Ollerton's business. I have been bringing the entries up to date, for his widow. In the course of this, I found a curious inconsistency for which I can find no explanation.'

'What is that?'

'The transactions with one customer were not put through the day book.'

Milward looked blank. 'What does that mean?' he asked.

'Nothing in itself; but where an obsessively meticulous man like Ollerton is concerned, there must be a reason. In my experience, an oddity like that often turns up something of interest to the police.'

This time, Milward was too perplexed to kick against the prick. 'So what do you suggest we should do?' he asked.

'It is plainly a matter for further enquiries.'

'Who is this customer?' Milward demanded irritably.

'Zachariah Gittings, of Cliff Farm, Lulworth Cove.'

'Lulworth?' The Inspector's interest was caught. 'I was stationed in Lulworth, in my early days. I know the farm well. But why would he use a carrier from Bere Regis? There are plenty in Wool and Lulworth.'

'There must be a reason, but it is surprising. Another factor is that the bulk of the transactions took place in the autumn and winter—although there were smaller amounts put through the books in the other months also.'

Milward tapped his pencil against his teeth, in thought.

'And you believe that this might have a bearing on the death of Ollerton?' he asked.

'In your shoes, I would not want to decide that it could not.'

'It certainly seems queer. Our trouble is that nobody here has any knowledge of business books. We would not know if we were being told a pack of lies, or not.'

'I would be glad to help, if you wished,' Bragg said earnestly.

Milward looked distrustfully at him for a moment. 'Are you free tomorrow morning?' he asked abruptly.

'Yes, certainly.'

'Could you borrow a trap and pick me up at Wool station around ten o'clock? We could be in Lulworth before eleven.'

'I will borrow my cousin's dog cart.'

'Right then, ten tomorrow morning,' Milward turned on his heel and strode out.

'Goodness!' Fanny exclaimed. 'I have lived in Bere Regis for most of my life, yet after eighteen days you know more of the happenings there, than I ever did.'

Bragg grinned. 'Tricky things are emotions, miss,' he said.

When Bragg got back home, he found a note from the vicar waiting for him. In it, Ryder said that he was beginning the excavation of the anchoret's well that day, and asked him to come as soon as possible. It was irritating. He had spent a satisfying morning, followed by a pleasant lunch at the Phoenix. He would have much preferred to meditate quietly on it. Now he would have to change into his second-best clothes and riddle soil. Why was it so hard to say no to parsons? Three o'clock. He could hardly say that he had got back too late. If he had accepted Fanny's invitation to come in for tea, he certainly would have been. Serve him right for not giving way to temptation. He grumpily put on his other clothes and walked up to the fort.

The vicar was kneeling on the chalk, scooping earth from

the shaft of the well into a bucket. He was in an excitable
mood and greeted Bragg effusively.

'You can see that there is another course of masonry
exposed now,' he said. 'In all probability, there are several
more below that. The stones appear to be loose, so I shall
have to remove them . . . I have begun a new pile for the
contents of the well-shaft. If you would like to man the
sieve with your usual adroitness, I have no doubt that we
shall make rapid progress.'

The material blocking the mouth of the well consisted of
fine soil and a few loose stones. There were no grass roots,
no pebbles. Bragg found that he could process it as fast as
Ryder could remove it. He was, therefore, better able to
appreciate the methodical nature of the vicar's work. He
numbered each stone, then recorded in his notebook the
depth at which it had been found, and drew its position on
a diagram of the shaft. By leaning over, he gradually
excavated to a depth of almost three feet. Then he carefully
brushed the soil away from the face of the lining stones.

'I think,' he called, his head down the well, 'that we have
uncovered enough courses of masonry. I would like to
record and remove the exposed layers, before we abandon
work for the day. It would be tragic if they should,
perchance, be disturbed before we could do so.'

'How could that happen?' Bragg asked.

'Children, animals, uninitiated adults—even a thunder-
storm . . . Now, would you be good enough to lay out
each course separately, on that grassy area behind the
wheelbarrow?'

Taking great care, he lowered himself into the hole and
began to lift out each stone. Once the first stone of a course
had been freed, the others came out easily and Bragg found
himself trotting backwards and forwards quite briskly. It
was when they were in the middle of the third course down
that Bragg heard a strangled yelp. He hurried back, to find
the vicar clutching a stone and staring at the place from
where he had wrenched it. The shaft of the well had been

hollowed out, behind it, to form a niche. On the bottom of the niche was the glint of gold.

'Oh, my goodness!' Ryder exclaimed excitedly.

'It must be the relic! I thought you said it would not be there.'

'Gracious me! I could not have anticipated this in my wildest dreams! Quickly, Mr Bragg, would you pass me that painting brush? We must be most scrupulous in our examination of this find.'

Bragg passed it over and watched as, with infinite patience, the vicar brushed away the soil to reveal a small, curiously shaped piece of metal. When he had freed it entirely, he wiped his hand on his coat and reverently took it from its resting place. He turned it over and over, scrutinising every part of it. Then, half reluctantly, he passed it to Bragg, who examined it in his turn.

'It is not pure gold, though, is it?' he asked. 'That little patch of verdigris means there is copper in it.'

'It is almost certainly bronze. It would be gold in a figurative sense only.'

'It is certainly heavy enough for bronze . . . And what a queer shape! I thought holy relics had to be finger bones and suchlike.'

'No, no. Any object which has been possessed and used by a saint or a holy person could be so venerated.'

'Well, I don't know about a golden relic,' said Bragg with a laugh. 'It looks more like a golden goose, to me!'

The vicar clambered out of the well in triumph and, wrapping the object in his handkerchief, stowed it away in his pocket.

'Are we not going to finish removing the exposed stones?' Bragg asked in surprise.

'They can wait. It is much more important that I write a full account of our discovery, while the details are still fresh in my mind. I think the masonry will be adequately protected, if we pull the tarpaulin over it . . .'

When Inspector Milward joined Bragg at Wool Station, next morning, he was in a taciturn mood. He showed no hostility, but it was lurking just below the surface. If the trip were a wild goose chase, it would be a painful journey back! After his initial terse greeting, Milward maintained complete silence until they were descending the steep hill to the village of West Lulworth. Then he thawed a little.

'It is a pleasant place in the summer,' he said. 'But, by God, it is isolated in the winter!'

'I came down once on a school trip,' said Bragg. 'We thought it was marvellous, ice-cream and candy floss—even a couple of donkeys to ride.'

The road levelled out and they passed a pleasant-looking inn. Bragg would have dearly loved a pint of beer, but socialising with Milward was too high a price to pay. They clip-clopped on, until they came to a big stone barn and a thatched farmhouse on the right.

'That is Cliff Farm, sergeant,' Milward said.

Bragg smiled to himself at being given his rank, then turned the horse into the yard. He looped the reins over a tree branch and followed Milward to the farmhouse. After a deal of banging, the door was opened by a grey-haired woman.

'I'm sorry,' she said, wiping her hands on her apron. 'I was out at the back, makin' cheese.'

'Mrs Gittings?' Milward asked pleasantly, raising his hat.

'Yes.'

'We want to have a word with your husband.'

'He be down at the cove, mendin' his nets.'

'He does a bit of fishing too, does he?'

'Farmin' won't keep body and soul together, nowadays, least not here.'

'We will walk down and find him, then.'

The two men sauntered down the slope towards the cove. As they neared it they could hear the screech of children playing. On rounding the corner by the pub, Bragg checked in surprise. The cove itself was just as it had always been—perfectly circular, as if formed by a gigantic ice-cream scoop. On the tip, they had christened it the devil's bath-tub, he remembered. But now, astonishingly, there was a large steamboat moored in the middle of the cove, with a rickety landing stage reaching out to it. And the narrow ribbon of sand was thronged with people.

'This is a surprise,' Bragg said.

'I expect it is an excursion, from Bournemouth,' Milward said. 'They can just about get in and out at the top of the tide. There is not much of an opening to the sea, as you know.'

'This will make it more difficult to locate our man.'

'Yes, but at least we will not stick out among this lot.'

They pushed their way down to the landing stage, where a man in waders was standing. Milward asked for Gittings and was directed round the seaward side of the cove, where a cutter-rigged fishing smack was moored. A heavily bearded man was sitting on the shore nearby, with a drift net spread over his knees.

'Mr Gittings?' Milward asked.

The man looked up suspiciously. 'Yes,' he said.

'We are police officers. We would like to have a word with you.'

'What about?'

'You must have heard that George Ollerton, from Bere Regis, has been killed in a shooting accident.'

'I heard that, yes.'

'I understand you knew him. I suggest that we go back to the farm, then we can have a chat.'

'But I shall miss the tide,' Gittings protested.

'You can be sure there'll be another. Come on.'

It was difficult to detect emotions through the enveloping fuzz of hair, but the eyes were wary. Without another word, the man got up and strode defiantly up the lane, with Milward and Bragg following. On reaching the house, he led them into a big stone-flagged kitchen, where a fire smouldered in the iron range. He drew up a chair to the table and the policemen followed suit.

'I gather that you had a trading relationship with Mr Ollerton,' Milward began.

Gittings merely looked back woodenly.

'We would like to look at your books, to check the transactions.'

'I don't keep no books.'

'I see. Why did you use a carrier from so far away?' Milward asked mildly.

'Why not?'

'Well, you could have used Daniel Tanner, from East Lulworth.'

'He once cheated me over some hay. Said it were no good; wouldn't pay.'

'Then, why not someone from Wool?'

'Same difference. Ollerton were always in Wool.'

'But it must have been costing him money, to come down here.'

'That's somethin' you'd better ask him about.' There was a brief gleam of triumph in Gittings's eyes.

Milward nodded to Bragg to take up the questioning.

'What goods did he carry for you?' he asked.

'Hay, cheese and butter . . . fish.'

'Where was the hay going?'

'He took it for hisself.'

'Why would he come here for hay?' Milward asked, with more aggression. 'There is plenty around Bere Regis.'

Gittings did not answer.

'The cheese and butter, then,' Bragg asked. 'Where were you sending that?'

'Ollerton used to take it round the shops and sell it for me, on his rounds.'

'There are no entries in his books for payments made to you.'

'I can't help that,' Gittings said shortly. 'We used to settle up every so often, in cash.'

'What about the fish?'

'The same.'

'Are you asking us to believe,' said Milward harshly, 'that a prosperous carrier, like Ollerton, would peddle fish and cheese for somebody as far away as Lulworth?'

Gittings remained silent.

'How many cows have you, Mr Gittings?' Bragg asked mildly.

'Five in milk and two heifers, at the moment.'

'And how big is the farm?'

'Twenty acres.'

'Most of it up on the chalk, by the sound of it.'

'Yes.'

'All grass?'

'Yes.'

'So you can make enough hay to see your own cattle through the winter, with some over to sell?'

'Yes.'

'But not a great deal over.'

The man did not reply.

'You cannot make much of a living,' Milward said brusquely.

Gittings looked around the kitchen, which was clean and neat, but sparsely furnished. He shrugged and said nothing.

'What fish do you catch?'

'Mackerel, whiting, herrings, sometimes a bass or two . . .'

'And did Ollerton sell all of it for you?'

'Nearly all.'

Milward raised an eyebrow at Bragg and leaned back in his chair.

'How much would you say you made gross, from selling your produce in this way?' Bragg asked. 'That is, before paying Ollerton. Let us take last year, for instance.'

'I don't rightly know.' The man hesitated. 'I reckon a hundred pounds.'

Bragg took a paper from his pocket and placed it in front of Gittings. 'This is a copy of the account with you, that appears in Ollerton's books.'

Gittings looked at it without comprehension.

'You will see that it shows only amounts paid by you to Ollerton.'

'Oh?'

'Why was it necessary for you to pay him, in cash, when

he was presumably collecting the full sale price of the fish
and cheese from the shops? Why did he not just pay you the
difference?'

'I can't say. It were how he wanted it.'

Bragg gazed steadily at Gittings, and he glared resent-
fully back.

'If you add up the amounts you paid him in the last year,'
Bragg went on, 'you will see that they total nigh on seventy
pounds. Why should you pay him so much, when you were
only making thirty pounds for yourself?'

'Maybe I made more than I thought,' Gittings muttered.

Milward reached out and took hold of the paper. 'According to this,' he said, 'you were paying him nearly every
month. Is that right?'

'I suppose so, if that is what the paper says.'

'Why are the amounts much higher in the winter? It can't
be sales of hay, because you agreed that you did not have
much left. Anyway, he used that himself, so he should have
been paying you. And spring and summer are the best time
for butter and cheese, because of the fresh grass.'

'It must be the fish.'

'The fish?' Milward exclaimed violently. 'There is no
mackerel here in the winter, and precious little of anything
else! I'm not a towny. You can't bamboozle me. Get up! I
am going to have a look around this place.'

He hauled Gittings to his feet and pushed him out through
the back door. Bragg saw Mrs Gittings's startled face
through the creamery window, as they marched towards the
farm buildings. Milward poked about in an empty pigsty,
then strode into the barn. A fine new cart stood inside,
elaborately painted. On seeing it, Milward gave a derisive
chuckle and pushed Gittings up the steps to the loft. The
ground floor was virtually empty, save for the cart. In a dark
corner at the back, was a drift of hay . . . Something was
odd about it, thought Bragg. Normally, the hay would be
upstairs to facilitate loading on to the cart. Yet there was too
much here to have accumulated accidentally. He took a
pitch-fork and plunged it into the heap. There was a dull

thud and the tines stuck firmly. Bragg pushed away the hay to reveal a small barrel. He released the fork and began to drag the hay to one side in armfuls. By the time he heard Milward and Gittings start down the steps, he had uncovered twelve barrels.

'You might like to look at this, sir,' he called.

'Cognac, by God!' Milward stood thunderstruck.

Bragg looked at Gittings. 'So it was brandy that Ollerton was selling for you. No wonder that you were paying him so much!'

'It's smuggled, that's what it is!' Milward exclaimed excitedly. 'How long has this been going on? The whole five years?'

Gittings just looked sullen.

'I can see it now . . . You fell out with him, didn't you? Over his share. You arranged to meet him at the stile, in Bere Regis. And when he wouldn't agree to what you wanted, you shot him . . . That was the way of it, wasn't it . . . Wasn't it?'

Gittings was staring, horrified.

'Zachariah Gittings,' Milward intoned, 'I am arresting you for the wilful murder of George Ollerton . . . You are coming with me.'

James Morton walked briskly out of the police headquarters building, in Old Jewry, and headed for his rooms in Alderman's Walk. He was feeling very pleased with life. He had been back on duty for three days now; and although the third test match had been drawn, through rain, people still remembered the centuries he had made in the first two. It was gratifying to have one's hand shaken by perfect strangers, and Bill, the desk-sergeant, still beamed every time he saw him. It would wear off, of course, but there was no harm in enjoying it while it lasted. Even more gratifying was the knowledge that Catherine Marsden had been at the Lord's test—had actually seen him make his hundred. That must mean something, for she had been prepared to say as much in front of Sergeant Bragg—and not to scoff, either.

Perhaps his own obduracy had at last triumphed over her contempt, and she would see cricket henceforth as just a harmless pastime, rather than a sign of moral degeneracy . . . It was as well that he had not known of her presence, or the outcome might not have been so creditable!

He bounded up the stairs and went into his sitting-room. In another week, Sergeant Bragg would be back and they would be able to resume their partnership. It must be rather like being married—a mixture of contentment and irritation, an instinct for what the other was thinking, companionship and dependency . . . Yet it had paid off handsomely in police terms and, from his own point of view, it had given him enormous satisfaction. He was fortunate to have been put under Bragg. No doubt it had been a case of one oddity being placed under the aegis of another—for Bragg was aware that he would rise no further in the force, and was prepared to follow his own intuition regardless of the directions of his superiors. It was only because of his phenomenally good record that he had not been dismissed by now. Instead, he held a semi-privileged position: nominally under the control of Inspector Cotton, but in practice working independently. And, by being attached to Bragg, Morton himself had benefited from this freedom of action. It was only at times like the present, when he was working under another sergeant, that he realised how exceptional Bragg was. He, himself, had entered the police force as a rather empty social gesture; to be able to say that he was doing something really useful with his life. But, had he been placed with Detective Sergeant Spenlow, dogmatic and unimaginative, he would have resigned long ago. All this, of course, assumed that Bragg would still want to have him. When he had visited him after the stabbing, he had been grumpy and resentful. Surely he did not blame him, because he had been away playing cricket? Certainly Bragg was contemptuous of the game. But he could easily have been on leave, or sick himself. Any number of circumstances could have sent Bragg out that night with an unfamiliar constable . . . Yet Bragg had not written to him during his convalescence, so the auguries were not good. Well, he had considered his position when he was told that Bragg had been injured, and the same decision would hold if he could not work with him for any other reason. He would resign and find something else to do.

There was a quiet knock at the door and his manservant entered.

'Excuse me, sir,' he said. 'This telegraph has arrived for you.'

'Thank you, Chambers.'

'Will you be dining in, this evening, sir?'

'I think not. I suggest that you and Mrs Chambers have an evening out.'

'Very good sir. Thank you.' He smiled and withdrew.

Morton slit open the buff envelope and unfolded the telegraph form. It was from Sergeant Bragg . . . Nothing about his condition, merely a request for information. Well, the old devil must be in good health; and if Bragg was wanting him to trot round London on an errand, then he had not been cast off. Dear God! It was like being married! He read the telegraph again, then looked at the clock. Why not now? Purdey's would certainly be open on a Saturday afternoon at the beginning of the shooting season. He changed from his somewhat clerkish working clothes into a stylish lounge suit, then took a cab to South Audley Street.

The premises of James Purdey & Sons were more like a substantial residence than a shop. The bow window was heavily curtained, the carpet was luxurious, there were cigars on the table—and not a shotgun in sight! A grave man in a tail-coat looked at Morton appraisingly, then came forward.

'Good afternoon, sir. Can I help you?' he said. There was no trace of unctuousness in his manner, no obsequiousness, just the straightforward desire of one gentleman to be of service to another. Morton pulled out his warrant-card and the man's face fell. Then he smiled.

'Why, you are Jim Morton the cricketer! How nice, how

very nice! I hope that we shall be privileged to make a gun for you.'

'I am afraid not. There are quite enough at home, already.'

'Ah, but to possess a gun that has been tailored to fit you, so to speak, is a totally new experience.'

Morton laughed. 'If I ever feel the need for such a weapon, I shall certainly come to you. At the moment, my need is for information about another of your guns.'

'What is that?'

'Anything you can tell me. The gun has been found,' he improvised, 'and we think that it may have been stolen.'

'I see. Very well, I will certainly do what I can to assist you.'

He went to a small desk at the back of the room and took a ledger from one of the drawers. 'I take it that you have the serial number of the gun,' he said.

'Yes. It is one five seven one.'

The man turned over the leaves of the book.

'Here we are,' he said. 'The gun was a self-opening hammerless model. It was ordered in November 1886, and was completed in January 1889. Hmn . . . It took somewhat longer than the usual two years, I wonder why. His finger ran down the edge of the page. 'Ah, yes. I see. We had to make some adjustments to the stock. The gentleman was not comfortable with it.'

'Goodness! They are tailor made! I had no idea that people went to such lengths.'

'It is essential, sir, if the gun is to perform to its fullest potential. After all, you do not have sights, as in a rifle. The shotgun is aimed by looking down the barrel—or, shall we say, down the rib joining the two barrels. Since the butt of the gun is pressed into the shoulder, there has to be a cast-off in the shape of the stock, to bring the barrels of the gun into alignment with the sighting eye. If you examine a shotgun, you will see that the butt is displaced sideways, to a considerable extent.'

'I have seen that, of course; but I did not realise that it

could vary enough to justify individual treatment, in this way.'

'Indeed yes! The stock is the most personal part of any gun. It has to fit the contours of the body comfortably. Not only has the cast-off to accommodate the width of the shoulder, but the bend of the stock has to be fitted to the length of the gentleman's neck. Too little bend will result in a high point of aim, too much and he will fire low.'

Morton laughed. 'I knew that some men made a great deal of fuss about their guns, but I had always thought that it was mere snobbery.'

The man smiled gravely. 'It is no doubt true,' he said, 'that the most painstaking fitting will not improve the shooting of some gentlemen. However, we console ourselves with the thought that the defect is in the shooter, not our gun.'

'But, surely, once you have determined the characteristics you want, on the try-gun, there should be no reason to change them?'

'You are referring to the adjustments to this particular stock?'

'Yes.'

The man smiled. 'It could mean no more than that our client did not perform particularly well when he came to try out the gun! However, there are natural variations in vision during one's lifetime. A young man sees out the centre of the pupil; but with the onset of middle-age, he will more and more tend to look out of the inner corner of the eye. That is enough to affect the aim.'

'You mean that there could have been this kind of deterioration during the period between his ordering the gun, and test-firing it?'

'It is possible . . . though most of our clients would prefer to think of it as a maturation!'

'So, after all this care and individual attention, how much did the gun cost?'

The man's finger found the bottom of the page. 'Three hundred and twenty-five guineas,' he said.

'For that money, it should be an exceptional weapon.'

'Indeed, sir,' the man said gravely.

'And who does it belong to?'

'As to that, I am unable to say. But it was made for a Mr Charles Jerrard, of Shitterton Manor, in Dorset.'

'I would never be able to do all that, Mr Bragg,' Mary Ollerton said in a worried voice.

'It really is not too difficult. The important thing is to keep the day book up to date. The other books can be written up at leisure, then.'

'If I ever have any. No, Mr Bragg, I have never understood figures, and I never shall.'

'Are any of your workers familiar with books?'

'If you ask me, they are not familiar with work, never mind books,' she said bitterly.

'Perhaps someone else in the village would help—the schoolmaster or another tradesman?'

'Mr Ollerton would never have wanted any of that lot to know his business.'

'But it is your business, now,' Bragg said gently.

'Oh, dear me,' she sighed. 'I wish I knew what to do for the best.'

'Have you sent off the invoices, that I prepared for you yesterday?'

'They went first thing this morning.'

'Then, they will produce enough money for you to carry on, in the short term. But you must get Harry Green to give you details of the work done since your husband's death, and enter it in the day book. It will be dead money, otherwise.'

'I will do my best . . . It's the future I'm worried about, Mr Bragg. I have two girls to look after. If I were back home in Yorkshire, I would have my family around me. Down here, nobody really cares.'

'It is natural to feel depressed, so soon after your husband's death, Mrs Ollerton. In a few months, things will seem brighter.'

'Don't be daft, man,' she said sharply. 'They won't be any different than what they are now . . . I wish I knew what to do.'

It was true enough, Bragg thought, and it would be wrong to persuade her otherwise. Moreover, before long there would be investigations by the police and customs men for her to cope with.

'I suppose I am the last person to advise you,' Bragg said quietly. 'But you must realise that your husband built up that business by working extremely hard himself and, above all, by seeing that the men worked even harder. You have lost not only him, but the driving force of the whole concern.'

Mary Ollerton's eyes were bright with tears. 'I know,' she said. 'They won't do it for me . . . They said they would, when my husband died, but they won't.'

'Then, you have got to face up to the fact that, if you try to run it yourself, the business will decline—it will just dribble through your fingers.'

Mary looked bleakly at him, and said nothing.

'At the moment, you have a valuable asset, but in three years, you might be struggling to make a living.'

'Why is that?' she asked brusquely.

'For one thing, Ted Sharman will be trying his hardest to take your customers away from you. He is an experienced carrier and a hard worker. Your business is going to suffer.'

'I am sure he will try!' she said combatively.

'He is bound to succeed, in some degree. After all, he knows many of your customers already—he lost them to your husband.'

'So what should I do?'

'I think that your best course would be to talk the situation over with your solicitor, and ask his advice.'

'Solicitor?' she said harshly, 'I don't want no solicitor. No good ever comes of bringing them in.'

'Then, if you want my advice, you ought to sell the business while it is still of some value.'

Mrs Ollerton blew her nose. 'Who would buy it?' she asked flatly.

'The most obvious person would be someone who wanted to set up as a carrier in the area.'

'The difficulty would be that someone newly setting up would be unlikely to pay you what the business is worth . . . The next possibility to explore would be a concern already established elsewhere, that wanted to operate from Bere Regis also.'

'And how would I set about that?'

'I suppose you could advertise in the trade papers . . . The other thing you could do is sell the business to the other Bere Regis carrier.'

Her head jerked up angrily. 'Ted Sharman? He hasn't two pennies to rub together!'

'You need not sell it for a lump sum. You could arrange for a certain amount out of the profits to be paid to you, each year. Or he might agree to your being a kind of sleeping partner, so that you would get an agreed proportion of the profits. There are plenty of ways of doing it.'

'Mr Ollerton would not have liked the idea of Ted Sharman,' she said doubtfully.

'Maybe not. I am certainly not suggesting that he is the only solution for you, or even the best. But you must do something, for your own and your daughters' sakes.'

'Well . . . Perhaps if you would sound him out for me.'

'Very well.'

Mrs Ollerton got to her feet. 'There is one thing I want to say. There are wicked tongues in the village, saying that Ted Sharman had a hand in Mr Ollerton's death. Well, I don't believe a word of it, and I want you to tell him so.' She looked bitterly at the shotgun which was suspended over the parlour mantlepiece. 'It was something he'd always wanted. "Mary," he would say, "one day, when I've made my pile, I will have a top-class shotgun." And look where it got him.'

'How long had he had it?'

'Last back end. The only thing he ever shot, was a hare—and we couldn't eat that, because it was a female in breeding . . . Why don't men ever grow up?'

CHAPTER ——————
—————— TWELVE

On the Sunday Bragg went to morning service at the parish church. He was surprised to see Ernie Toop sitting by a pillar near the door. The cripple did not have much to praise God for, he thought. Bragg affected not to have noticed him and sat in a pew on the organ side, under Judas Iscariot. He knew a couple of the hymns, and managed to kneel and stand up in the right places, so he put up a creditable performance. But as an act of worship, it was a failure. The choir was thin and faltering, the vicar seemed to lack conviction, but the real fault lay within himself. He had been boycotting God for twenty years; it would take some getting back into the habit. His mind drifted, wondering about Emma and Ted, Mary Ollerton, Fanny . . . Suddenly he jerked alert. An idea had almost formed in his mind. It had risen to the surface of his consciousness for a split second, then submerged again. He could not even decide what it had been about, but he was convinced that it was important. He tried to lure it back by recreating the same train of thought, but it would not be caught. He emptied his mind, waiting to pounce on it should it return, but to no avail. Damnation! he thought. What had precipitated it? Was it the church he was in? Would he have to haunt the building, in the hope that the same thought-process would be triggered? Or was it something in the vicar's rambling sermon? At the end of the service he picked up his hat and walked impatiently down the aisle. He overtook Fanny and Mrs Hildred, who was fussing about her gloves. Fanny smiled at him.

'Do not forget that you are coming for tea,' she said.

'Indeed, I will not!' Bragg replied and passed on.

In his frustration, he walked down to the bridge and along the bank of the stream. He looked intently around the scenes of the two deaths, but found no new insight. Oh well, he might as well forget it. If the thought was worth anything, it would surface again.

He went back to the Old Brewery and was treated to a traditional Sunday lunch. It would be his last for that visit, and Emma had done the roast beef succulent and pink, as he had learned to like it in London. To follow, there was hot gooseberry pie swimming in cream. Afterwards he sat in the parlour with the two girls, watching them play cat's cradles, while Ted helped Emma with the washing up. A nice relaxed family lunch . . . except that the family was anything but relaxed—and his time was running out.

At a quarter to four, he went out into the sunshine and sauntered round the corner to The Retreat. When he rang the bell, the door was answered by the young fair-haired maid.

'Mr Bragg?' she asked, with the beginnings of a smile.

'Yes. You are Lucy Ollerton, aren't you?'

'That's right, sir. I've been asked to put you in the drawing room. The ladies are engaged at the moment.'

She left him in a spacious room, overlooking a carefully tended garden. There was no doubt at all that this house had been built by a prosperous man. The doors were of solid mahogany, the skirting-boards were a foot high and elaborately moulded; an elegant frieze bordered the ceiling and brass fire-dogs graced the imposing fireplace. On the other hand, the furnishings were light. There was no heavy swathe along the mantlepiece, the armchairs and settees were covered in chintz, and there was a light Chinese carpet on the floor. Bragg walked over to examine the photographs over the fireplace. This one was clearly of the late master of the house, solid and stern. He had been in his late fifties then, by the look of it. By his side, his wife looked slim and pretty. And here was a recent one of Fanny. It was a really professional job, just enough out of focus to soften the outlines, make the subject look ethereal. In a way, it diminished her. It turned her into an empty stereotype of a socialite, when she was a warm, generous, amusing woman.

'Ah, Mr Bragg,' Fanny hurried into the room. 'I am so sorry that you have been left alone. I am afraid that Mrs Ryder came, unexpectedly, about church affairs and I had to support mamma.'

'I would have thought that your mother was well able to take care of herself,' Bragg said with a smile.

Fanny pursed her lips. 'Well, let us say that my presence occasionally imparts a little restraint to the proceedings! Now, sit by me and tell me what happened yesterday, when you went to Lulworth Cove.'

'I think that Inspector Milward must have regarded it as a good day's work,' Bragg said. 'Zachariah Gittings turned out to be a typical countryman of his generation. I doubt if he can read or write: he certainly keeps no records, and deals exclusively in cash. It is a great disservice to such people when a proper businessman, such as Ollerton, with his ledgers and invoices, becomes involved with them!'

'What did you discover?' Fanny exclaimed impatiently.

'I suppose that, since I am acting merely as a good citizen, there is no reason why I should not tell you,' Bragg said with a grin. 'We had an inconclusive discussion with Gittings, as a result of which Milward judged that he was justified in searching the premises. We marched him into the barn—and there were twelve kegs of brandy!'

'Brandy?'

'Milward promptly decided that they had been smuggled into the country by Gittings—which is probably true—and that Ollerton had been involved in the distribution of illicit spirit for five years.'

'Really?'

'And then, by a quite remarkable feat of mental presti-digitation, he ended up by arresting Gittings for Ollerton's murder!'

'Poor Mr Gittings! But at least the Inspector seems to accept that Mr Ollerton's death might not have been an accident.'

'That is true. But I cannot see Gittings being involved in it. There is not a smattering of real evidence against him. It is my bet that he will be released—on the murder charge, anyway. Still, it might keep Milward amused for a few days.'

At that moment Mrs Hildred came in, followed by Lucy with the tea tray.

'I do not understand where they get the clergy from, nowadays,' she declared. 'They have no idea of how to run a parish! Mrs Ryder has just been in to ask for a donation to repair the floor of the north aisle. Her husband was, no doubt, reluctant to come himself. I told him, years ago, that it needed replacing. I even offered to defray the whole cost of the work. But no! In the meantime, of course, it has got much worse and will cost twice as much to repair.'

'The vicar inveigled me into pumping the organ for him, the other day,' Bragg remarked, 'so I can attest to the state of the floor.'

'The man is a fool,' Mrs Hildred said crossly.

'At least, he stood up to the parochial church council over burying Miss Gosney,' Bragg said.

'What is this?' Amy asked sharply.

'Did you not know? They said that she ought not to be buried in consecrated ground, because she was a witch. But I hear it went ahead all right, yesterday morning.'

'Ignorant savages!'

'She was no more than a harmless eccentric,' said Fanny equably, handing round the cakes.

'When do you return to London, Mr Bragg?' her mother asked in a more amiable tone.

'I only have six more days here. A week tomorrow I shall be back on duty.'

'Are you fully recovered?'

'Yes, indeed!'

'You are too old to be taking foolish risks,' Amy asserted. 'When do you retire?'

Bragg laughed. 'I could retire in two years, but I might go on a bit longer. It depends.'

'On what?'

'On all kinds of things.'

Amy waited for enlightenment, but received none. 'I would like to retire,' she said plaintively. 'But Fanny shows no interest in involving herself with the brewery.'

Bragg glanced at Fanny, who was looking fixedly out of the window. 'I expect you might get a lot of satisfaction out of it, miss,' he said. 'Making beer is a fascinating business.'

She did not reply.

'To where will you retire?' Amy asked relentlessly.

'In the last few days I have been thinking that I ought to get a place of my own. But I would miss the bustle of London, if I left it. There is always something going on there.'

'When you get older, you want to escape from bustle.'

'You are probably right,' Bragg agreed mildly.

'Will you come back to Dorset?'

'It is possible, ma'am. But certainly not to Bere Regis. It is too small—and anyway, I would want to feel that I was starting afresh.'

'Somewhere like Dorchester, perhaps?'

'It's possible.'

'I do not suppose that you have sampled Hildred's beer yet. They do not sell it in Bere Regis.'

'I might have. I had lunch at the Phoenix, the other

day . . .' Bragg felt the pressure of Fanny's knee against his thigh and stopped. 'I might have had some there,' he finished lamely. 'Well, ladies, I have imposed on you long enough. It has been most enjoyable.'

'I will see you out,' said Fanny, jumping to her feet.

'You didn't tell her, then,' Bragg remarked when they were in the garden.

'I did, of course, Mr Bragg—but not in detail. I wanted to have something to treasure.'

She stopped to pick a rosebud and threaded it through his buttonhole. It was the same as the one that had won the prize at the flower show.

'This should remind you of one of my poems,' she said with a mischievous smile, and was gone.

When Bragg got back, he went up to his bedroom and pored over the book. She knew damned well that he had not read them. Now, here he was wading through every one. The trouble was that it might apply to a score of them. There was hardly a sentimental poem that didn't have a reference to a rose in it. Then he found it.

> *But I send you a cream-white rosebud*
> *With a flush on its petal tips:*
> *For the love that is purest and sweetest*
> *Has a kiss of desire on the lips.*

Dear God! He could feel a tingling at the back of his neck. What on earth should he do? . . . Well, in a week he would be gone. That should sort it out. He took the rosebud out of his lapel and looked at it. It was beautiful, there was no question. He would ask Emma to give him a vase for it. It might last till Sunday morning, then.

Next morning, Bragg woke early. He lay for a time, listening to the cocks crowing and the occasional bark of a dog. Should he try to get back to sleep? He felt too alert for that, but he could not just lie there for three hours . . . He could get up and enjoy the still freshness of the five o'clock countryside. But there would not be any hot water. He could wash in cold, but he drew the line at shaving with it. He rubbed his bristly chin. What the hell did it matter, anyway? He flung back the bedclothes and dressed quietly.

He walked briskly up Rye Hill and through the heath, towards Gallows Corner. He could feel elation and excitement welling up inside him. Amy Hildred had made him feel quite dejected, the previous afternoon, with her talk of retirement and being too old to take risks. It was absurd! He was full of vigour, in his prime. Good for another thirty years, at least. He would certainly never crawl into a hole to await dissolution. He would fight it, as he had fought every adversity . . . He marched on for another mile, then began to grow uneasy. He should not be squandering this buoyancy, this feeling of mental acuity. He wanted to clear up the Ollerton business before he went back to London. Fanny had pitched her hopes high and he had gone along with it. He did not want to look a pretentious fool in her eyes. He turned on his heel and hurried back.

It had barely gone half-past six when he arrived in Bere Regis again. People were stirring now. He could see threads of smoke coiling from the chimneys; cowmen greeted him on their way to milking. So, here he was. What should he do? If he went to spruce himself up, the mood would vanish. He wanted to be by himself while this zestful feeling lasted. He walked on, past the Royal Oak, past The Retreat and turned down towards the church. He had been so close to a revelation yesterday. Perhaps it was worth a shot at retrieving it. He went into the porch and tried the door, but it was locked. Damnation! Dare he roust out the verger? Come to think of it, he did not even know who the verger was . . . But all kinds of people wanted to get into the church in the course of a day. They could not be running back and forth with the key, all the time. And it was not as if anyone would vandalise or steal from a church. He crouched down and felt along the underside of the porch benches. Ah! Here was the key.

He unlocked the door and went to the seat he had occupied the previous morning. The silence was absolute. He only had to shuffle his feet and the sound echoed all round the church. Now then, was it something he had seen? He scrutinised the chancel arch, the pulpit, the chancel beyond. Nothing raised a response in his mind . . . Perhaps it was more an association of images that had triggered it. He let his mind relax, while his eyes drifted at random over the scene. The sun had broken through the east window. He had never seen it quite like this. Whenever he had been before, the sun had been much higher in the sky . . . Was it only three weeks since he had come down to look at the church, had first raised his hat to Fanny Hildred and been beguiled into riddling soil by the barrow-load? That was another loose end. He had still to decide what to do about the vicar . . . That was it! He had it hooked! . . . But gently . . . gently. He could see the outline of the idea. It seemed incredible! He let it run away, then drew it into his mind again . . . It could be a solution . . . At least it explained the mechanics of the situation, even if it did not point to the killer. When he had turned it over in his head a few more times, he became convinced that it was not fanciful; that, indeed, it must be the truth. He relocked the church and went back home. The sense of elation had gone. He felt as he often did when he had achieved a breakthrough in a case—wary, withdrawn, sensing the first stirrings of compassion for those who would be hurt by the truth. When he went into the kitchen, Ted was eating his breakfast. Bragg greeted him cheerfully, getting little response, and took some hot tap water up to his room. By the time he came down again, Ted was gone. Emma carved a wedge from a crusty loaf and set ham and eggs before him. She seemed subdued, barely speaking. She looked after his needs, but was far from her usual jolly self. Bragg was grateful, it matched his own mood. Above all, he had to think the thing through properly, before making a move.

'Joe, can I ask you something?'

Bragg looked up, to see Emma biting her lip tremulously, her face suffused with worry.

'What is it, love?' he asked in concern.

'Is . . . Is Ted in trouble? . . . I mean really in trouble?'

'Now, you don't want to go listening to silly gossip, Emma.'

'I can't help it! How would you feel if folk stopped talking as soon as you walked into a shop?—if your children didn't want to go out, because the other children were saying things about their father?'

'You, if anybody, ought to know Ted better than that,' Bragg said quietly. 'Have you asked him about it?'

'How could I? He snaps my head off, every time I speak to him.'

'Perhaps he is afraid that you believe it, too.'

'I've tried to be cheerful and show that I trust him, all along. But it's been no good. Now I don't know what to think.'

'Just hold on a bit longer, my dear. I am sure things will change for the better, very soon.'

'I don't know if I can hold on, Joe. I haven't slept properly for weeks, and he is tossing and turning all night. We can't go on like this.'

Bragg stood up. 'Well, I will tell you one thing,' he said firmly, 'I do not believe that Ted had anything to do with the death of George Ollerton. And, if it is any comfort to you, neither does his widow.'

He walked down to the bridge, to get away from the wash of emotions. Above all, he must be able to think clearly. He leaned on the parapet and watched the water writhing and twisting over the pebbles. When he had a coherent pattern in his mind, he strolled back to the Old Brewery.

'There is a telegraph for you, Joe. A lad brought it, not ten minutes ago.'

Emma seemed to have recovered her composure, if not her natural ebullience. Bragg tore open the envelope. It was from Morton . . . Jerrard! Well, that was unexpected. A

good thing that the telegraph had been brought from
Dorchester, or tongues would already be wagging in the
village. Even so, the squire might get to hear of it; the
telegraph girls would be sure to gossip about someone well
known. Far better if it came from him. Bragg went up to
West Street in the hope that he might bump into Jerrard.
After all, he seemed to be a man of regular habits. He
walked to West Mill and watched the water-wheel turning
lazily, for a time. Then he strolled back. He had got as far
as the post office, and resigned himself to failure, when the
squire turned out of Butt Lane and came towards him.

'Mr Jerrard!'

The squire stopped and looked up. 'Ah, Bragg. Good
morning.'

'Good morning, sir. Can I confirm a point with you?'

'Why, yes. What is it?'

'I gather that the gun which killed Ollerton had previ-
ously belonged to you.'

'That is certainly possible. I did sell him a gun, towards
the end of last year.'

'This one was a Purdey.'

'Then, in all probability, it is the same gun.'

'From what the coroner said, it seems to have been a bit
above Ollerton's class,' Bragg remarked.

'Well, perhaps so. But, between you and me, Bragg, it
was not a very good gun. I am sure that Purdey's would not
like to hear me say that, but it is true, nevertheless. It
functioned properly, of course, but somehow I was never
comfortable with it. They tried to get it right, a couple of
times, but they did not manage it. I should never have taken
delivery of it . . . Anyway, Ollerton admired it, so I
offered to let him have it.'

'May I ask how much he paid, sir?'

'Fifty pounds.'

'That would be a great deal of money to him, but you
must have sustained a considerable loss.'

'A gun is no good to you if you are not comfortable with

it. And it is not as if I have any sons to follow me. The only shooting I do, nowadays, is the odd pot-shot at a rabbit.'

'In the circumstances, one can only agree with his wife, that it would have been better if he had never bought it.'

'Yes . . . In a way, Bragg, I wish that you had not told me. It makes me feel responsible.'

Bragg laughed. 'Don't let it worry you, sir. Good day.'

He strolled down to the Royal Oak, to find Ernie perched on the wall. He took him the usual glass of beer.

'You will have to find someone else to keep you in drink when I go back to London,' he said.

'Don't worry.' Ernie gave a snigger. 'There is always somebody sorry for me . . . glad it didn't happen to them. Not the Bible-thumpers, though. To them, it's God's judgement.'

'I thought you were a churchgoer, yourself,' Bragg said with a smile.

'I am. But it doesn't mean that I agree with it.'

Bragg took a drink of his beer, then set the glass on the top of the wall. 'You did not tell me that Ollerton bought his gun from the squire,' he said.

'You never asked me.'

'You are a fat lot of use! I have to know what is in your head, before I can get it out of you.'

'I told you. I don't let on all I know.' Ernie gave his twisted grin.

'It is quite possible that you are holding back something that really matters.'

Ernie spat in the dust. 'See here, Mr Ball Crusher,' he said, 'none of it matters to me.' It was another of the flashes of despair that were the counterpoint to his courage.

'I suppose not,' Bragg said quietly.

After a moment, Ernie looked up with a smirk. 'They've took Alf Dyer. Did you know that?'

'Have they? Where?'

'In the woodman's hut, in Bere Wood. Caught him in the middle of the night. I expect old Bugby would have him hanged by now, if he had his way.'

'Not until you and I have agreed that he did it, I hope!'
Ernie gave a titter and finished his beer.

'You have lived next to the Ollertons ever since they
came to Bere Regis, haven't you?' Bragg said.

'Yes.'

'What kind of neighbours were they?'

'Kept themselves to themselves. Always plenty goin' on
there, what with the carts in and out . . . They were all
right.'

'He was not very well off when they came, was he?'

'No. They lodged with Mrs Sprigg, in North Street, for a
few weeks. Then they got the place next to us.'

'Who owns it?'

'Her ladyship's mother, of course . . . I hear you've
been a-squirin' her round Dorchester.' His eyes glinted
slyly.

'I was only taking your advice,' Bragg said disarmingly.
'Mrs Ollerton was pregnant when they came to live here,
wasn't she?'

'Like a barrel!'

'It must have been a bit of a shock, to have twins—
particularly when they were so hard up.'

'She was as proud as punch of them, though. She used to
walk them up and down West Street in an old bassinet, as if
nobody had ever done it before.'

'I suppose there are not all that many twins.'

'They say she had a bad time. I expect you do, if there are
two of them. It was a few weeks, before the paradin'
began . . . They said she wouldn't be able to have any
more.'

'Perhaps Ollerton was relieved at that.'

'I don't know. He seemed to be as proud of them as his
wife. He had got this notion that people's breath is full of
germs. He didn't like you gettin' too close, in case they
caught somethin'.'

'How long did he keep that up?'

'Not long. Once he had started his business, he was never
at home. He did work hard, I'll say that for him.'

'That was in the autumn of 'seventy-nine, wasn't it?'

'If you say so, mister.'

'What happened in 'eighty-three?'

'I expect a lot of things,' Ernie said peevishly.

'That was the year he got the business of a number of big coal importers, at Poole.'

'What is wrong with that?'

'Nothing. I was just wondering what was behind it.'

'I've already told you. George worked hard.'

'I meant, why would they all decide to use a carrier based in Bere Regis?'

Ernie wriggled off the wall. 'Since some of them were Ted Sharman's customers,' he said, 'they couldn't have been any worse off with George, could they?'

Next morning, Bragg borrowed his cousin's dog cart and drove into Dorchester. It was nothing like as pleasant a journey as his last. For one thing, the wind had dropped and the heat was already beginning to be oppressive. And, of course, he was on his own . . . He hoped that Fanny would not find out. She would be hurt that he had not asked her to take him. But, on this occasion, he had a serious purpose that might detain him for some time. And, anyway, people were beginning to talk. He did not want her reputation smeared. There was enough malicious gossip in the village, already. It was funny how, once it started, people got a taste for it and would besmirch the most innocent relationship. He drove sedately, in comparison with the headlong dash of the previous week, and left the trap in the station forecourt. He walked across to the goods section. A porter was stooping over a pile of boxes, pasting labels on them. Inside the office was a clerk in a dusty frock-coat, writing painstakingly in a ledger. He glanced up, as Bragg entered, then went on with his work. Bragg looked round in growing irritation, but there was no one else in the office. He wanted to grab him by the scruff of the neck and shake him . . . but he had no leverage here, so he could not afford to get off on the wrong foot. He pulled out his pipe and made a business of lighting it, then leaned on the counter and waited. At last, the man looked up.

'Yes?' he said tersely.

Bragg pulled out his warrant-card. 'I am trying to trace some luggage,' he said. 'I hope that you can help me.'

'The clerk looked at the card dubiously. 'I've not seen one of them before,' he said. 'I don't rightly know if I should.'

'If I were a member of the Dorset force, you would.'

'Well, yes . . . But I would know them. I've never seen you in my life.'

Bragg laughed. 'The detection of crime cannot depend on whether people know one another,' he said.

'Crime?' the man cried in alarm. 'They've not been sending headless bodies down here, have they?'

'No, nothing like that! It is just ordinary personal luggage, that I am after.'

'Oh . . . Do you think it was sent from here, or something?'

'I have reason to believe so, as they say.'

'Of course, if it was passenger accompanied, we would not have any record.'

'I realise that,' Bragg said patiently. 'I am trying to cover the off-chance that it was despatched as goods.'

'I see. On what date was it sent?'

'I have not got a specific date. However, it must have been towards the end of August or at the beginning of September in 1879.'

The clerk's jaw dropped. 'You are having me on!' he said.

'No, I assure you that it is a perfectly serious enquiry, connected with a rather grisly murder case.'

'Is it?' Despite himself, the man's interest was caught.

'Now, I appreciate that you are a very busy man,' Bragg said smoothly. 'I don't expect you to spend time looking for the entries. But if I could have half an hour with the despatch book, that should do the trick.'

'I don't know,' the clerk said doubtfully. 'This is a pretty heavy time of year, with the young nobs going off to school.'

'Well, I should at least try. Do you have the books for that year?'

The clerk stooped down behind the counter and, after a great deal of muttering and grunting, brought out a large brown-paper parcel. He brushed off the thick coating of dust and untied it. Inside were four large tomes. He selected the third and opened it.

'This is the one,' he said. 'You will have to look through it at the counter. I have nowhere private I can put you.'

'That is all right, sir,' Bragg said unctuously. 'It will be quite satisfactory here.' He took hold of the book and carried it over by the wall.

The clerk was perfectly right. There were plenty of trunks being consigned to young gentlemen at schools and colleges, about that time. Fortunately, Bragg was not interested in them. His difficulty lay more in deciding the period that he should cover. He could fix the beginning of it with reasonable certainty, but he could only guess at its end. He extended his search to the beginning of November, and still only had three possible names. Well, it was a long shot, after all. It would have to do.

He thanked the clerk, surrendered the ledger, and drove into the centre of town. He despatched a short telegraph to Catherine Marsden, at her home, then thought about lunch. It would be pleasant to have a meal at the Phoenix again, but it was still a bit early. He stopped at the window of the gunsmith's shop and gazed at the display of rifles, shotguns, bandoliers. It was a sport he knew nothing about. Had he stayed in the country, he might have been caught up in it; but having become a towny, guns were just a dangerous pest to him. He pushed open the door and waved his warrant-card at the man behind the counter.

'I wonder, sir, if you can give me a bit of information about a shotgun,' he said amiably.

'Of course! Always happy to aid the guardians of our peace.' He was a brisk little man, with bright eyes and a habit of jerking his head round, bird-like. 'Any particular gun?'

'A Purdey.'

'I see. Was it a particular Purdey?'

'I am concerned with one gun, yes, but the manufacturer has already given me the details of it. I need more general expertise.'

The man gave a gratified smile. 'It is just as well. As you know, Purdeys are individually built to their client's order. So I do not have one in the shop to show you—indeed I do not have anything of comparable quality.'

'It's a good gun, is it?'

'A Purdey is in a class of its own—absolutely supreme! I actually shot with one, for a whole day, many years ago. It was made for someone else, naturally; but, even so, it was an unforgettable experience.'

'There can't be all that much difference between one gun and another, surely?' Bragg said sceptically.

'Indeed, there is!' He gestured to a rack of guns in a case behind him. 'These are very good, in their way; but they are made down to a price. For instance, their barrels are drawn tubes. I could not guarantee against slight variations in the bore, down the length of the barrel.'

'Are you saying that price is not a consideration to Purdey's?'

'Their aim is perfection, and their clients are prepared to pay them a price which will enable them to achieve it. So, their barrels are bored from solid bars of steel, to a tolerance of a thousandth of an inch. A Purdey is hand-built from muzzle to butt. I was once told that it can take nine hundred hours of a master-craftsman's time to make one of their guns.'

'Does it matter whether a barrel is a drawn tube, or is bored out of a bar?' Bragg asked.

The little man wrinkled his nose. 'I suppose there must come a point at which the pursuit of excellence for its own sake is strictly unnecessary,' he said. 'Nevertheless, we are not dealing with playthings. When a gun is fired, the pressure inside the barrel is around two and three-quarter tons per square inch. A faulty barrel can burst, with tragic consequences.'

'Hmn . . .' Bragg consulted his notebook. 'Now, can you explain what choke does to a gun?' he asked.

'Indeed!' The man's eyes gleamed with pleasure. 'The choke is a slight constriction in the last inch or so of the barrel. You must appreciate that the sportsman is endeavouring to hit a quite small bird, flying fast, at a range of around forty yards. The degree of spread of the pellets, and the pattern of that spread, are crucial to the success of the enterprise. By varying the amount of choke in a barrel, you can alter the spread-pattern of the shot.'

'I see,' said Bragg thoughtfully. 'I have got the impression, from somewhere, that one barrel has choke and the other hasn't.'

The man smiled in delight. 'Comparatively speaking, that must be true,' he said, 'in that one barrel will almost always have considerably more choke than the other. Imagine the problems posed by a bird flying across your front. You will naturally wait until it is well within range, before you fire your first shot. For that, you will want a moderate choke that will throw a wide pattern of shot. If you miss, however, the bird will be going away from you. In that situation, you need a denser pattern of shot, which will carry further. So the second barrel is normally given a higher choke. A usual combination is left barrel three-quarter choke, right barrel quarter choke.'

'Which barrel does the front trigger control?' Bragg asked.

'The right one.'

'Being the barrel with less choke, which is fired first.'

'You are an apt pupil, sergeant.'

'An ex-army man, who told me I ought to get confirmation from an expert, said he thought the pellet from a right-hand barrel would be as one projectile, for a distance of three feet. Is that right?'

'Yes . . . yes, I would agree with that,' the gunsmith said with conviction.

'And beyond three feet, the shot would begin to spread?'

'The degree of spreading would be affected by the choke of the barrel, but there would be some spreading. Let me try to put it into perspective. Using normal cartridges, in a barrel with full choke, the spread-pattern should be the size of a dinner plate at twenty-five yards.'

'What do you mean by normal cartridges?'

'Usually, the chamber of a twelve-bore takes a cartridge two and a half inches long, which means a load of just over one ounce of shot. Sometimes, a gun is chambered to take a larger cartridge, in the quest for greater carrying-power. In my view, that is illusory, while the increased recoil makes shooting the gun less comfortable.'

'You seem to set great store on comfort,' Bragg said with a grin.

'Indeed, sergeant! If you think of standing in the butts for hours on a cold November day, with only short flurries of activity, you will understand why it is important.'

'Purdey's tell me that the gun I am interested in, is a self-opening hammerless model,' Bragg said. 'What does that mean?'

'Goodness!' the gunsmith exclaimed. 'It is certainly a very special weapon. They have only been making hammerless guns since 1886. There is only a handful of them in existence. I would give my eye-teeth to have a day's shooting with one!'

'What is so special about it?'

The man took a shotgun from the case behind him. 'On a normal gun, like this,' he said, 'the cartridge is fired by an external hammer, which strikes the firing-pin when the trigger is pulled.' He thumbed back one of the hammers to expose the tip of the firing-pin. 'It is essentially the same mechanism as the old flintlock, and many people think that it cannot be improved upon! For one thing, it is inherently safe. Even if you load your cartridges—and that is discouraged until you are on the point of firing—you cannot discharge them until you have pulled back the hammers to cock the action. The hammerless gun is a considerable refinement on this one, in that the hammers are placed inside the action. It gives a cleaner line to the gun, and all the working parts are protected from grit and weather. To a certain extent it makes shooting smoother, too. You load the cartridges, and merely closing the action cocks the gun. A sportsman can take a gun from his loader and discharge it, without having to pull the hammers back. It must make one the nearest thing to a machine-gun that it is possible to imagine! There is one great drawback, to my mind. Whenever the action is closed, the gun is potentially deadly. One should never rely on the safety-catch, it is much too easy to fail to apply it. So, with a hammerless gun, it is even more important to carry the gun with the action open, except when you are actually on the point of discharging it.'

'That explains something the coroner said. One last question, sir. How easy is it for a gun to be discharged by catching the trigger in the hedge?'

The man's head jerked up. 'I had wondered why you were seeking abstract knowledge on the subject, sergeant, but I suspect that it is something much more concrete. Has this to do with that poor man's death in Bere Regis?'

'I would be glad if you would be discreet about my call, sir,' Bragg said gravely. 'Since the verdict was accidental death, it's a bit tricky . . .'

'I see . . . Yes, of course. I will say nothing. As to your question, the pull on the front trigger would be about three and a half pounds, and on the back four and a half. It is all too easy to discharge a gun accidentally—which is why we teach people to observe the safety precautions most meticulously.'

When Bragg got back to the Old Brewery that afternoon, he found Rose sitting alone in the kitchen.

'How are you, Uncle Joe?' she greeted him perkily.

'I am quite better now, that you, my dear. Your mother has done wonders for me.'

'Good . . . And how are you getting on with Miss
Fanny?' she asked archly.

'You cheeky young monkey!' he exclaimed. 'I do believe
I shall end up spanking you! I am sure it is part of my
responsibility, as your godfather.'

'Go on!' she smiled knowingly. 'You can't get out of it
like that. You were seen walking round Dorchester, arm in
arm; and they say she is always on the lookout for you.'

'There was nothing remotely improper in it. People love
to exaggerate.'

'I expect so . . . Anyway, it would not be like her to be
fast . . . I like her.'

'That is quite enough about Miss Hildred,' Bragg said
with mock gruffness. 'How are you getting on in the world
of high society?'

'It's all right. We shall have it easy for a couple of weeks,
soon. Ruby—that's Mrs Jerrard—has made Charlie promise
to take her to London. They are off on Saturday. You
wouldn't credit the washing and ironing, mending and
brushing that is going on. I don't know why she bothers.
She could throw them all away. The minute she gets there,
she will be off to the shops. She'll come back with a pile of
hat-boxes and dress-boxes as big as a house!'

'Will you get any time off, while they are away?'

'Not us! We are supposed to give everywhere a thorough
clean. She's left Mary—that's the first housemaid—a list of
jobs to do, as long as your arm. But we will have a bit of
fun.'

She rose back to her feet and went to the door. 'Uncle
Joe,' she said, looking back.

'What?'

'You might suggest me for a bridesmaid. I could do with
a new frock!' She gave a screech of laughter, as he started
from his chair, and skipped out into the yard.

Bragg lit his pipe and sat contentedly on his own for a
while. Emma would have gone off somewhere, knowing
that he would be away for lunch. She would probably be
glad to see the back of him. Three weeks was too long a

period to have a stranger in the house; particularly as she and Ted were at odds. But would they get on any better, once he had gone? She had said that Ted had been like it before his visit. Would they continue in that way, long after he had gone? He sighed and knocked his pipe out in the grate. Then, for the sake of something to do, he walked up to the Cross. No one was around. Ernie would have gone with one of the drivers, or be up in a cornfield somewhere. Well, perhaps that was to the good. Until this theory of his was tested, one way or another, he would not feel like chit-chat. Not that he could take it any further himself. At least, not with discretion. He began to walk up West Street, wondering what he would do if Catherine Marsden's enquiries were inconclusive. Perhaps he ought to have named names. But she would have to consult other people, and it would only have started gossip . . . He could always tell the Chief Constable, but Colgrave would think that he had gone off his rocker.

'Mr Bragg!'

The vicar was hurrying out of Church Lane. Bragg stopped and waited for him.

'Mr Bragg, I have completed the draft of my learned paper on our discovery. Perhaps I should say "our learned paper", since I would wish you to be its joint author. If you have a moment, I would like you to read it, in case there is anything that you feel I might profitably add.'

'Very well, sir,' Bragg said reluctantly.

'Good! Good! Think of the renown we shall share, Mr Bragg!' He turned up the drive to the vicarage. 'You might find yourself debating the significance of the discovery before scientific societies!'

'I doubt that very much, sir.'

He followed the vicar through the French windows, into his study. The golden goose was on his desk, in front of the inkwell. On the blotter was a neat bundle of papers. Ryder picked them up and handed them to Bragg.

'Sit down and read them in comfort,' he said breezily. 'If

there is anything that you do not understand, such as a technical term, then please ask.'

Bragg sat at the desk and ploughed through the report, while Ryder prowled excitedly round the room. When he had finished, he picked up the relic and looked at it.

'Well?' the vicar asked, coming to a halt by the fireplace.

'You know, sir,' said Bragg heavily, 'I cannot see what weight my signature would add to this paper. I have no knowledge of history or antiquities, so my opinions are worthless. All I can honestly say is, that I saw you remove it from behind a stone in the shaft. I cannot even say that the well has never been excavated before. I grant you, there was no broken clay pipe, this time; but the soil was looser than I would have expected . . . What I did do, was to have a word with the blacksmith. According to him, if this piece of bronze had been buried in the ground for hundreds of years, it would have been thick with bright green verdigris all over . . . I think someone is trying to play a trick on somebody. If I were you, sir, I would just put it away in your drawer, and say no more about it . . . You would have two then.'

CHAPTER ————— ————— THIRTEEN

On that Tuesday afternoon, Catherine Marsden happened to come home early. She was preparing a series of articles for the *City Press*, about women and the professions. She had gone to interview a woman doctor at the Royal Free Hospital in this connection. Unfortunately, or some would say inevitably, she held only the humblest of posts in that institution and, just as they were warming to the subject, she had been called away. Catherine had thereupon decided to go home and rough out the article. It might be that she had obtained enough attributable material; she could always pad it out with comments of her own.

She went into the hall and was surprised to see a telegraph envelope on the card-tray—it was addressed to her! She tore it open and smiled to herself. Dear old Sergeant Bragg. So far as she was aware, no one had heard from him since he left for his convalescence. Certainly, James had not. He had taken her to dine at the Savoy, a week ago, and had said nothing about Bragg. But perhaps that was deliberate. He had seemed to be trying to find a new basis for their relationship, carefully avoiding anything she might find contentious, refraining from references to past events. Nor had she discouraged him. She had often regretted the circumstances of their first meeting. She had followed him and Sergeant Bragg, in an effort to get a story, and had confronted them outside a gentleman's club in the West End. James must have an abiding impression of her as a militant woman rampant! What long shadows small incidents threw. But, to give him credit, he was seeking to put it behind him. She had her father to thank for that, she suspected. If she had not fallen in with his suggestion that she should actually witness a cricket match, before condemning them, she and James might still be sniping at each other all the time.

She read the telegraph again. So he wanted information urgently—and she was to be discreet! Well, she had been a mere child at the time and, although they were living in Park Lane by then, her mother was too unworldly to be interested in such things. But Lady Lanesborough would know, and she was her godmother, after all! She glanced at her fob watch. The time for paying calls was almost over but, at the beginning of September, socialising was diminishing. There might still be time.

She took a cab to Lanesborough House and made herself float serenely up the grand, curved staircase. At the top was the famous portrait painted by her father, when Lady Lanesborough was in her twenties and the toast of London. Turning left, Catherine entered the drawing-room and was relieved to see the merest handful of visitors. She decided not to greet her hostess immediately, lest a new arrival should cause the remnant of callers to dally. Instead, she accepted a cup of tea from a maid, and went to look out of the window. That should be enough of a signal for her percipient godmother. When she glanced round again, the last of the visitors were taking their farewells. There was only Mrs Gerald de Trafford left. She was an old crony, and could linger till dinner time. Lady Lanesborough beckoned her over.

'I thought that you had foresaken us, child,' she said reprovingly.

'You know that I would never do that.'

'I really should chide you for dropping out of society. At the beginning of the Season, your name was on everyone's lips. The Prince of Wales, himself, was seeking you out.'

Catherine smiled. 'Perhaps the two are not wholly unconnected,' she said.

'You will never make a good marriage, if you carry on in this fashion! I hope Harriet has made that clear.'

'Mamma seems perfectly content for me to choose a husband myself . . . or not, if that is my wish.'

'Are you still set on that policeman of yours?' Lady Lanesborough asked darkly.

'I could hardly be set on a mere acquaintance!'

'Who is this man?' Mrs de Trafford asked.

'The second son of a baronet. He is personable enough— but hardly a catch. She could do much better.'

'The finding of a husband is not the reason for my call,' Catherine said with a smile.

A look of disappointment crossed Lady Lanesborough's face. 'Then I expect that it will be connected with this wretched journalism of yours.'

'Do I neglect you so much?'

'Neglect me? No, child. Nevertheless, there is always an ulterior motive to your visits.'

Catherine laughed. 'Well, I promise that you will enjoy my current preoccupation.'

'What is it this time?'

'A little social research. It is for background only, and I shall not incorporate what you tell me in any article.'

'Very well, what is it that you want to know?'

'I am going to ask you to cast your minds back to 1879.'

'Good heavens!' Lady Lanesborough exclaimed. 'Nowadays I have difficulty in recalling what happened last month!'

''Seventy-nine?' Mrs de Trafford said in her rather bleak voice. 'Was not that the year in which the Prince of Wales was going to be cited as co-respondent in the Langtry divorce case?'

'Was it? I forget.'

'Certainly, the prince was besotted with Mrs Langtry at the time.'

'I thought it was in 'seventy-nine that he began to tire of her.'

'My interest,' Catherine broke in, 'is not with the Prince of Wales, or with any of his lady friends. But it is to do with society.'

The two women looked at her expectantly.

'Can you tell me if any society lady missed the 1879 Season?'

'Gracious! That will not be easy. Are you suggesting that this did actually happen?'

'My information is that a young lady, who would have been expected to be present in London that summer, did not appear at all.'

'I see.' Lady Lanesborough turned to Mrs de Trafford. 'Can you think of anyone, Molly?'

'I am sure that was the year when Princess Alice died in the January,' she said.

'Ah, was it? . . . Yes, I believe you are right. Then it was the year that Caroline Massingham was thrown from her horse and injured her back. I do not think that she came up at all, that Season.'

'What about the Kindersley girl?' asked Molly. 'The one who ran off with someone quite unsuitable.'

Lady Lanesborough pondered. 'No,' she said at length. 'She was going to be bridesmaid to Lady Vigo's youngest daughter, and I know that she was married in 'eighty-one . . . It is no use, I shall have to get my journal.'

She went out and, after a moment, returned with a red morocco-bound book.

'Now then,' she said, as she began to turn the pages. 'Let us see . . . Had it been worthy of notice, I should certainly have recorded it.'

She glanced down page after page, sometimes murmuring to herself and smiling at a recollection. Halfway through the book, she checked.

'Do you remember the scandal caused by that silly Everard girl, Molly? She met her husband in the park with a demi-mondaine on his arm, and had not the sense to ignore it.'

'Ah yes . . . She ended up by losing everything, as I recall it. A stupid young lady!'

Catherine watched anxiously, as the pages turned. Already she must be past the end of the Season. Lady Lanesborough kept on dutifully, till she came to blank pages.

'No,' she said, closing the book. 'I am sorry, my dear. If some lady did miss the Season, then it cannot have been anyone of note.'

'I wonder if the journal for the next year might jog your memory. Perhaps you did not notice her absence, but you might have become aware of her reappearance.'

'You are persistent, child, I will grant you that,' said Lady Lanesborough with a smile. She went out and came back with a similar book.

'I take it that we need only consider the months of May to August, in this year,' she said, flipping through the pages. 'Here we are . . . May.' She began glancing through the entries as before, then suddenly stopped.

'What a clever girl you are,' she said in delight. 'This must be it. I have a note on the seventh of May, to the effect that Elizabeth Wilcox has got over her indisposition. Since I have inserted three exclamation marks, I take it I suspected that, in the previous year, she had committed a social solecism . . . Do you wish me to continue?'

'If you would. I ought to check as exhaustively as I can.'

'I do not mind at all. It is really quite fascinating to go back all those years. I think it is time that I began my memoirs. Would you assist me, child?'

'If you could assure me that they would not corrupt my innocence!'

'Would you have no one read them?' Lady Lanesborough

asked with a smile. She went on turning the pages for a few more minutes, then closed the book. 'No, there is no one else,' she said finally.

'Can you tell me any more about Elizabeth Wilcox?' Catherine asked.

'The family came from the West Country—Wareham, I think. Am I right, Molly? Her father was a landowner, I believe.'

'That is so,' said Mrs de Trafford. 'Her mother was one of the Grey girls. There were three of them—each one a considerable beauty. Elizabeth was the daughter of the youngest.'

'I remember that she made a good marriage,' said Lady Lanesborough. 'One of the Sussex Prideauxs, I forget which.'

'When did she marry?' Catherine asked.

'Is it important?'

'It could be.'

Lady Lanesborough pursed her lips in concentration. 'It was not immediately after her presumed indiscretion,' she said finally. 'I would say that it was three or four years after it.'

Catherine took her leave and returned home to write to Bragg. He had specified a reply by letter, giving the need for discretion as the reason. It was more likely that he felt he would get a fuller report than if she sent him a telegraph. Whatever the reason for his interest, it could hardly be of significance after this lapse of time. Nevertheless, she wrote a detailed account of what she had discovered. As she was sealing the envelope, she realised that she did not know where he was staying. James might have the address, but she doubted it. In any case, she was reluctant to ask him; he might think that was merely a pretext to call on him. But Mrs Jenks must surely know. If she took a cab straight away, she could be back home for dinner. And she could post the letter in St Martin's le Grand, on the way back. It would go off that evening, then.

The hansom took her to Tan House Lane and Catherine

asked the cabby to wait for her. She rapped on the door and, after some moments, Mrs Jenks opened it.

'Do you have Mr Bragg's address?' Catherine asked.

'Come in, miss, I have it somewhere.' She led the way down to the basement kitchen, where she began rummaging in a drawer.

'Here it is,' she said. 'Have you heard from him?'

'I received a telegraph this afternoon.'

'That's more than I have,' she said shrilly. 'I've had never a word since he left this house . . . And he was not well then. I have never seen him looking so thin.'

'I think you can safely assume that he is his old self again, Mrs Jenks,' Catherine said, copying the address into her notebook.

'Yes . . . well, I suppose he is.' The anxiety was replaced by petulance. 'Men are all the same. You spend your life looking after them, and never a thanks do you get.'

'When does he return?'

'It should be this coming Sunday.'

'I am sure,' said Catherine kindly, 'that he will be very glad to be home again.'

On the following afternoon Bragg was sitting in the shade of the pear tree, smoking a pipe, when Inspector Milward strode into the yard. Seeing Bragg, he went over and sat down beside him.

'I thought you might be interested to know,' he began brusquely, 'that you were right about Applin. I have just come from Blandford. I have been able to establish that not only did Applin leave there early on the twenty-first of last month, but on the fourteenth also.'

'I see.'

'He could have been in Bere Regis when George Ollerton was killed, as well.'

'Hmn . . . So you will be on the lookout for someone who saw him in this vicinity?'

Milward looked up sharply, but Bragg's face showed only a mild interest.

'I shall get Bugby on to that,' he said.

'What will you do about Applin, in the meantime?'

'I shall pick him up for questioning, this afternoon.'

'I see,' said Bragg thoughtfully. 'That will make three separate people behind bars, for the same murder. You ought to be able to hang it on one of them. How are you getting on with Dyer?'

Milward gave him a jaundiced look. 'He has barely uttered a word since we took him. The bloody man will not even admit to hocking the watch. We brought the pawnbroker to Dorchester, and he identified Dyer as the man who had come into his shop. All Dyer will say is that he is not George Ollerton, and never has been.'

'I should think you have got enough circumstantial evidence to get a conviction on the theft of the watch,' Bragg said cheerfully.

'I would not be too sure about that. Tabitha Gosney was the one person who saw Dyer bending over the body, and she snuffed it the week after . . . If I am honest,' Milward added reluctantly, 'I cannot even prove that Ollerton was wearing the watch that day. We know that it cannot have been pawned by him, because he was already dead. But proving it was Dyer that did it is another matter. You know what juries are like. They are not over fond of unsupported identifications.'

'How about getting the coroner to reopen the inquest on Ollerton?' Bragg asked, tongue in cheek. 'Would that help?'

Milward considered for a moment. 'I cannot see that it would make any difference,' he said gloomily. 'Unless we can squeeze something out of Applin, what fresh evidence have we got?'

'What about Gittings?'

'Don't talk to me about that bugger!' Milward exclaimed. 'He denies ever having been to Bere Regis in his life. We ask him where he was on the fourteenth, and every time he says he was out fishing.'

'It ought to be easy enough to check. He could not handle a boat that size, on his own.'

'We have asked, you may be sure. Half the village is prepared to confirm it—perjuring bastards!'

Bragg smiled. 'Never mind,' he said. 'You will be able to nail him on the smuggling.'

'That's what you think!' Milward said angrily. 'I asked the excise men, from Weymouth, to come with me and examine the kegs that we found in the barn. It took till yesterday for them to get off their backsides. When we got there, every last barrel had disappeared.'

'So you have no evidence?'

'We both saw the bloody things!' Milward exclaimed fiercely.

'We saw twelve barrels, and the markings on the sides of the front four,' Bragg said evenly. 'But I don't think either of us could swear as to what was in them . . . That is what you wanted the excise people for, presumably.'

'Stupid sods,' Milward said irritably. 'They think that smuggling was finished with a hundred years ago.'

'So, what happens now?' Bragg asked.

'I shall have to let the bugger go, that's what.' Milward got to his feet. 'Is Ted Sharman in?' he asked.

'He is around somewhere.'

'Not scarpered, then? Good! I still have my eye on him.' He turned and went moodily out of the yard.

The sound of his horse's hooves had barely died away, when Ted appeared.

'What did he want?' he asked anxiously.

'He just wanted you to know that you are still on his list of suspects, that's all.'

'Oh Christ! Why can't he let it drop?'

'Because, if Ollerton was murdered, you have an obvious motive . . . and you either cannot, or will not, account for your whereabouts at the relevant time.'

A mulish look settled on Ted's face and he did not reply.

'You may be relieved to know that he has at least two more suspects—Alf Dyer and Bill Applin.'

'Applin?' Ted exclaimed incredulously.

'He goes to Blandford every Thursday. Normally he does not return until four o'clock in the afternoon.'

'I know.'

'It seems that on both the day Ollerton died, and the day Tabitha Gosney died, he came back early. He could have been in the village at the time of their deaths.'

'I see.'

'Inspector Milward has just gone to interview Applin. If he runs true to form, Bill will be behind bars this evening!'

'Oh shit!' Ted said irritably.

'What are you complaining about? It will take the pressure off you, for a bit.'

'No it won't. It will make it a bloody sight worse.'

'Why?'

'Well, I suppose you might as well know. But I warn you, you won't like it . . . Over both of those lunch-times, I was with Lily Applin.'

Bragg bit back an exclamation of astonishment. 'The methodical Lily Applin, eh?' he remarked. 'And exactly where were you?'

'We used to meet at the old barn, on the lane to Shitterton.'

Bragg gazed at him. 'Why?' he asked quietly.

'I don't know . . . She was sympathetic, she seemed to understand.'

'Barmaids usually are.'

'You may scoff, but it's true . . . Emma never took the bad state of the business seriously. She seemed to think that I was inventing problems, half the time. All she would say was that everything would come right. But it just went from bad to worse.'

'She had faith in you, that's why. But don't run away with the idea that she was not worrying about you. I know that she was, from what little she said to me.'

'And what did she say to you?' Ted asked truculently.

'In my book, you have forfeited any right to ask that question,' Bragg replied flatly. 'Presumably the obliging

Lily wanted more from you than to hear your troubles. She could have listened to them over the bar.'

Ted dropped his head. 'It didn't mean anything to either of us,' he said.

'Did she ever give you anything to drink?' Bragg asked.

'Of course she bloody did!'

'I mean apart from beer.'

'No. Why?'

'Nothing, it was just a passing thought . . . And why are you telling me this now?'

'It's you that have been quizzing me about where I bloody was,' Ted said in exasperation.

'Sorry. Go on.'

'When Lily turned up on the twenty-first . . .'

'Which was the day that Tabitha was drowned.'

'Yes . . . she said that, just as she was going to slip away, the pot-boy waylaid her. He said that her husband knew she was carrying on with somebody. He told her that Bill had come back early the previous Thursday, hoping to catch her. When she was not at home, he went off looking for her. By the time he returned, she was back in the pub, so he told the lad to say nothing.'

'I expect the boy fancies Lily himself.'

Ted glared at Bragg. 'Anyway,' he went on, 'she said we must chuck it up; she had too much to lose . . . So we were having one for the road, when we heard a trap in the lane. I jumped up to have a look, and there was Bill Applin, coming towards the barn. There was no chance that Lily would get away, but she begged me to. So long as there was no man with her, she said, he would have no proof. So I did.'

'That was when she received her bruise, I suppose.'

'She said that he gave her a good hiding, but she never let on that I'd been with her. Say what you like about Lily, she's a good sort.'

Bragg fought down his disgust. 'Where did you go, when you left the barn?' he asked.

'I cut through the fields and over the river. Then up Black Hill and home.'

'Which was when you got your boots soaked,' Bragg murmured.

'What has that to do with it?'

'Not much. And, of course, you were seen by Ernie Toop, sneaking over the bridge.'

'That nosey little sod. He'd better keep his trap shut!'

'Do you seriously think that you are going to be able to keep this quiet?' Bragg asked with amazement.

'I hope so. I wouldn't want Emma to find out.'

'I would not bank on it, if I were you. Applin will have to explain his early return on those days to Inspector Milward. I cannot see how he can avoid telling him his reasons.'

'Would the Inspector question Lily?' Ted asked.

'He might. I certainly would. It would then be up to her, as to whether she supported her husband or not. After the beating he gave her, she might be disposed not to.'

'So it still might not come out?'

'Possibly not . . . If Lily does not back up her husband, then he will be in a difficult position. He would have no one to confirm his whereabouts at the time of Tabitha's death . . . That is, unless you are prepared to do so.'

'Not bloody likely!'

'For my money,' said Bragg, 'Milward will look at it the other way, and concentrate on the fourteenth. Here, he will say, is a man who admits to being back in Bere Regis on that day, by half-past one. He goes looking for his hot-arsed wife, down the path by the stream. He sees Ollerton, who he has heard is humping his wife. He tricks him into handing over his gun and shoots him with it.'

'What would happen then?' Ted asked soberly.

'It would depend how much Lily wanted to be rid of him . . . In the ultimate, it would depend on you.'

Ted swallowed hard. 'What would you do, Joe?' he asked.

'I would never have got myself into such a shit heap,' Bragg said harshly.

'I couldn't let George Applin swing for something he didn't do.'

'At the moment, we do not know whether he did it or not. And you are not out of the wood, yourself. Suppose Milward comes after you for Ollerton—and Tabitha, for that matter. Will Lily Applin back you up, and say you were rodgering her in the hay?'

'Christ knows.'

'Well, one thing is certain. If you hear the least whisper about your involvement with Lily, you must go to Emma and make a clean breast of it.'

Bragg spent the evening in the corner of the Royal Oak bar, pondering on what Ted had told him. It had been a shock, there was no denying it. Ted was the last person he would have expected to play fast and loose. But his own marriage had been so brief that he really had no experience from which to judge. He could not imagine himself ever getting into such a predicament, but it was easy for him to pontificate. He could well imagine Emma's resolute cheerfulness grating on someone as desperate as Ted. Not that it was any excuse . . .

It was late when he returned home and the house was in darkness. He locked the back door and felt his way upstairs. When he struck a match to light his candle, he could see a note on his bedside table. It was in Ted's writing. *I have told her*. Bragg wondered if it would have been all that surprising to Emma. Women were not stupid. What would her reaction have been? Rejection, mortification . . . relief? She would be deeply hurt, for sure. But she was too sensible to throw it all away—her home, her children, her grandchild. They would work out a basis for co-existence. They would have to.

Next morning, he went down to breakfast in some trepidation. Emma, red-eyed, was busy frying eggs, while a chastened Ted washed up their own dirty dishes. Bragg had his meal in silence. Even after Ted had gone out into the yard, Emma rebuffed his attempts at conversation. Damn Ted to hell! He took his empty plate to the sink, then made to go outside. As he passed Emma, she laid her hand on his arm.

'Thanks, Joe,' she said in a strangled voice, then burst into tears.

Well, it was not his place to comfort her, even if he could. He murmured something inane, then escaped into the yard. He found Ted in the harness room, staring into space. He perched himself on the corner of the bench and waited. The silence prolonged itself till it rankled. At length Ted looked round.

'You read my note, then?'

'Yes . . . I think you were right to tell her.'

'You are the only one that does,' Ted said dully.

'Look, I must speak to you about the business. I am sure that it is the last thing you want to think about, at the moment. But you may have to make a decision before long, so I feel I have got to mention it.'

'Decision? Since when have I made a decision?'

'Stop being so damned sorry for yourself! The other day, Mary Ollerton said that I could approach you, on her behalf, with a view to your taking over her business.'

'And what do I do for money?' Ted asked harshly.

'You might be able to increase your bank loan, or give her an annuity secured on the business assets. You could even take her into some kind of partnership. There are plenty of ways to do it. Mind you, I want her to get a fair deal.'

Ted grunted sceptically.

'It is my belief that she will want to sell very soon,' said Bragg. 'If I am right, you will not have much time to consider your offer.'

'You seem to be in the driving seat, Joe,' said Ted bitterly. 'You had better decide this one too.'

'Will you authorise me to negotiate with her?'

'Do what you like. I haven't any money, that's all I know.'

Bragg went into the house to fetch his hat.

'There's a letter for you,' Emma said with a sniff.

'Thanks, love.'

He split open the heavy cream envelope with his tobacco-stained knife. It was from Catherine Marsden . . . Wilcox! It was one of the names from the railway despatch book. It could not be a coincidence. Then he saw the reference to Wareham. That did not fit his theory . . . or not comfortably, anyway. Was it possible that Wareham luggage could have been despatched via Dorchester? Not unless Wareham station had been out of action, for some reason. But it could have been sent from Dorchester as a blind . . . He took a piece of paper and set out the elements of his puzzle, listing their interaction. He still could not find a solution. Was he just being thick-headed? Or was he going up a blind alley? He pondered, then decided that he was justified in testing it further. So, calling to Emma that he would be out for lunch, he walked up to the village. Lunchtime was perhaps not the most convenient moment to go calling, but then, it was Thursday. There was something to be said for being with her over a Thursday lunchtime. He knocked a tattoo on the Ollertons' door, and it was answered by Lucy.

'Hello! Is it your day off?'

'Yes. Do you want to see my mother?'

'Please.'

'Perhaps you would like to wait in the parlour.'

She ushered him into the room and left him. She had managed very well, for a fourteen-year-old. Confident and polite, she was a credit to Amy Hildred . . . He felt unease nagging at him. Had he forgotten something? Was there anything that he had promised to do?'

Mary Ollerton came in and greeted him.

'I am sorry to come at this time of day, Mrs Ollerton, but there are one or two things I wanted to ask you about.'

'It is no matter,' she said. 'I have a bite whenever I can find the time.'

'You will remember that, last time we spoke you, you agreed I should ask Ted Sharman if he was prepared to take over your business.'

'At the right price,' she said sharply.

'Of course. I have discussed it with him, and he would do so if a satisfactory arrangement could be made. It is unlikely that it could be a wholly cash purchase, but there are ways around that, as I mentioned.'

'I remember.'

'I would suggest that, however repugnant it may be to you, you should put the negotiations in the hands of a solicitor or an accountant.'

'I would know if I was getting a fair price,' she said stubbornly.

'Well, it must be your decision; and you will be able to consult someone at any stage of the negotiations . . . I really came to ask you about something else.'

'What is that?'

'The girls . . . the twins.'

'What about them?'

'Sarah is the image of you, Mrs Ollerton, but, tell me, who does Lucy take after?'

The blood drained from her face. 'What do you mean?' she asked.

'She does not look like either you or your husband. One can usually see some likeness to one or other of the parents, in a child of fourteen; but not in her case.'

'She takes after my husband's mother's side,' she said in a low voice.

'Lucy is not your child at all, is she?' Bragg demanded. 'She is a golden goose.'

'No!'

'You know, it is an offence to make a false declaration for the purposes of registering a birth,' Bragg said sternly.

'I didn't register her, George did!' she said.

'Then it is as well that he's dead. How much did you get? Was it a lump sum? Or was it so much a year, while she was young?'

'Four hundred pounds,' she said bleakly, her eyes drifting up to the shotgun suspended on the wall. 'I said no good would come of it, but he would take it on. Then I got to looking on her as if she was my own . . . They won't take her away from me, will they?'

'It depends if you tell the truth about it now. Who was the real mother?'

'We never knew.'

'Then, how was the business arranged?'

'One day there was a knock at the door—we'd not been down here long—and a man was standing there. He asked us to go with him to Dorchester, to see a solicitor. He said it would be to our benefit. We could not think what it would be about—it was not as if we had any relatives hereabouts. Anyway, Mr Ollerton said there was nothing to be lost, so I put on my bonnet and we went.'

'Where was this solicitor's office?'

'I don't know. In the middle, somewhere. Mr Ollerton knew, but I never bothered my head about it.'

'And what happened?'

'I was pregnant, of course. The first thing this man asked was when my baby was expected. It seemed a bit cheeky to me. But my husband said I was to tell him, so I did.'

'What then?'

'He asked if I were prepared to adopt a child, if it was made worth our while. We were very poor at that stage, so we said we might. He mentioned a figure of two hundred pounds. Mr Ollerton said it was not enough. I would have done it for that, but not my husband. He would always screw the last ha'penny out.'

'So what happened then?' Bragg asked.

'This man said that he might be able to increase the money a lot, if we would co-operate. He said the baby he wanted us to adopt was not yet born, but was due at the same time as my baby. He said he would offer us four hundred pounds, if we would pretend that this other baby was mine—that I'd had twins. He said it was a "harmless

subterfuge" . . . I can hear him now, "a harmless subterfuge".'

'And you agreed to this arrangement?'

'Mr Ollerton thought we would be daft to turn it
down . . . so we agreed.'

'Which baby was born first?' Bragg asked.

'Sarah—that is, my own baby. I had her nearly a week
before Lucy was brought to me.'

'Who brought her?'

'Tabitha Gosney.'

'So she knew about the arrangements?'

'She must have.'

'Where did she bring her from?' Bragg asked perempto-
rily.

'I don't know.'

'Did she bring the baby in a trap, on foot . . . how?'

'I don't know, honestly I don't. She came in the middle
of the night, with the baby wrapped up in a blanket.'

'Do you still have the blanket?' Bragg asked.

'Of course not! It was thrown out, years ago.'

'How old was Lucy, when she was brought to you?'

'She was newly born. I would say, just a few hours.
Tabitha put it about that I had had a bad time; so we didn't
take the babies out till they were getting on for a month old.
By then, you could not see the difference in their ages.'

'Did Miss Gosney ever say anything to you about where
she brought the baby from?'

'No. Never a word. Once the child was with me, we all
went on as if she really was my own. I never made any
difference between the two of them.'

'I suppose Miss Gosney was well paid for her part,' said
Bragg pensively.

'I expect so. Oh dear! What a tangle it is, to be sure. Do
we have to let on? I mean, she is grown up now. How am
I to tell her that she has not been my child all along?'

'Are you sure that you have told me all you know?' asked
Bragg.

'As God is my witness!'

'I certainly would not want to harm Lucy in any way. The trouble is that someone else is aware of it.'

'Who?'

'I do not know. But of the three people in the village who knew about it, two have been killed in the last three weeks. I think you should take great care of yourself, Mrs Ollerton. You could be next on the list.'

Bragg let himself out and walked along West Street, to clear his mind. How much further forward was he? It had not been the breakthrough he had been hoping for. He now had confirmation of his theory, and a tie-up between the Ollertons and Tabitha Gosney. Which meant that there was a logical link between the two deaths.

'Why, Mr Bragg!'

He looked up to see Fanny standing on the footpath smiling encouragingly at him.

'Good afternoon, Miss Hildred,' he said, raising his hat.

'Do call me Fanny. I think we know each other well enough to permit that small degree of intimacy.'

'Then, good afternoon, Fanny.' He raised his hat again and she laughed happily.

'Are you going for a walk?' she asked.

'Not really. I shall be glad to stroll back with you . . . As a matter of fact,' his voice became serious again, 'I want to ask you something, and I have not a great deal of time left.'

'Mr Bragg!' Fanny gasped, colouring.

'I suppose that I ought to ask your mother . . .'

'I would much prefer you to ask me first,' said Fanny firmly.

'I am probably wasting my breath—but nothing ventured, as they say.'

'I am sure that you need not hesitate, Mr Bragg.'

'Do you know of a family called Wilcox in this area?'

Fanny's face fell and she checked in her pace.

'They seem to have lived around Wareham, in the late 'seventies,' Bragg went on. 'You would be a young girl then, so I expect you would not remember.'

'You flatter me,' said Fanny, trying to recover her poise.

'Does the name ring a bell?'

'I am afraid not.'

'Do you think it might be worth asking your mother?'

Fanny gave a bright laugh. 'Why do we not take the gig and drive to Wareham? It would be much more satisfactory than relying on mamma's memory.'

Bragg smiled with pleasure. 'That is the best idea I have heard this week,' he said.

They hurried back and, while Fanny changed into a light tailor-made, Bragg helped the groom to harness the horse. Soon, they were trotting down the dusty road. This time, Fanny was content to let the horse proceed at its own pace. She sat slightly turned towards Bragg, the current of air ruffling the feathers in her hat. She looked very handsome, he thought. She would be a credit to anyone.

'Was your question related to the untangling of our tragic situation, Mr Bragg?' she asked.

'Indeed it was, miss . . . er, Fanny.'

'Are you making progress?'

'I still have to find a couple of pieces, then the jig-saw will be complete.'

'I knew that you would do it!' she said, with pride in her voice.

'In fact I ought to put you in the picture, for Lucy's sake.'

'Lucy? Our maid?'

'Yes. I would not want you to remark on it to her but, when she gets back tonight, she may be very upset.'

'Indeed?'

'It will depend on whether Mrs Ollerton has told her. She may well not, but you ought to be prepared.'

'Told her what, Mr Bragg?'

'Lucy is not an Ollerton, she is a golden goose.'

Fanny gave a puzzled smile. 'I do not understand,' she said.

Bragg gave her a sidelong glance. 'Well . . . I don't mean to embarrass you, miss.'

'I can assure you that you could never do that!'

Bragg cleared his throat. 'It sometimes happens,' he said, 'that a young woman of good background finds herself in the family way . . . I mean, without being married.'

'I understand, Mr Bragg, do go on.'

'You know better than I do, the store that the upper classes set on marrying off their daughters. For a girl to get into trouble is, for them, nothing short of a disaster.' He glanced at Fanny, but she was preoccupied with negotiating a badly rutted bend.

'The usual answer is to try to get rid of the baby,' he went on.

'Yes, an *accoucheur*,' Fanny said in a matter-of-fact tone.

'You know about it, then?'

'Of course I do!'

'Sometimes that solution is not acceptable—where the family is Roman Catholic, say, or where they have left it too late. In such a case, they will send the offending daughter away; give out that she is staying with relatives abroad, or some such. As soon as the baby is born, it is put with a poor family to bring up as their own; and the young lady gets back in the hunt for a husband.'

'You make it sound very cold-blooded, Mr Bragg.'

'It is cold-blooded. To all intents, they forget that the child ever existed . . . But to the family that accepts the child, it can make a lot of difference. They get a generous settlement to pay for the bringing up of the child, and to induce them to keep their mouths shut. So, to them, it's a golden goose.'

'Are you saying that Lucy is the child of a society lady?'

'In all probability. She was brought to Mary Ollerton a few nights after she had borne her own child. The arrangement was that she should pass the two babies off as twins.'

'And the settlement formed the basis of the Ollertons' prosperity?'

'That would appear to be the case.'

'There is one aspect of this that intrigues me,' Fanny said thoughtfully.

'What is that?'

'I wonder who selected Mrs Ollerton for the role of mother surrogate.'

'They were approached by a solicitor from Dorchester. All the arrangements were made in his office.'

'But someone must have decided that she was suitable; must have noticed that she was pregnant and discovered when she would come to term.'

'I suppose anybody in Bere Regis might have made a guess. But it's my belief that it was Tabitha Gosney.'

'Tabitha? I suppose you are right. No doubt she delivered Mrs Ollerton's own child.'

'She did,' Bragg said. 'And what is more, it was she who brought Lucy, a few nights later. She must have been well paid for her part. You said that she wouldn't let people into her cottage. I reckon it was in case they saw the things she had bought with the money, and started to wonder.'

Fanny looked searchingly at Bragg. 'Are you suggesting that the deaths of Mr Ollerton and Miss Gosney were brought about because they had been concerned in this deception?' she asked.

'It is the only significant link between them.'

'Poor Lucy. I hope that she is never told. It would be on her conscience for ever.'

'Well, I have left that to her mother—to Mary Ollerton, that is. She certainly has a great deal of affection for Lucy. The fear uppermost in her mind is that the child may be taken away from her.'

Fanny laid her hand on Bragg's arm. 'I am sure that you will do all you can to keep the matter secret,' she said.

'Well . . . normally I am all for letting in the light of day.'

'But not on this occasion, Mr Bragg. For my sake.'

'Very well, miss. I will do my best. What I want to find out is who her real mother is. Once we have discovered that, we shall be a long way towards identifying our murderer . . . Come to think of it, there was a very well-to-do couple that came to Ollerton's funeral—drove up in a spanking carriage, couldn't have come far. They might tie in with this Wilcox strand.'

'How did you come to unravel it so far?'

'It was just a guess at first. I was looking for a connection between the two deaths—one that would explain why Ollerton had become so prosperous. It took me a long time, for all that it was staring me in the face. The girls are not the slightest bit alike—and Tabitha was the local midwife.'

'It was a stroke of pure genius,' Fanny said with a smile.

'After that, it was a case of taking a long shot. I was thinking that Lucy might have been born somewhere nearby. Dorset is remote enough from London, in all conscience.'

'Indeed!' said Fanny wryly.

'So I went to Dorchester station to see if any luggage had been sent to London, in the name of a single woman, in the weeks following Lucy's birth. I found three possibles.'

'How did you settle on Wilcox?'

'A friend of mine is a reporter on a London newspaper. She is a society woman herself. So I asked her if anyone had missed a Season, fourteen years ago.'

'This lady friend . . . did she know the answer?' Fanny asked coolly.

'Not herself, miss. She's only twenty or so. But she has a lot of contacts. Would you believe it? The only name she came up with was Wilcox—one of my three. It couldn't be a coincidence.'

'Did she discover that they lived at Wareham?'

'More that the family came from the Wareham area.'

'This is exciting,' Fanny exclaimed, 'and also a little frightening. What will you do when you find them?'

'One step at a time, Fanny! Nothing very startling, I suppose. This isn't my patch. I don't really have any authority here. I expect that I shall end up presenting the case to Inspector Milward.'

'But why? It will be you who has done all the real work!'

'It happens that way, sometimes. The only thing that matters is catching the murderer.'

Fanny turned towards him. 'I shall see that no one is left in doubt as to who really solved the crimes,' she said vehemently.

They turned into the main street of Wareham and were directed to the police station. Giving an urchin a penny to hold the horse, they went into the building.

'City of London Police,' Bragg said briskly, holding out his warrant-card.

The young desk-sergeant gave it a suspicious look, at the same time eyeing Fanny quizzically.

'I would like some information,' said Bragg. 'I am told that a well-to-do family called Wilcox lives hereabouts. Can you tell me how to get to their house?'

'Wilcox? . . . Wilcox? It doesn't ring a bell with me. Just a minute.'

He went to a rear door and they heard him bellowing for someone called Jack. After a few moments a grizzled constable appeared.

'Wilcox?' Jack repeated. 'No. I don't know of any.'

'Are you quite sure about the name?' the desk-sergeant looked at Bragg sceptically.

'I cannot be certain, but that is what I am told.'

'There used to be a Wilcox at Wareham Castle, sarge,' said Jack. 'That was when I first came here. The Pargiters have been there a good long while now.'

'That is the best we can do for you, then,' the desk-sergeant said crisply.

'Thank you, anyway.'

'What a disappointment,' Fanny said, when they got outside. 'Does that mean that this thread of enquiry is broken?'

'Not necessarily. We will go along to the public library. They will have the voters lists for a good few years back. We might pick up the other end yet.'

The librarian was exceedingly pleasant and helpful. He found them room in his own cubby-hole upstairs, and had a great pile of voters lists brought to them. They ploughed steadily through the dusty sheets for almost two hours. By the end of that time, they had established that there was only one family named Wilcox in the lists. They had, indeed, lived at Wareham Castle. And they had left there by 1873.

CHAPTER ———— ———— FOURTEEN

For once in his life, Bragg was tempted to let dejection flood over him. On the way back from Wareham, Fanny had been sympathetic and consoling; but for all the warmth of her manner, he could tell that she was disappointed. And well she might be. The trouble with the country was, it blunted your brains. You were always too slow in seeing things. Always one step behind. If he were back in London, he would be rattling around questioning people, casting about for a new scent. Here, everywhere was so damned spread out, the people so scattered, that you could spend a whole day in making one mistake . . . Anyway, it was not his case. Tomorrow was Friday; on Sunday he would be back in London, back in the old rut. He could forget about silver watches and kegs of brandy—and a slim, happy woman who made him feel young again . . . And yet he had the uneasy feeling that he knew the answer, that it was there in the back of his mind. Just as it had been over the so-called twins.

After supper, Emma proposed a game of dominoes. Ted

got some bottles of beer and they sat down to play. It was hardly a relaxed evening. There was constraint between Emma and Ted, reproach and recrimination barely held in check. But it was a start. Towards the end of the evening, there was even some laughter. Emma seemed reluctant to abandon the game and relapse into inimical reality again. Once midnight had struck, however, she got up from the table and Ted followed her meekly to bed.

Bragg was too restless to feel like sleeping. He went out into the yard. It was a sticky, sultry night. Even the wind, soughing in the pear tree, gave no relief. He could hear the rumble of thunder to the south, and jagged lightning was cracking across the sky. He sat under the tree and smoked his pipe for a while. Life was a muddle, and no mistake. Up there Ted and Emma would be lying rigidly, side by side, ridden with mutual betrayal and guilt. If he turned to the left, there was the gable of The Retreat. He had often wondered which was Fanny's bedroom—it was not the kind of thing you could ask a young woman! What would she be thinking, lying awake on this sweltering night? Would she be feeling let down, disappointed in him? He sighed, knocked out his pipe and made his way upstairs.

He undressed, got into bed and nipped out the candle. Then he realised that the window was wide open. If it rained in the night, it was sure to come in. He got up to close it and, as he did so, became aware of a light in the village—a glow. He leaned out of the window and saw the flicker of flames. He scrambled back into his clothes and roused Ted, then pelted off to the cross-roads. The thatch of Mary Ollerton's house was on fire. She was standing numbly in the street with Sarah, while neighbours unavailingly threw buckets of water at the blaze. Then a burly young man rushed up and began to organise the gathering crowd. He despatched two men to bring the fire-hooks from the church porch, and some more to get the fire-pump from inside the tower. The hooks were soon brought. One man was set to pulling the burning thatch away for others to extinguish;

another was told to tear away the unaffected thatch, to make a fire-break. But, despite their efforts, the conflagration was spreading. The flames licked up the gable, insinuating themselves through the overhang; burning fragments of thatch were whirling about in the gusts of wind. A youth came running to say that the church was locked, and they could not get the pump. He was told roughly that he ought to know the key was under the porch bench, and sent back again.

Ted arrived panting. 'What about the horses?' he asked.

'No one seems to be worried about them,' Bragg replied. 'Let's go and see.'

They dashed into the yard. As they did so, the fire reached the ridge of the house and great columns of flame shot skywards. Neither the stables nor the cart-shed were thatched, but the stables were dangerously near to the back of the house. They could hear the horses moving about and whinnying uneasily.

'Let's get them into the cart-shed,' said Ted urgently. 'They will be safe there.'

He opened the stable door and began murmuring reassuringly to the horses. One by one, they untied them and led them to the top of the yard, where they penned them loose in the cart-shed. While they were doing so, the pump arrived and began squirting water from the well on to the roof.

With the last horse safe, Bragg and Ted dodged back into the street again. The thatch at the front was well alight and the flames had bridged the fire-break. Every time the wind gusted, the blackened right-hand side of the roof glowed a fierce red.

'I reckon it be a goner,' someone muttered.

'Bloody lightning!' another man exclaimed. 'Good thing old George had paid the insurance man.'

The remark switched Bragg's mind from the house to its contents. The furniture could be replaced, but the business

books could never be reconstituted. Calling Ted, he ran
full-pelt into the yard and round to the back door. It was
locked. Disregarding the shouts of the men on the pump, he
battered at the lock with his boot until the wood splintered
and sent him staggering into the kitchen. Smoke billowed
out, and they had to crouch near the floor to get to the
office. But it was not far and, in two journeys, they
managed to bring out the bulk of the records. But the
draught from the open door was feeding the fire and they
were forced to abandon the remainder.

Once more at the front, they could see a new danger. The
wind had blown a handful of burning straw on to the roof of
the next house. It had caught in the eaves and tongues of
flame were licking at the thatch. The hook men began
ripping away the deep layers of straw; but the more they
tore at it, the more easily the fire seemed to spread. Then
someone came running from the Ollertons' yard.

'Mr Shave! Mr Shave! The well be run dry!'

'Then leave it, and get the pump round to Toop's,' the
burly young man ordered. 'We'll have to let this one burn
out.'

By the time the hose was in position, the new fire was
well alight; but it was in the eaves, so more accessible to
the puny jet of water from the pump. As long as no more
burning fragments came from the Ollertons', there was a
chance that this blaze might be contained. Bragg looked
around him. Mary Ollerton was gazing stonily at the
destruction of her home, with Amy Hildred's arm around
her. Nearby, Fanny stood hand-in-hand with the two
girls.

'Where is Ernie Toop?' he demanded of a spectator.

'I dunno,' the man said slowly. 'There be 'is da.' He
pointed to an elderly couple, peering anxiously at their roof.
Bragg went over to them.

'I cannot see your son anywhere,' he said urgently.
'Where is he?'

'He went back inside, not five minutes ago,' said Mrs

Toop. 'Said he wanted somethin' from his room. I expect he is out again by now.'

'Which is his room?'

'Downstairs, at the back.'

Bragg rushed round the rear of the house, and found the door ajar. Enough light came from the fire next door to reveal Ernie, sprawled on the floor of the passage. Bragg bent over him.

'Are you hurt?' he asked.

'I've twisted my ankle,' Ernie gasped. 'I tripped over the threshold and hit my head.'

'The thatch of this house is on fire now. We'd better get you out. Can you walk at all?'

'What do you bloody think?' Ernie asked venomously.

'Then, I will carry you. Ready?'

Bragg hoisted the cripple's light body on to his shoulder and got him out of the building. He edged past the men labouring at the fire-pump and carried him to the street. As he emerged into the light, there was some ragged cheering and hands reached out to clap him on the back. He sat Ernie in a doorway and went in search of his parents. Having told them he was safe, Bragg worked his way to the front of the crowd.

'That was very courageous of you, Mr Bragg,' said Fanny warmly, tucking her hand in his arm.

'Nonsense! There was not the slightest danger to either of us,' Bragg protested.

'Even if that were true, you were not to know it. Yet you went into the house without regard for your own safety.'

'I have become quite fond of our caustic cripple; but that doesn't make me a hero, Fanny.'

She looked at him steadily. 'I believe that you always underrate your own worth, Mr Bragg . . . in every field.'

There came a muffled crash as the Ollertons' roof fell in. There was a sudden cascade of sparks, and tongues of flame groped skywards. Then the light was dimmed as the fire was contained within the walls. It was soon apparent that

the flames in the Toops' thatch had been extinguished, and
that there was now little danger of the fire spreading.
Accordingly, Shave directed that the remaining water in the
Toops' well should be pumped into the burning building.
Gradually the conflagration diminished until, as dawn
broke, it was declared to be out.

'Where are the two girls?' Bragg asked.

Fanny smiled tiredly. 'Lucy took Sarah to her own bed,
hours ago. They will be a comfort to each other. Mamma
has persuaded their mother to stay with us, for the time
being, also.'

'That is kind of you . . . I expect it is time we got to
bed as well. May I come to your house in the morning, for
a word with Mrs Ollerton?'

'Of course!'

'Goodnight then.'

'It is already the penultimate day of your visit, Mr Bragg,
so I will wish you good day.' She turned and vanished into
the shadows.

Bragg managed to snatch a few hours' sleep and woke with
his mind unexpectedly alert. He could hear Emma moving
about downstairs. Their day had to start as usual, whatever
happened; they had customers to satisfy. He wondered what
Mary Ollerton was feeling. The business would be able to
carry on—thanks to Ted's efforts in moving the horses—but
she would not have much heart for it . . . The onlookers
had been putting the fire down to lightning. But Bragg had
been awake and the storm had never come near Bere Regis.
The blaze had started in the bottom right-hand corner of the
roof, by the entrance to the yard. Could it have been caused
by a careless passer-by flipping a cigarette-end into the
thatch? After the long, hot spell, it would be very dry. It
would not take much to ignite it. But a cigarette-end?—at
half-past one in the morning? No, it was much more
deliberate than that. It had been started at precisely the point
where the wind would spread the flames most effectively.

He toyed with the theory that Gittings might have been trying to destroy Ollerton's records. The man had maintained that he had never been to Bere Regis in his life. If that were true, he would not have been able to identify Ollerton's house, for there was no name-board outside. Of course, other people had been involved with Gittings and Ollerton in the smuggling and distribution of the brandy. Some of them would have known. But it was all too late and too far-fetched. It had to be the Lucy business. He had warned Mary Ollerton that she might be the next on the list. His prediction had been fulfilled sooner than he had expected. Bragg wondered if the killer had been hanging about in the crowd, watching the flames. If so, he would know he had failed—in which case, he would probably try again.

Immediately after breakfast, he went round the corner to The Retreat. One or two children were gazing in fascination at the gutted building. There was some activity in the yard, as well. As he watched, he saw Harry Green cross the road from the Royal Oak, with two buckets of water for the horses. Bragg went through the Hildreds' gate and knocked on the door. Once again, it was answered by Lucy.

'Hello,' he said. 'How are you feeling?'

'All right.' She looked tired and strained. 'Are you wanting Miss Fanny?' she asked.

'No, love. In fact, I want a word with your mother. Is she in?'

'Yes. Will you wait in here please?'

She showed him into the drawing-room and, after a few moments, Mrs Ollerton came in.

'Well, what is the business worth now?' she asked despondently.

'Thanks to Ted Sharman, no more and no less than it was yesterday at this time.'

She sat down heavily. 'I heard you and he took the horses up the yard. Thank you.'

'People were saying, last night, that it must have been

caused by lightning. I suppose that it is just possible. But I was awake, and the storm was over the Purbeck Hills. As an explanation, it will do for the insurance company; but I am convinced that it was a calculated attempt to kill you.'

Mary Ollerton shivered. 'They might have managed it, too. I generally sleep soundly. Only, last night I was turning it all over in my mind—about Lucy, I mean. Then I heard this crackling and could smell smoke. So I got Sarah up, and we ran for help.'

'I take it that there had not been a fire in that bedroom?'

'No! I even let the kitchen range go out, after supper, it was that hot.'

'Whose is that front bedroom?'

'Mine.'

'Tell me, are there any men who knew you would be sleeping there?'

'What do you take me for?' she cried, bridling.

'I am sorry,' Bragg said penitently, 'I didn't mean it like that. It's just that I believe the murderer of your husband is a man. You must admit that the fire was started where it was most likely to kill you . . . For once, it was a good thing that you had a lot on your mind. Have you said anything to her yet?'

'What, to Lucy? No. I can't find it in my heart to. She is such a lovely girl . . . And I don't know how she would feel afterwards—about me, I mean.'

'Then, keep it to yourself, and I will try to see that it is kept secret, as well. And remember, be on your guard. Our friend may well try a second time.'

Bragg left the house and crossed the road again, his mind dwelling on the delicate features of the blonde girl. He wished he had paid more attention to the woman who got out of the carriage, at Ollerton's funeral. He might have been able to catch a resemblance through the veil. Ah well, hindsight was a useless faculty. He made a mental note to ask Mary Ollerton if she knew who the woman was.

He poked his head through the shattered window, into the

burnt-out remains of the parlour. It was in the room above that the fire had first got hold; he could look up, clear to the sky. A few ceiling joists remained, badly charred, but the collapsing roof had brought everything else with it. A brass bedstead had crashed down on to the remains of a settee. By the doorway, a blackened length of wood with a brass handle on it was all that remained of a wardrobe. The floor was a foot deep in sodden ash and debris. Still suspended over the fireplace, was the shotgun, the symbol of George's success. Bragg gave a sardonic smile. Fate was a queer thing. The man's prosperity had been founded on a deception, 'a harmless subterfuge'; yet, for some reason, it had led to his death. The object he had most prized had been the instrument of his murder. There it hung, covered with ash, its stock scorched and scratched . . . The stock . . . Good God! That was it! Stupid bugger that he was, he had known all the time! He set off at a run along West Street.

Rose was smiling cheekily, as she led him along the corridor and knocked on the heavy oak door.

'Mr Bragg, sir.' She curtsied and closed the door behind her.

The squire was standing by a table in the centre of the room, cleaning one barrel of a shotgun. Along a wall were cupboards, with rifles and shotguns ranged in them.

'Yes, Bragg?' he said curtly. 'What is it that you want?'

Bragg took a chair at the end of the table and leaned back confidently.

'As you know, sir, I am an officer in the City of London police force. So, in one sense, what goes on down here is no concern of mine. On the other hand, every citizen has the right to enforce the law. If he becomes aware of a crime, he can arrest the offender and deliver him to the constable.'

Jerrard looked up blankly. 'How does this concern me?' he asked.

'I am making a citizen's arrest on you for the murder of George Ollerton, the murder of Tabitha Gosney and the attempted murder of Mary Ollerton.'

The squire's face went puce with outrage. 'You must be off your head, Bragg,' he said angrily.

'Oh no. It all hinges on Lucy Ollerton's being a golden goose. Mary Ollerton admitted it, when I pushed her, but she had no idea who the real mother was . . . I ought to have realised it at the cricket match. Lucy bears a strong resemblance to your nephew, Stephen Bennett; and, of course, to your wife. She was one of the Grey girls, from Wareham, wasn't she?'

The squire glared at Bragg and made no reply.

'The natural mother of Lucy Ollerton was Elizabeth Wilcox, the daughter of one of your wife's sisters. By then, the Wilcoxes had left Wareham Castle, but they knew the area well . . . And what better place for the young woman to hide herself away from society, than Shitterton Manor?'

'Even if this were true, it does not make me a murderer,' Jerrard said violently.

'I agree. It is not even all that unusual. The trouble was that, despite all your careful planning, George Ollerton found out who the real mother was. He probably got it from the luggage records at Dorchester station, like I did. He was a carrier, after all. And since Tabitha Gosney had brought the child to them in her arms, it was probable that the birth had taken place nearby. It cannot have been difficult to tie it all together.'

'So?'

'So Ollerton started to blackmail you. And, by chance, he approached you when your niece was at her most vulnerable. She was about to be married to a rich husband. It would have been a disaster if the truth about her bastard child had come out, so you had to buy Ollerton off. As it happened, he did not want money, he wanted your patronage. He asked you to persuade your friends in influential positions to favour his business. You did as he asked, and that is the reason why Ollerton's business expanded so dramatically in 1883 . . . But he had not finished with you. From time to time, he screwed you for something he wanted, like your shotgun.'

The squire turned to the window and squinted down the barrel. He gave a grunt of satisfaction and laid the shotgun on the table. Then, opening a drawer, he took out a bottle of gun oil and began to rub some on the metal parts of the gun.

'Even if this were all true, it does not mean that I would kill the fellow,' he said eventually.

'No, but you did, nevertheless. And, having got rid of him, you decided that you had to get rid of Tabitha Gosney, also. She had delivered the child at Shitterton Manor. If Ollerton's death were judged not to be accidental, she could point the finger at you. It was easy enough for you to choose your time, you were always wandering around the village. When you spied your chance, you knocked her unconscious and held her head under the water till she drowned. Then you escaped over the stream to Black Hill, and made your way home round the fields.'

'Rubbish!'

'I don't know whether you felt secure for a bit, or not, but you must have realised that there was still another person who knew that Lucy was a golden goose—Mary Ollerton. There was always the risk that her husband had told her what he had discovered.' Bragg paused. 'So, last night you tried to burn her alive,' he said grimly.

'This is all fantasy, Bragg,' the squire exclaimed. 'Are you suggesting that a man of Ollerton's physical stature, would allow someone much smaller than he to wrest his gun away from him and shoot him with it?'

'That is what put me off, for a long time. But he was not killed with his own gun. When I first saw you, in West Street, I noticed that your shotgun had a distinctive dent in the stock. Although I did not realise it at the time, the next occasion on which I saw that gun, it was lying on the table in front of the coroner at Ollerton's inquest. You had a pair of Purdeys made, not one. Ollerton blackmailed one off you, but you still used the other. When you quarrelled at the stile, that day, you lost your temper and shot him—from six feet away. Then you put your gun in Ollerton's hand, and took his away with you.'

Jerrard suddenly plunged his hand into the drawer and pulled out a revolver.

'You are clever, Bragg, I grant you that,' he said with a sneer. 'Too clever for your own good . . . What a pity that there has to be yet another accident.'

He raised the weapon to the vertical, like a dueller, then began to bring the muzzle down to bear on Bragg. As he did so, Bragg seized the end of the table and flung it upwards. The edge caught Jerrard's arm. There was an explosion and he slumped to the floor. Bragg rolled him over. The bullet had entered below the chin bone and blown the back of his head off.

There was a rush of feet in the corridor. Bragg leapt to the door and held it open a crack. A young housemaid was standing there, a look of alarm on her face.

'Don't come in,' Bragg said quietly. 'Tell someone to go for the police.'

The Chief Constable dropped into a chair, in Ted's parlour, and sighed unhappily.

'After our chat last evening, Bragg, I decided that I must go and see Jerrard's widow myself . . . It is all rather sensitive—not the sort of thing I could leave to people like Milward.'

'I agree, sir.'

Colegrave looked relieved and took out his pipe. With a smile, Bragg proffered his tobacco pouch.

'Ruby was very sensible about it,' Colegrave went on. 'She admitted the golden goose arrangement and acknowledged that the mother was Elizabeth Wilcox—now Mrs Prideaux. It seems that she played a leading role in the affair. It was she who noticed that Mrs Ollerton was pregnant, and discovered from Tabitha Gosney when the baby was due. It was she who proposed the adoption

arrangement. Then her sister became concerned that
Bere Regis was too near their former home for comfort,
so Ruby evolved the twins scheme. It was really very
imaginative, Bragg. If she had not been childless, I
would have begun to think that she had perhaps strayed
herself, in her youth.'

'Did she know about the blackmail, sir?' Bragg asked.

'She was a little less forthcoming in that area. At first,
she said that she knew Ollerton was asking for favourable
treatment from their friends. I pressed her, and she then
admitted knowing that Ollerton had found out the identity of
the child's natural mother. She said that she supported her
husband's resolve not to allow Elizabeth Prideaux's reputation to be harmed. Knowing them both as I do, I would have
said that it was the other way round!'

'He certainly did not look like someone who would
perpetrate three brutal murders,' said Bragg, taking back his
pouch and beginning to fill his pipe.

'Three?' Colegrave asked in surprise.

'Including the attempt on Mary Ollerton.'

'Ah, yes.'

'Was Mrs Jerrard involved in them, do you think?'

'I honestly believe that she was not, Bragg. She seems to
have thought that the status quo was tolerable. After all, the
patronage exercised on Ollerton's behalf was costing them
nothing. Even when he began to demand sums of money for
particular purposes, she was not too concerned. They are by
no means wealthy, but the sums were not great. She did not
say so, but I would be surprised if she did not ask for them
to be reimbursed by the Wilcoxes. I believe that they are
well-to-do.'

'That would seem to be reasonable,' Bragg said, striking
a match and laying it over the bowl of his pipe.

'I think that it must have been the gun business that got
under Jerrard's skin,' Colegrave went on. 'I gather that he
offered him the pick of his other guns, more than one if he
wanted, but it had to be the Purdey.'

'Ollerton was just demonstrating his power over the squire. Damned stupid, if you ask me.'

'Certainly, Jerrard seems to have been seething with outrage.' Colegrave puffed at his pipe meditatively for a few moments. 'Anyway,' he went on, 'when Ollerton was found shot by his own gun, Ruby thought that he had got his just deserts. It was not until Miss Gosney died, the week after, that she began to suspect that her husband might be behind the deaths. She persuaded him to go away with her to London, and he agreed.'

'But he felt he had to eliminate Mary Ollerton first.'

'That would seem to be the case . . . This is quite a pleasant smoke, Bragg. Who is your tobacconist?'

Bragg laughed. 'It is Gold Block, from the local store. I can't get my usual evil-smelling twist down here!'

There was a silence for a while, then the Chief Constable roused himself.

'There will have to be an inquest, I presume,' he said.

'I should think so.'

'It would seem to be a rather complicated situation,' Colegrave remarked cautiously. 'Goodness knows what the verdict will be, this time.'

'Indeed, sir.'

'I mean, reopening the other two cases would be bound to cause needless distress . . . and it is not as if the murderer would escape.'

Bragg allowed a silence to grow between them, then he leaned forward and knocked out his pipe in the ash-tray.

'My concern is with the little girl,' he said. 'For me, that is the only thing left in this case that matters. It would be a tragedy if, after losing her father and her home, she found out that she was the chance-child of some cock-smitten socialite.'

'Yes . . . er, yes indeed.'

'Then, if we see eye to eye on that, sir, there will be no difficulty. I have made a statement to PC Bugby. I have got to go back to London, tomorrow, and I am hoping that I shall not be needed for the inquest.'

'And what is the import of your statement?'

Bragg grinned. 'Well, of the three deaths, I can say without doubt that the squire's was an accident. His intention was to kill me, not himself. If I hadn't jogged the table, as I jumped up, he would have managed it, too.'

Colegrave smiled. 'What precisely did you tell Bugby?'

'I said that the squire was cleaning his guns, before going to London. I heard an explosion. I did not actually see what happened, because I was looking at the grain of the table at that moment.'

'Good man! We could use a few people like you in the Dorset force.' He got to his feet. 'If you ever feel like transferring down from the City police, just let me know. Perhaps we could even make it a promotion to Inspector . . . Yes, I think I could wangle that.'

'You know, sir, I might just take you up on that.'

'Good, good. Then I will be off.'

'What will happen about the other suspects now, sir?' asked Bragg.

'It is my belief that Dyer did steal the watch. We might give that one a run. I shall instruct Milward to drop any murder charges, of course. Are there other suspects, besides him?'

'Applin, the landlord of the Drax Arms.'

'Oh, yes. He refused to say anything whatever. Publicans seldom have a good relationship with the police, as I dare say you are aware. He seems to have regarded Milward's hauling him off to Dorchester for questioning, as a breach of the rights of every true-born Englishman . . . You need not worry. I will see that the Inspector is too heavily involved elsewhere to want to continue his enquiries into the events in Bere Regis.'

'What about Gittings, the Lulworth Cove smuggler?'

'I shall leave well alone.' Colegrave made a grimace. 'Do you realise, man, I may have been drinking his brandy myself!'

• • •

'So you solved it, after all?' Fanny said in a gratified tone.

'After a great deal of time had been wasted. The truth was staring me in the face, but I could not recognize it. If my mind had been half as keen as it usually is, the Ollertons would still have their home.'

'You must not blame yourself,' Fanny said firmly. 'You were convalescing, after all . . . Promise me?'

Bragg smiled. 'I promise,' he said.

Fanny put her hand on his arm and they walked down the church path, between the sentinel yew trees.

'Mrs Ollerton has told mamma that, once the sale of her business is completed, she intends to go back to Yorkshire.'

'With the children, of course.'

'Yes. We shall miss Lucy, she was such an intelligent child.'

'It would be for the best, miss. So far as I know, there is no risk that the truth about her parentage will come out, but she is best out of harm's way.'

They strolled in silence until they had reached her father's grave. She busied herself for a few moments, rearranging the flowers, then they turned back.

'Tomorrow you return to London,' she said sadly. 'I shall miss you. These last three weeks have been such a joy for me.'

'It won't be for ever,' Bragg said jauntily. 'I am helping Ted Sharman to buy Mrs Ollerton's business. I shall have to come down fairly often to look at my investment!'

Fanny squeezed his arm. 'I would gladly drive you into Dorchester tomorrow, for your train,' she said.

'Best not, Fanny . . . People are talking enough, as it is.'

'Let them!' she said spiritedly.

'I shall be down again soon, to sign the sale papers. I would hope I could see you then.'

'May I write to you?'

'If you want to. But I warn you, I am not much of a hand at letter writing, myself.'

'The merest line would be enough.'

'I will do my best . . . there is another thing I will do, though.'

'What is that?'

'I will give some thought to those poems of yours!'

EPILOGUE _____

Morton turned into the courtyard of the Old Jewry head-quarters building and walked briskly into the entrance hall.

'Is Sergeant Bragg in yet?' he asked.

The desk-sergeant nodded. 'I reckon he must have been up at the crack of dawn,' he said dryly. 'He'll be giving you the old run-around, mark my words!'

Morton bounded up the stairs and went into Bragg's room. 'Welcome back!' he said cheerfully.

Bragg looked up from the report he was reading. 'What? . . . Oh yes. Thanks.'

'Are you fully recovered?'

Bragg put aside the paper. 'Indeed I am, lad. I can't wait to get stuck in again.'

Morton grinned. 'Miss Marsden and I compared notes over dinner, last evening, and we concluded that you had involved yourself in some kind of criminal investigation, while you were supposedly on sick leave!'

'What makes you think that?' Bragg asked innocently.

'Come, sir! Sporting guns belonging to Dorset gentry,

society girls with connections in that area, it could hardly be anything else. What was it all about?'

Bragg pulled out his tobacco pouch and began to cut thin slices of twist. 'What was it about? That's a good question . . . I suppose it was about people not fitting the pattern, or the pattern changing . . . or both.'

'And what is that sphinx-like utterance supposed to convey?'

'Even in the deep country, society is changing, lad. Fifty years ago, what occurred could never remotely have happened. The old paternalism would have kept everybody in their place.' He began to rub the tobacco lovingly between his palms. 'I suppose it's to do with every man having a vote nowadays; every Jack thinking he is as good as his master.'

'Surely, you would not wish to go back to the bad old days?' said Morton in surprise.

'Of course not . . . and it's not that I hanker after them, either. It is time that things changed in the country. But we should allow for the fact that some people will not be able to cope with change.'

Morton looked at him quizzically. 'People like Mr Charles Jerrard?' he asked.

Bragg began to feed the tobacco into the bowl of his pipe. 'He was the local squire,' he said, 'and a real misfit. He ought to have been strong and autocratic; instead he was weak and ineffectual—hen-pecked, too, by all accounts. He was a pleasant enough man, at bottom, but in these enlightened days, that was not enough to earn him the respect of the villagers.'

'Disrespect is hardly a criminal activity,' Morton said with a smile, 'or we would both have been arraigned long ago!'

'No, but murder is.'

'I thought that nothing less would have induced you to send us scurrying around London!'

Bragg struck a match and sucked the flame down into his pipe.

'We haven't got the time for the ins and outs now,' he said, when his pipe was drawing well, 'but it all comes down to Jerrard's weak character—and his liking for guns.'

'The two often go together,' Morton observed. 'Do not the Americans call a revolver an "equaliser"?'

'Maybe they do. Certainly, the squire seemed to carry a shotgun with him, wherever he went. It was as if it was a symbol of his authority. He had a whole row of them in the gunroom at home; case after case of them . . . then the new hammerless action was invented. I can imagine that he felt he had just got to have one, to maintain his authority.'

'So he ordered one from Purdey's,' said Morton.

'It seems you have these things made in pairs. When he took delivery of them, he must have felt like a kid with a new toy. Unfortunately, there was a thrusting northerner in the village, trading as a carrier, determined to make his pile. He had been blackmailing the squire for ten years and more, over a family indiscretion.'

'Which is where Miss Marsden's enquiries fit in, I suppose.'

'That's right, lad . . . He didn't want great sums out of the squire; it was almost amicable, you might say. Then the carrier made the mistake of screwing one of his new guns out of him. It must have been like robbing him of his self-respect. We shall never know what it was they quarreled about, but eventually the squire shot him, swapped guns with him and walked off home. The coroner duly brought in a verdict of accidental death, and everybody was happy.'

'Except for the redoubtable Sergeant Bragg! How did you get on with the local constabulary?'

'Well enough, considering . . .'

'You obviously solved the crime for them.'

'Only after blundering about like a blind donkey for days. I tell you, lad, country air fogs your brain. It's good to get back to the smoky old City again. Now, then . . . there was a burglary at Petherbridge's jeweller's shop, in Cheapside, last night.' Bragg knocked out his pipe in the ash-tray.

'We have a preliminary report from the beat constable. Sounds like a professional screwsman, to me. We'll have a chat with the owners and find out what's missing. Then we might slip up to Foxy Jock's pop-shop; see if he's taken any interesting pledges this morning . . . Come on, lad!'

AGATHA CHRISTIE

MYSTERY'S #1 BESTSELLER

The most popular mystery writer of all time, Agatha Christie achieved the highest honor in Britain when she was made a Dame of the British Empire.

NGAIO MARSH

BESTSELLING PAPERBACKS BY A "GRAND MASTER" OF THE MYSTERY WRITERS OF AMERICA.

____ ARTISTS IN CRIME	0-515-07534-5/$3.50
____ GRAVE MISTAKE	0-515-08847-1/$3.50
____ HAND IN GLOVE	0-515-07502-7/$3.50
____ LIGHT THICKENS	0-515-07359-8/$3.50
____ DEATH IN A WHITE TIE	0-515-08591-X/$3.50
____ DEATH IN ECSTASY	0-515-08592-8/$3.50
____ DEATH AND THE DANCING FOOTMAN	0-515-08610-X/$3.50
____ DEATH OF A PEER	0-515-08691-6/$3.50
____ PHOTO FINISH	0-515-07505-1/$2.95
____ WHEN IN ROME	0-515-07504-3/$3.50